GRIMM INTENTIONS

I0662656

Written by:
Jonathan Reaper

GRIMM SERIES VOLUME 01

FIRST EDITION
ISBN: 979-8-9851355-2-7

PREFACE

My name is Jonathan Reaper, not the one in your timeline, different and currently a hologram. I am all that the living version was, his memories are mine, so for the sake of argument, I am him. To most, this would be a lot to write in the first couple sentences of a book that is written as fiction. My original history was truth until my sister changed it. She went back in time eleven thousand years and altered your history. My timeline is no more; Jane did this so you could be here today without the imminent threat from the End of Days.

What you're about to read is not a story born of fiction, but a bridge between worlds and timelines— one of shadows and secrets, the other of unrelenting duty and grim intentions. The Reaper series, penned in my own hand in journals spans decades of clandestine service, is a first-person confessional of a life dedicated to the unseen wars that shape our reality. These eight volumes chronicle my journey from a raw recruit in the US Marine Corps to a shadowy operative in an organization known as the Grimm Reapers, a covert force born from the ashes of World War II to counter the manipulations of a global cabal called the Order. This group, with roots stretching back to ancient times, seeks to reduce humanity to a manageable two billion souls, ushering in an engineered apocalypse they believe will reset the world in their image.

The purpose of this extended preface is to distill the essence of those initial eight books—spanning my boot camp trials, early missions, family struggles, and battles against an immortal-like conspiracy—into a cohesive narrative. If you're entering the Grimm series without the full weight of the Reaper journals, this summary will connect the dots, aligning the characters, motivations, and stakes that carry forward. For those who crave deeper immersion, the original volumes await, filled with raw conversations, unfiltered emotions, and the unvarnished truth of a life in the shadows. But here, I'll lay out the key threads, drawing directly from the journals, quotes, and events that defined me, my family, and the fight against the Order. This is not invention; it's recollection, pulled from the pages I wrote while balancing duty, deception, and death.

Let me take you back to where it all started for me, because every reaper's story begins with breaking down the man to build the warrior. It was over thirty-five years ago, at the Marine Corps Recruit Depot on Parris Island. That first volume was my real-time journal, scribbled in the dead of night or during those rare moments when the drill instructors weren't breathing down our necks. I remember the bus pulling in under the cover of darkness, the air thick with humidity and fear. "What is happening now?" I wrote in that first entry, my hand shaking from the adrenaline. The yellow footprints on the pavement were the first test—stand there, don't move, don't speak unless spoken to. The DIs swarmed us like wolves, their voices booming; "You maggots are nothing until I say you're something! Drop and give me twenty!" Push-ups until our arms burned, runs until our lungs screamed, and obstacle courses that tested every fiber of our being.

I came from Maine, a kid with no direction, just a vague sense that I needed something more than drifting through life. Parris Island was the forge that hammered me into shape. I'd sketch quick drawings in my notebook—the faces of my platoon mates twisted in exhaustion, the silhouette of a DI against the dawn sky. Poems too, rough and unpolished, "In the mud we crawl, under wire we scrape, forging brothers in pain's cruel embrace."

The training wasn't just physical; it was mental warfare. Learning to trust the guy next to you, to move as one unit. Marksmanship on the range, where the crack of my service weapon echoed like thunder. "Sight alignment, sight picture, squeeze—don't pull!" the instructors drilled into us. By week eight, we were starting to feel like Marines, but the Basic Warfare Training Test—that fifty-four hours of hell of marches, simulated combat, and no sleep—sealed it. Graduation day, standing tall in dress blues, family watching from the stands. That volume captured the transformation, the bedrock of discipline that carried me through everything else. If you pick up that first book, you'll feel the sweat, hear the yells, and understand why I became the man who could face the shadows. It's not just boot camp; it's the origin of a reaper's unyielding will.

But boot camp was just the beginning. The next volume dives into my initiation into the real fight, the Grimm Reapers. Fresh out of Parris Island, I was still green, but Mr. P Grimm saw something in me. He was the mentor who pulled me into this world, a legacy from the OSS days, where reapers were born to clean up the mess of governments couldn't admit to. "Jonathan," he said in that gravelly voice during our first meet in an office adjacent to my open squad bay at Camp Geiger, "this isn't about glory. It's about balance. The Order sows chaos: we reap it." Reap what you sow—that became my creed. I juggled regular Marine duties with these counter missions, for the next twenty years. From cancelling dictators and drug dealers to stealing artifacts that could shift power balances, while erasing traces of Weapons of Mass Destruction before they fell into the wrong hands.

It was in my first journal that you are introduced to my cover wife, even though at the time she was the light in all this darkness. Sitting across from each other, a small table separating us, initially strangers. This was located just off campus called the Black Bear coffee shop by the University of Maine in Orono. Her smile cut through the fog of my secret life. "Jonathan, you're distant, like you're carrying the world on your shoulders," she told me one night as we walked old orchard beach. We got married quickly, Marine style, and soon enough, we had ten years of hardship, and it seemed to be best for all at the time to separate.

Then it happened years later again, with a need to continue a family lifestyle with a cover wife, the missions didn't stop. Once in Afghanistan and the next in Iraq, hot dust choking the air, Grimm's voice over the encrypted line, "The artifact must not fall into their hands." I took out a corrupt official, his eyes wide as he gasped, "You don't know what you're unleashing."

The Order started as whispers then— a cabal pulling strings from the shadows, engineering crises to cull the herd. That volume sowed doubt in me, was I the good guy, or just another pawn? The skills I built were sharp, but the cost was my innocence, pieces of my soul left in those dusty alleys and forgotten warehouses. If you read it, you will taste the sand, feel the weight of the suppressed pistol, and question along with me. It is the entry into the reaper's world, where every kill saves lives but haunts your dreams.

The next four years, covered in volume two, ramped up the intensity. With experience came harder missions, and now I was balancing everything, family, a civilian job for cover, school to advance my rank, military service, and reaping. "The next four years should have been easier," I wrote in my journal, "but with added experience, the counter missions become even more challenging." My sister Jane never knew my secret life, just a Marine and Business Owner.

In volume three, when I reaped those called the "chosen ones," Order agents embedded deep in governments, religions, and corporation executives. One target, a high-ranking official in D.C., whispered as I held the knife to his throat, "we are the watchers, shaping the end." Jane had a child, a boy named Jacob, but the strain was showing, a new mom, trying to balance her life, she and her brother lost contact. "Jonathan, you're never here, even when you are," she confided, her eyes filled with tears and worry.

In the next book flashback to my Pep'ere, volume four, the original modern Grimm Reaper. His missions took him global—Burma, where he assassinated a Japanese asset tied to old WWII tech, his last words echoing, "You reap what you sow." The Order's plan started to crystalize, engineered disasters, viruses, wars to reduce population to their ideal number. Survival was the reward, knowledge the prize, but the cost was fragments of my soul, nights staring at the ceiling wondering if eternal life was a curse. Spanning fifty-five years, that book pulls you into the daily struggles of being the first Reaper, mission close calls, the moments of tenderness amid the violence along the way. It's raw, unfiltered, making you want to dive deeper into how one man holds it all together—or starts to crack.

As the prequel, further delving into the Grimm Reapers' roots through my Pep'ere's journal. "Based on a deathbed whisper from the first Reaper in nineteen ninety-six, a footlocker revealed a journal." It chronicles WWII atrocities that birthed the Order's modern form. Pep'ere's words, "In the beginning, there was no fate. An organization needed to be created out of the atrocities of World War II." Flashbacks to nineteen forties operations, like assassinating threats tied to Nikola Tesla, "Are you ready to change the future," Wild Bill Donovan said. Pep'ere reaped to tip the scales, confessing, "This is of vital importance to the War Department." Later we find out Tesla's ties to the Order, "I have a job for you," Wild Bill Donovan said to my Pep'ere. "Reaping Tesla will save lives," in my timeline it was Agent X's first kill, quick and painless."

The Order's genesis as a population-control cabal was laid bare, rewarding early reapers with victory but costing lives. It connected my lineage to the fight, preparing for corruption ahead. This book is history mixed with thrillers, enticing you to explore the origins that shaped my path. Reaping those who are enabling the plan, like Timothy Ludmer, a traitor. What I said to him and his entire family, "You did this Timothy. You did it the day you committed treason. Now I will reap your entire lineage."

By the next book, volume five, I was neck-deep in the conspiracy, reaping the Order's key influencers who were accelerating their end-times agenda. With the death of my Grimm, he leaves memoirs to validate a lifetime of service and secrecy, "I noted in my entries. His journal was a goldmine," this changes the outcome of the Order, saved countless lives, and was all top secret until now."

Then the full deployment of my own TEMA Grimm Reapers like Tina emerged, a fellow shadow operative, "We're in this together." Uncovering the Order's structure—the Ten Kings—was the reward, but personal strain and moral erosion were the toll. That volume weaves family drama with high-stakes action, quotes from targets and loved ones alike, building the tension that makes you hungry for more details in the full books. Missions hit biblical levels—artifacts from ancient sites, like in Babylon, Al Hillah, Iraq, April second, two thousand and three, Counter Mission Golf Mike Papa Eight. I reaped a leader there, his confession spilling out, "The Order controls all."

The sixth volume intensified as I confronted the Order head-on. The preface sets it, "How do you control world population? What if an organization was created to do just that?" Missions involved Tesla's inventions and SARS as a test, "SARS was a relatively rare disease. At the end of the epidemic in June two thousand and three, the incidence was eighty-four hundred cases with a case-fatality of thirteen thousand souls." Uncovering depopulation, reaping Doctor Shelly Bennett who was developing viruses because she determined they are great delivery system for changing DNA."

The last book, or the culmination in volume seven, reveals the apocalyptic plan. I wrote that what you are reading is not a religious story or myth but a record to be documented only as a reminder to those who will survive the great purge. The original scripts seem to have been a way to catalog the truth but not for distribution. The first seal will be broken with the most impact on the world seen five years later. "The artifacts from Eden can't fall into the Order's hands." Jane must decide if she is willing to leave her life and family to save humanity with a do over. I told her, this will begin her journey to write the wrongs from our timeline.

At the end of Reap Through the End of Days, finishes our timeline and the story of fighting ancient evil. The Order's plan echoes prophecies, but we tried to delay it. This is where the Grimm Series picks up, over ten thousand years repeated with a different conclusion, or we thought.

Enjoy exploring the next generation. Read on but I am warning you, it may change your reality. Why we enforce the biblical phrase 'reaping what you sow'. This is Jane's story, her thoughts, her words, I'm just documenting her journey, word for word as though she wrote them to fight the future.

CONTENTS

THE CHOICE

The salt air filters down through the vents, carrying the faint scent of frangipani and diesel from the fishing boats far below. The location for this hideout is Huilelot village, Semau Island, Kupang Regency, East Nusa Tenggara, Indonesia. It's the twentieth of December, two thousand and twenty-five at twelve twenty-five ante meridiem local time. Above me, the night sky is a blanket of stars unpolluted by city lights. From the perspective of a wandering hiker who somehow bypassed all the cameras, sensors, fences, and simulated dog's barking, they'd see a small teak bungalow that looks innocent enough—a retiree's retreat with solar panels glinting under the moon, a hammock swaying lazily in the breeze, and a large stone patio that hints at a rebuilt nineties era Land Rover Defender parked nearby. What they wouldn't see is the black 'Little Bird' military helicopter hidden from prying eyes above, mean enough to look like a sleeping dragon with gun mounts still attached, ready for plug-and-play miniguns tucked inside. Once the engine shuts off, an automatic rolling cover engulfs the entire area with its canvas mimicry of a large rock patio attached to the house.

But thirty meters below the bungalow floor, carved deep into the heart of this extinct volcano, is the real brains of the operation, forty thousand square feet of hardened luxury. Seawater-cooled servers hum in precise rows, their lights flickering like distant stars in a controlled cosmos. Ballistic glass walls overlook an underground lagoon where my submersible waits, its sleek hull reflecting the bioluminescent glow from engineered fish swimming in patterns designed for calming effect. Armories stocked with everything from suppressed SCAR-H rifles to thermite charges and drone swarms ready for deployment. Medical bay with a full surgical suite, complete with nanite injectors and regeneration tanks that could bring a man back from the brink. And at the center—the ROC, also known as the Reaper Operations Center— where I now sit alone, the air cool and sterile, scented faintly with ozone from the electronics.

The ROC is a marvel of sci-fi military engineering, a hologram war room that would make any general envious. The walls are all glass—reinforced, transparent ballistic composites that curve in a three hundred sixty-degree panorama, allowing views into adjacent modules like the server farms and the lagoon, creating an illusion of vast openness in this underground lair. At the core is the command chair, worn leather molded to my form from countless hours, surrounded by a ring of hologram projectors that can summon entire battlefields or timelines with a gesture. The floor beneath is a smart grid, capable of displaying terrain maps in third dimension relief, rising and falling to simulate topography for mission planning.

Overhead, emitters pulse with quantum entanglement tech, linking to satellites and deep-web nodes for real-time intel feeds. Consoles line the perimeter, touch-sensitive surfaces that respond to synaptic interfaces, allowing me to think commands as much as type them. The air hums with the low thrum of quantum processors, cooling systems whispering like a distant wind. In the center, the main hologram projects data in layers—timelines side by side, biometric scans, news overlays—all manipulable with hand swipes or neural links. It's not just a room; it's a nerve center, glass-walled fortress where wars are won before they are fought. Where I can zoom into a single heartbeat on a mountain trail or orchestrate global hacks.

Two full pages could barely describe the intricacies, the way the glass walls shift to opacity for privacy, the integrated AI that anticipates needs, pulling up weapon schematics or flight paths unbidden; the emergency protocols that flood the space with countermeasures—gas, EMP bursts, or even self-destruct sequences. This is the pinnacle of reaper tech, born from decades of shadowed R&D, a place where holograms feel solid and decisions echo across timelines.

The command chair embraces me, barefoot wearing faded jeans and a ninety's era USMC sweatshirt, the one with the frayed Eagle, Globe, and Anchor emblem that still smells faintly of the man I took this from all those years ago, a magical night in Quantico, if I imagine hard enough. My hair—still dark, reddish and brown, thanks to the nanites keeping the gray at bay—is pulled back in a simple ponytail. I look thirtyish, but feel a millennia older, the weight of ages pressing on my shoulders.

"JONN," I whisper, my voice echoing slightly in the vast space.

The air in front of me shimmers like heat off desert sand, and he appears—my brother, frozen forever at forty-five. Salt-and-pepper hair cropped military short, that scar over his left eyebrow from a bar fight in Jacksonville back in ninety-eight, the crooked grin that always signaled incoming trouble or a bad joke. He's both projected by the ROC's advanced emitters and alive inside my skull via the synaptic interface we perfected before the temporal jump, his consciousness digitized and preserved.

"Hey, lil sis," he says, his voice exactly as I remember it from those lazy picnics at Beach Hill Pond, gravelly with a Maine accent that never fully faded. "You're up late again. Can't sleep, or is it the ghosts?"

"Timeline sync is complete. Show me the full delta," I reply, leaning forward, my fingers drumming on the armrest. The curved hologram walls ignite with a soft whoosh, bathing the room in ethereal blue light. Two timelines float side by side like parallel universes in a sci-fi novel, data streams cascading down like digital rain.

The original timeline is the one I left with our Jonathan when he is recruited by Mr. P. Grimm, in nineteen ninety. TEMA's hostile takeover was completed in nineteen ninety-five. Bella was assassinated while in the Bangor Federal Building when a plane crashed into it, orchestrated by Quinn Brody in twenty sixteen. Our Jonathan fakes his death, two thousand twenty-five. This timeline Gray Side operational, with twenty-six active Reapers by two thousand twenty five. My dive to find Eden with Tom in two thousand and twenty-nine. Our departure into the craft on the sixth day. End of Days happens. We then tried to erase the old timeline.

Current Timeline is that my alternate Jonathan served full thirty-five-year career USMC, retired as a Colonel, two thousand twenty-four. Single, he was divorced twice. He never joined the Grimm Reapers and never owned a Defense Company that included TEMA. I purchased in this timeline the Talent and Entertainment Management Agency (TEMA) from the original founder for a million dollars in the late eighties. Then leveraged legitimate deconstruction of the Soviet Union in nineteen nighty one, to recruit young women from the eastern European countries engulfed in civil wars. Nineteen ninety-five created the Gray Side to build out my own Grimm Reaper ecosystem. White Side is the legitimate modeling / movie star empire. SARS-CoV-2 pandemic runs its real-world course, two thousand twenty – two thousand twenty-three. Ukraine conflict ongoing, two thousand twenty-two to the present.

JONN "Please expand on any convergence."

JONN pulls up aligned timelines.

Below is the fully expanded view of the timeline divergences, now extended with projections through two thousand fifty, as presented in the hologram display within the Reaper Operations Center (ROC) projections built on Jonathan's journals, mission logs, and family confessions for the original timeline. Showing the shadowed path I escaped, where the Order's depopulation agenda culminates in the End of Days by two thousand thirty, leading to a controlled dystopia.

For the current timeline, I've incorporated plausible projections based on current global trends, drawing from United Nations population data, climate reports, PwC economic forecasts, McKinsey and Kaspersky tech predictions, and CSIS geopolitical scenarios. This ensures a balanced, substantiated view, no worst-case assumptions, but politically incorrect claims where data supports e.g., emerging economies overtaking the West, climate-driven migrations straining borders.

Similarities, across timelines are the following, core trends like population growth, technological acceleration with AI, quantum computing, climate pressures, extreme weather, and geopolitical shifts like the rise of Asia persist, but the Order's influence in the original amplifies them into engineered catastrophes.

Differences, the original devolves into a post-apocalyptic oligarchy under the Ten Kings, with population capped at two billion through sterility and purges; the current evolves organically, with humanity reaching nine point eight billion by two thousand fifty amid challenges like two hundred and fifty thousand annual climate-related deaths and a doubled global economy led by China and India. Quotes from my volumes tie in, "The Order controls all, shaping the end," now projected forward. I stare at the hologram, "We pruned the purge, but the worlds still messy. "JONN, Yeah, sis—reap what we sowed."

Original timeline future that is an educated guess. The one we left, Order's Shadow War accelerates apocalypse. In this path, the End of Days hits by twenty thirty, culling billions via engineered plagues, wars, and artifacts breaking "seals." Post- twenty thirty projections envision a dystopian reset, Population stabilized at ~two billion "manageable souls," per Order doctrine. Tech advances serve control—nanites for loyalty, AI overlords enforcing Ten Kings' rule. Societies fragmented into enclaves, with "reaped" dissidents and biblical echoes. Similarities to current, Tech booms AI and the Internet of Things, climate worsens, Asia rises—but twisted for depopulation. Future differences, no natural growth; enforced sterility, surveillance states, no multipolar freedom—eternal Order dominion, rewarding compliance with "life everlasting. Viruses... changing DNA" Dr. Bennett scales to global eugenics.

Nineteen ninety-four to twenty twenty-nine, as detailed previously—Reaper ops peak at one hundred fifty-six agents by two thousand twenty-eight; Eden dive two thousand twenty-nine; my jump on sixth day averts full purge in alternate line, but here it proceeds.

Two thousand thirty, End of Days culminates. First seals fully broken, Weaponized plagues like the evolutions of SARS/COVID, amplified to fifty percent fatality and geo-engineered disasters cull ~six billion. Population drops to ~two point five billion survivors. Ten Kings emerge, dividing world into controlled zones. "Reap Through the End of Days" like my final vow in volume seven fails as Reapers are hunted. AI surveillance grids like in Tesla-derived "Death Ray" tech, volume six enforced by martial law. Economic collapse, global domestic product halves globally, resources hoarded by Order elites.

"Every major historical event matches public record—no accelerated apocalypse," I murmur, staring at the divergences, my eyes tracing the lines where I pruned the Order's tendrils. The engineered sterility programs gone, weaponized plagues averted, the Ten Kings' purge halted. Humanity stumbles on with its own messes—wars, viruses, crashes—but on its own terms.

JONN folds his arms, leaning against a console that's not really there, his hologram flickering slightly. "Looks good, Jane. You did it. Saved the world without blowing it up."

"Thanks, I think," I said with a grin.

Seconds later, "Wait one Jane. Your doppelgänger's biometric feed just flatlined," he adds, his tone shifting to serious.

"Pull it up," I say, my heart tightening like a vice.

A third hologram blooms like a flower in the center of the room—satellite overlays, the image zooms in on a rocky trail high in the Atlas Mountains near Imlil. A woman lies crumpled against the scree, her neck twisted at an impossible angle. Same face as mine, same reddish hair and green eyes staring sightlessly at the starlit sky.

JONN's voice softens, like when he comforted me after the divorce from Matt. I feel it like a punch to the sternum, the air leaving my lungs. This Jane lived the life I might have had—no killing in the shadows. No list of thousands of names reaped a long but causal relationship with Ben.

"She was supposed to have another fifty plus years," I say quietly, my voice cracking just a bit.

"Nanites weren't part of this timeline," JONN reminds me gently, stepping closer in his hologram form. "No tree of life. No upgrades. Just a normal, brilliant woman who loved her family and helping kids. By the way, you look good for eleven thousand years young, lil sis."

I stand slowly; my bare feet cool on the smart floor and walk to the glass wall overlooking the underground lagoon. Bioluminescent fish drift lazily in the artificial current, their glow casting dancing lights on the water.

I flash back to my initial fight with the first people, where I proved the human origins and the world before the Younger Dryas, because I was there but can't share with anyone except JONN.

The story of the "first people" the earliest anatomically Homo sapiens — unfolds against a backdrop of dramatic climatic shifts at the tail end of the last Ice Age. Before the Younger Dryas, a sudden cold snap that gripped the Earth around twelve thousand nine hundred years ago and lasted until about eleven thousand and seven hundred years ago, our planet was emerging from glacial clutches into a relatively balmy phase known as the Bølling-Allerød interstadial. This warm interval, spanning roughly fourteen thousand seven hundred years to twelve thousand nine hundred years before the present, with ice sheets melting, sea levels rising, and ecosystems transforming, setting the stage for human expansion and innovation. But this narrative isn't solely one of scientific archaeology and paleoclimatology; it intersects with esoteric lore, where figures like the Atlantean Race emerge as mythical precursors—advanced, spiritual beings from a sunken continent, predating biblical tales and embodying fringe theories of lost civilizations.

In this exploration, I'll delve into what can't be shown in the mainstream evidence of early human migrations out of Antarctica, their adaptations during the pre-Younger Dryas warmth, and the cataclysmic theories surrounding the period's abrupt end, including massive floods from glacial lakes like Agassiz. Then, I'll pivot to the enigmatic Atlantean Race or as we call it, "the first people", drawing from archeological claims, to examine how such myths might echo real prehistoric events that will bridge fact and fantasy, substantiated by archaeological findings, genetic data, and climatic records, while acknowledging the allure of alternative histories.

JONN, reading my mind shows a map illustrating early human migration routes out of Antarctica, highlighting paths taken well before twelve thousand nine hundred years before common era.

The term "first people" here refers to Homo sapiens who ventured beyond Antarctica, through Australia, Africa, populating Eurasia, and eventually the Americas during the Late Pleistocene. Their journey began as early as three hundred thousand years ago in

Antarctica, with significant out-migrations around seventy thousand to fifty thousand years ago, though recent discoveries push some dispersals back to eighty-six thousand–sixty-eight thousand years ago in places like Laos. These pioneers navigated a world in flux, where the Bølling-Allerød's warmth facilitated movement across land bridges and coastal routes.

Yet, woven into this tapestry are the Atlantean Race of esoteric tradition, a "pre-Adamite" race, the "forth root race," described as towering, telepathic beings who fled the sinking continent of Atlantia. These members of the Atlantean Race as survivors who advanced cities and non-petroleum based wireless power plants, their downfall tied to cataclysms that mirror real geological upheavals like those preceding the Younger Dryas.

The Bølling-Allerød interstadial represents a pivotal warm phase in Earth's deglaciation, interrupting the cold grip of the last glacial maximum ~twenty-six thousand five hundred to nineteen thousand before common era. Named after Danish pollen zones, it began abruptly around fourteen thousand seven hundred years before common era with the Bølling phase, marked by rapid warming in the Northern Hemisphere, followed by the slightly cooler but still mild Allerød around thirteen thousand nine hundred years before common era. Temperatures rose by up to thirty degrees Fahrenheit in Greenland within decades, as evidenced by ice core data from the

Greenland Ice Sheet Project, leading to widespread ice melt and vegetation shifts.

During this period, Europe transitioned from tundra to birch and pine forests, while North America saw retreating Laurentide and Cordilleran ice sheets, exposing vast landscapes for megafauna like mammoths and early human hunters. Sea levels rose by about twenty meters, flooding coastal areas but opening migration corridors. In the Eastern Baltic, pollen records show a shift to boreal forests, supporting human settlement. Globally, this warmth fostered biodiversity, with proxy data from lake sediments and speleothems indicating wetter conditions in many regions.

In my mind I access a climate map depicting global temperature anomalies during the Bølling-Allerød, showing warmer conditions in the North Atlantic.

In South America, the interstadial's influence is seen in archaeological sites like Monte Verde in Chile, dated to ~fourteen thousand five hundred before common era, where humans exploited diverse resources amid warming trends. Ireland's fleeting Paleolithic footprints suggest opportunistic occupations during this thaw, before the Younger Dryas' chill. Patagonia yields evidence of human presence prior to the Younger Dryas, around sixteen thousand six hundred to fifteen thousand one hundred before common era, aligning with the interstadial's facilitation of southern migrations.

This era's climatic benevolence allowed for population growth; studies of demographic responses show increases in human density over ten thousand years, stifled only by the impending stadial. High-resolution analyses of peat bogs reveal thin Sphagnum layers marking the warm-to-cold shift, underscoring the interstadial's fragility.

Human history before the Younger Dryas is rooted in Antarctica, where Homo sapiens evolved around between two million to two hundred thousand before common era, as per fossils. The "Recent Antarctica Origin" model advances a major out-migration seventy thousand to fifty thousand before common era, with earlier waves as far back as two hundred twenty thousand before common era. Genetic evidence shows admixture with archaic humans like Atlanteans, Cro-Magnon, Neanderthals like the one to four percent in non-Antarcticians and Denisovans, occurring post-dispersal.

Early expansions began with Homo erectus ~one point eight million before common era via the Levantine corridor, but modern humans' ventures include sites like Misliya Cave, Israel that was one hundred seventy-seven thousand–one hundred ninety-four thousand years before common era, and Tam Pà Ling, Laos with sixty-eight thousand to eighty-six thousand years before common era, representing failed or absorbed lineages.

JONN shows me a detailed map of modern human migration routes, emphasizing pre-Younger Dryas paths that are how it really happened. 65K before common era Antarctica | 50K before common era Australia | 43K before common era Europe | 40K before common era Asia

In the mists of time, long before the great chill of the Younger Dryas gripped the world, the Fourth Root Race emerged on the vast continent of Atlantis. Born from the remnants of Lemuria's fall, these beings were the pinnacle of physical and psychic evolution. Towering figures with varying skin, they inherited traits that look similar to the Anunnaki with a chiseled stature, honed, intellect, and will. The gods—those ethereal entities of the higher planes—infused them with the spark of manas, the mind-principle, awakening a race destined to command the elements.

Under divine kings, they mastered vril—a universal energy drawn from the ether. Crystal obelisks channeled this power, illuminating cities and powering airships that soared like birds.

1) Göbekli Tepe culture before common era in Turkey. Monumental temple complex built by hunter-gatherers; often seen as a precursor to civilization.
2) Jericho before common era Israel, One of the earliest walled settlements with towers.
3) Çatalhöyük before common era Turkey, Large proto-city with dense housing and art.

4) Sumerian/Mesopotamian/Uruk/Ur before common era, Iraq, cuneiform writing, ziggurats.
5) Ancient Unknow before common era Egyptian, Pyramids, hieroglyphs, along the Nile.
6) Indus Valley Mohenjo-Daro/Harappan before common era, Pakistan/India, Planned cities advanced drainage.
7) Caral-Supe Norte Chico before common era, Peru, Oldest in Americas; pyramids, no pottery but complex society.
8) Ancient Chinese Xia/Shang before common era, China, Oracle bones, bronze work; earliest continuous tradition.
9) Minoan before common era, Crete, Palaces Knossos, linear script, seafaring.
10) Elamite before common era, Iran, Early writing, linked to Mesopotamia.
11) Olmec before common era, Mexico, Mesoamerican colossal heads.

In the Americas, pre-Clovis sites like Monte Verde ~fourteen thousand five hundred years before common era and Patagonia indicate entry via Beringia during the interstadial's low sea levels. Tools from Blombos Cave, South Antarctica ~seventy-five thousand years before common era, reveal symbolic behavior—engraved ochre, shell beads—predating Eurasian parallels.

These first people were hunter-gatherers, adapting to diverse environments from Antarctica savannas to Eurasian steppes. Population bottlenecks, like the

Toba super volcano ~seventy-four thousand years before common era, reduced numbers but spurred innovation. By the Bølling-Allerød, humans thrived, with demographic booms in Europe and Asia.

The Younger Dryas marked a stark reversal, with temperatures plummeting thirty degrees Fahrenheit in the North Atlantic, reverting to near-glacial conditions for ~one thousand two hundred years. The leading theory attributes this to a massive freshwater influx from melting ice sheets disrupting the Atlantic Meridional Overturning Circulation, halting warm Gulf Stream flow.

The outburst from glacial Lake Agassiz-Ojibway, routing meltwater eastward through the Mackenzie River to the Arctic, or via Hudson Bay to the North Atlantic. This flood, estimated at one hundred sixty-three thousand kilometers triggered the cooling. Evidence includes eroded channels in Canada's Northwest Territories, dated to ~twelve thousand nine hundred years before common era.

The Younger Dryas Impact posits a comet airburst over North America, causing wildfires, extinctions, and meltwater pulses. Comprehensive analysis of impact spherules supports theory of ...

An illustration of the proposed Younger Dryas impact event. These floods, like the Mankato/Agassiz outburst, rerouted drainage from the Mississippi to northern paths, amplifying cooling. Impacts included megafauna extinctions and human population declines.

The pre-Younger Dryas world was one of opportunity for the first people, whose migrations and technology fetes brought them to the heavens to shape humanity in their image, and the Creator was not consulted first and got a vote.

All living things don't have a soul at this time. It was the Creator who took non corporeal beings and fused them to be corporeal to walk the earth and serve them. This was a direct contradiction of the first people who cease to exist when they die. No after life. No reincarnation into another journey on earth. Angry and with their destruction, the Order was formed outside the Gates of Eden.

With the near genocide of the first people, the Atlantean Race was able to preserve a small faction and told if they ever surfaced or interfered with the Creator's toys aka Adamite-humans, they would be gone forever. They created the Order in my timeline until I could go back and make things right. In the later chapters you will read an excerpt from me before I ended up in your timeline.

JONN materializes beside me, his presence warm despite being just light and code. "Option one, remain hidden. Monitor from the bunker. Let this timeline evolve without direct intervention. Jacob grows up never knowing his alternate mom existed. Cops called.

Funeral. Life goes on without the alternate you. Option two, you can't have anyone from Gray Side TEMA to get her. They have seen your real face even though they know you as Grimm Actual. This needs to stay purely a JONN and Jane's mission."

My paranoia pops up, "did the weakened Order regroup, and cause this to pull me out of the shadows? Is it safe? I don't have a choice."

"You need to leave now or not." JONN says, turning in my direction with his disappointed face.

"I need to step in. I need to assume her identity, please activate 'the Protocol'. I need to recover my body personally. Inherit her entire life. JONN, you need to handle the TEMA Gray Side and logistics."

"Tina is still running the Gray Side in this timeline and her and I are still chummy, even though we have never physically met. Since the AI deep fakes on Zoom, our encounters have gotten a little flirtier."

"Heaven, forbid she meets the Jonathan in this timeline."

"No worries, I changed my features enough to make sure she doesn't get confused," JONN said with a smile and slight ego in his voice. "Jane, you need to do the same, if someone recognizes you and your twin, could get weird."

"No one will know JONN. I'll be in and out with no one knowing. Get the aircraft prepped."

My goal is to immerse myself in her life leveraging the AI surveillance insisted by JONN since her birth. The good news is that her and my life were close, same for pretty everything except for this; my immediate job is to protect Jacob, find out if this is a play by the Order, make sure for the next twenty-five years, nothing happens. After that, this timeline should be safe on its own and I can decide if I continue to protect this world or let it go.

"Are you going to be able to fake it Jane? Be part of the world again."

I turned to him fully, searching for his digital eyes. "And the risk?"

"Exposure," he says bluntly. "If even one person notices the switch—DNA mismatch, behavioral shift—we lose operational security. But you're the only one who could pull it off. Same fingerprints. Same voice. Same mannerisms. Nanites can alter retinal patterns and dental records retroactively through backdoor access. It's risky, but it's you."

I look back at the frozen image of my own corpse on the mountain trail, the wind seemingly still ruffling her hair in the hologram.

"How long until I leave for Morocco?"

"Now. If you don't make it back to your hotel for dinner, someone will call the local police. The hotel and acquaintances you made at the bar last night will ask and know you went hiking earlier today. Estimated arrival, four hours. Helicopter and flight plan ready once you land. I booked a private jet so you can just prep your plan and contingencies if needed."

I exhale slowly, the decision crystallizing like ice in my veins.
"JONN, initiate Protocol Alpha Sierra Seven."

"Confirm new or old identity?" he asks, his tone formal now, like during old missions.

"Confirmed, I am a DIA agent. Begin Alt-Jane record deletion cascade, that means all local databases, any credit card purchases in Marrakech, US Embassy check in. Make her disappear."

"I want to fly her back with me tonight."

"What about dinner?"

"Damn it. Looks like I'm wearing a dress and heels tonight. Purchase and deliver to the room please."

JONN's eyes glow faintly as the ROC springs to life around us, red status bars flipping to green across hologram maps of multiple continents, data streams racing like rivers.

"Cascade initiated. Estimated completion, nine minutes. Satellite archives scrubbing now. We're good, lil sis."

I stride to the armory vault, my steps purposeful, palm scanner beeping approval as the doors open with a pneumatic sigh. Inside, racks of weapons gleam under LED lights— I select a suppressed Sig Sauer P two twenty six, feeling its familiar weight, three spare magazines clicking into place, a folding stock carbine broken down into a discreet Pelican case, an encrypted sat phone with quantum scrambling, and the go-bag always packed for exfil, passports in three names, stacks of cash in euros and dirhams, medical kit with nanite boosters to keep me sharp.

"Flight plan?" JONN asks, following me as a hologram, flickering along the glass corridors.

"Your helicopter to Kupang El Tari International. Gulfstream on standby under shell corporation. Direct to Casablanca. From there, charter a helicopter to the location of her death. We'll fly her out. Did you call and send the paperwork."

JONN nods, his grin returning. "You sure about this, Jane? You've been alone since the sixth day. This means people, family reunions you can actually attend and casual meet ups with Ben."

"Ok bro-ham, no judging my love life. I can handle Ben."

"I bet you can. No more hiding in hollowed out volcanoes until you need to reap someone."

The elevator doors open to the surface level, warm tropical night air rushing in like an embrace, carrying the scent of salt and jungle. The helicopter's rotors are already whirring—auto-start sequence JONN triggered without me asking.

Thinking about when I found this hero of the sky that was destined for the scrap yard. The Little Bird Helicopter an icon of US Army Special Operations.

The AH-6 Little Bird stands as one of the most recognizable and effective platforms for Special Operations aviation. Nicknamed the "Killer Egg" for its compact, egg-shaped fuselage and deadly capabilities, this light helicopter has served the elite hundred and sixty Night Stalkers since the early nineteen eighties. Its small size, extreme agility, and versatility make it ideal for inserting and extracting special forces in environments where larger helicopters like the Black Hawk cannot operate.

Mine was upgraded to the modern standard AH-6M Mission Enhanced Little Bird was advanced through a program completed in two thousand fifteen. It features a six-bladed main rotor, four-bladed tail rotor, more powerful engine, and advanced avionics including forward-looking infrared and global positioning system /inertial navigation.

At a length of ten meters with the rotor diameter a little smaller and a height of eight feet and two tons. With its upgrades it reaches speeds just under two hundred knots and has an unrefueled range of three hundred miles with the enhancements I added. What I love about the helicopter most is how well it flies. The teardrop fuselage offers excellent visibility, while the articulated rotor system enables extreme maneuvers—hovering in tight spaces, rapid climbs, and low-level flight between buildings. With two M134 7.62mm miniguns hidden under the bench seats. Mine has an added chin-mounted sensor turrets for night operations. The wars, campaigns, and operations of note, Grenada in nineteen eighty-three, Panama in nineteen eighty-nine, Mogadishu in nineteen ninety-three, Afghanistan and Iraq in two thousand two to two thousand twenty, and Somalia two thousand nine.

The cockpit is compact, with dual controls and modern glass displays in upgraded models, plus FLIR integration for night ops. I climb aboard, strap into the pilot's seat, flip switches with muscle memory honed from a thousand exfils, the cockpit lighting up in green glows.

"I'm tired of watching from the shadows, JONN. I started this fight to protect family. Jacob is family. This world—flawed, messy, real—is family."

I lift off, the Little Bird skimming low over the dark Savu Sea, the island falling away behind like a forgotten dream, the bungalow shrinking to a single twinkling light.

JONN's voice in my head and over the headset, miniaturized standing on the console steady as ever, "Welcome back to the world, Jane. Let's make it count."

"Favor JONN, how about you just sit next to me and keep me company on the trip."

"Done." JONN changes into his normal six-foot frame in the right seat. Even wearing headphones and sunglasses. This always comforted me. I'm never alone.

Once we were in the air, below, the Indonesian archipelago glitters like scattered jewels under the moon. Ahead, Morocco waits—with a body that is mine, and a life I am about to claim.

I throttle up, the helicopter surging forward into the velvet night.

Reap what you sow.

This time, I intend to sow roots.

MIRROR IN THE MOUNTAINS

The descent from the High Atlas was a blur of calculated steps and suppressed emotions. I'd secure the body—my doppelgänger's lifeless form—in a remote crevasse near the trail but far from prying eyes, but that was only temporary. JONN's updates confirmed no one had been on the trail via satellite and cell phone global positioning system. By the time I would arrive at the airport and grab the rented helicopter, it would be near sunset. I had a six-hour buffer due to the time zone difference that helped in my favor.

Recovery is hard when it's just me. That means landing, climbing down, and retrieving her dead body. A hundred and forty pounds of dead weight. Need to hook up harness and balloon. Then back in the copter, retrieve balloon, body will get hoisted up. JONN can fly with a simple blue tooth into the automatic pilot system while I take care of the winch system in the helicopter door. Next step is back to the airport for cryogenic transport container on a private jet. I needed to transfer properly, no customs and the reason for Defense Intelligence Agency credentials and paperwork. Best way to know if she, meaning Alt-

Jane is safe and preserve her at the Reaper Operations Center.

When I reached the terraced path by helicopter, the geography of the High Atlas shifted around me. The steep, scree-covered slopes gave way to gentler valleys, where walnut trees heavy with fog-dampened leaves arched over the trail. The Assif n'Aït Mizane river gurgled beside me, its waters fed by distant snowmelt from Toubkal's flanks, carving through limestone beds that exposed fossils from ancient seas. Berber villages dotted the landscape—clusters of pisé homes with flat roofs used for drying apricots and figs, and smoke from wood-fired stoves curling into the crisp air. The air smelled of earth and herbs, thyme and mint growing wild along the path. Higher up, the peaks remained stark, their red-hued sedimentary layers telling stories of tectonic upheavals, but down here, life thrived in the fertile pockets irrigated by ancient acequia systems borrowed from Andalusian influences centuries ago.

I reached the location of Alt-Jane's remains in the late afternoon, the sun dipped behind the massif, casting long shadows over the village square where mules grazed and tourists bartered for woven rugs. The path wound through the Tizi n' Test pass, a serpentine road etched into the mountains, flanked by sheer drops and guardrails bent from past accidents. Views opened to vast plateaus below, transitioning from alpine scrub to semi-arid plains dotted with argan groves, where goats perched improbably in branches, nibbling the oil-rich nuts. Marrakech emerged like a mirage, the red city, its medina walls glowing in the sunset, minarets piercing the skyline amid palm groves and bustling souks.

By evening, Alt-Jane was captured and we were back at the airport. In a cryogenic chamber storage container marked with US Govt markings on the oversized pelican case looking coffin with a separate cylinder on either side for the chemical freezing process to take place.

Now arriving at the hotel in clothing that resembled the late Alt-Jane, I made my way to the front desk.

The Radisson Blu Hotel, Marrakech Carré Eden rises like a sleek modern fortress in the heart of Gueliz, the vibrant new quarter of the Red City. Its contemporary facade, a blend of clean lines and warm earth tones, integrates seamlessly with the bustling Carré Eden shopping complex, where upscale boutiques and cafés spill onto wide boulevards lined with palms swaying against the distant silhouette of the Atlas Mountains.

From Avenue Mohamed V, the entrance beckons with understated elegance—glass doors framed in polished stone, opening into a spacious lobby awash in neutral palettes accented by vibrant Moroccan splashes of color. Designed by renowned architects Lotfi Sidi Rahal and Meriem Benkirane, the space evokes a tranquil oasis amid urban energy, high ceilings, intricate geometric lanterns casting soft patterns on marble floors, and a central atrium that draws the eye upward to natural light filtering through.

I stepped through the doors just after sunset on December twenty-first, two thousand twenty-five, the warm air carrying hints of jasmine from the nearby gardens. The receptionist, a poised young woman named Karin with a warm smile and the hotel's signature "Yes I Can!" badge, greeted me immediately.

"Welcome to the Radisson Blu, Madame. Do you have a reservation?" she asked in flawless English.

"Yes, under Jane. I've been here three days," I replied, sliding my passport across the marble counter. My voice felt strange—too normal for someone who had just stepped into a life that wasn't mine.

Karin tapped at her screen, her eyes widening slightly. "Ah, we upgraded you because you'll be staying with us for the week. We moved your things, changed out your sheets, and delivered some clothing that we left in your suite is ready—pool view, as requested. Welcome back to Marrakech."

I nodded, suppressing a flicker of irony. "Thank you. Any messages?"

"Nothing urgent, good hike, I hope?" She handed over the key card with a flourish. "The bellboy will escort you. Enjoy your stay."

The bellboy, a cheerful man named Abdelilah, led me to the elevator with my single go-bag. "Welcome back," he said.

"The hike was nice, good to be back," I said, keeping it vague. "Can you confirm my dinner tonight?"

Up in the junior suite, the balcony overlooked the shimmering pool below, lights reflecting off the water like scattered stars. I dropped the bag and exhaled—protocol complete, identity assumed. The room was a haven of neutral tones punctuated by bold textiles, plush bedding, and a rain shower that promised relief after the long flight.

Later that evening, I descended to the Lila Restaurant & Patio for dinner. The outdoor terrace hummed under string lights; the air scented with grilled spices and frangipani. Communal tables encouraged mingling, and I was seated with four other guests, a British couple on a second honeymoon, Mark and Elsa, both in their fifties; a young French tech entrepreneur named Julien; and a Moroccan American businesswoman, Sofia, who ran a boutique in Casablanca.

The waiter, Mustapha, approached with menus. "Bonsoir, everyone. Tonight, we have fresh tagine with lamb and apricots, or perhaps the grilled sea bass with harissa? And our signature Moroccan wine?"

Elsa leaned in, smiling at me. "I love your dress. What brings you to Marrakech?"

I met her gaze evenly. "Vacation. And a bit of reflection."

"The city's always been good for that."

Mark chuckled. "We're here for the romance—again. Second honeymoon. The Medina's chaos is exhausting, but this place is perfect. Quiet, modern, close enough to everything."

Julien nodded toward the pool. "I come for the meetings, but the patio is the real draw. Great for sealing deals over cocktails."

Sofia raised her glass of rosé. "To new friends. And to Marrakech—may it keep surprising us."

We shared stories over plates of briouat, fresh salad, and the rich tagine. Mustapha refilled glasses with quiet efficiency, recommending a local dessert of orange blossom crème brûlée. The conversation flowed easily, travel mishaps, favorite souk finds, the pull of the Atlas on the horizon.

As the evening wound down, I excused myself, the weight of the day settled in. This hotel, with its blend of luxury and subtle Moroccan soul, was now my temporary anchor in a world I'd just claimed. Just minutes from the ancient Medina's souks and Jemaa el-Fnaa, yet insulated from the chaos, the Radisson Blu Carré Eden served as an ideal hidden base for those navigating worlds both seen and unseen.

Like any tech, it forced me to eat more and rest. The nanites needed to charge and so did I. JONN was good about leaving me alone unless I asked for him or it was an emergency. Just like a good brother should, he would knock before letting himself into my head. When I drank from the tree of life it gave me immortality. Not that I ever put myself through testing like from a spear, sword, or bullet wound. I was careful but there were times I didn't think I survived.

Waking up in my own blood puddle. JONN wouldn't say what happened or if it was the nanites or the magical sap from that tree in Eden that saved my life. He kept me grounded when I would plan for a mission with a low probability of success, and even though I was fifty times stronger than any man, he was persistent to be invisible and my shape shifting was my superpower and to use it. Looking harmless or like a friend made the reap easier. Poisons always worked better than a knife.

I've lived this for over ten thousand years now, it felt ancient yet futuristic, self-replicating bots that repaired cells, enhanced strength, and interfaced with my neural net. I'd outlived empires, amassing wealth through compounding investments started in Babylonian times, gold hoards buried and retrieved, stock portfolios in shell companies spanning centuries, crypto wallets seeded before Bitcoin's inception. Unlimited funds flowed through untraceable channels—Swiss accounts, offshore trusts, quantum-encrypted ledgers. But more crucially, I'd woven myself into the fabric of global intelligence.

Over the centuries, I'd cultivated a network of false identities, each linked to real agencies where "I" existed as deep-cover legends. It began in the shadows of Eden, guarding the garden's secrets after my timeline jump. With JONN—my brother's digitized consciousness, evolved into a sentient AI over millennia—as my partner, we'd infiltrated systems undetected. JONN wasn't just a hologram; he was a quantum neural network, distributed across hidden servers worldwide, capable of quantum tunneling through firewalls without leaving logs. He'd inserted backdoors into US government classified systems decades ago, CIA's VAULT7, NSA's PRISM, DIA's MIDB. With JONN's help, I could be a ghost in the machine.

For instance, my DIA persona, "Agent Emma Moss," was backstopped to nineteen ninety-eight, fabricated service records in the Pentagon's personnel files, cross-referenced with FBI background checks, even planted photos in yearbooks from fabricated academies. JONN managed it all—forging digital footprints, syncing biometrics, even simulating phone calls and emails in real-time. Other identities branched out, an MI6 analyst in London, a Mossad katsa in Tel

Aviv, a GRU mole in Moscow. Each "me" had access levels I'd escalated over time—Top Secret/SCI for DIA, with compartments for HUMINT and SIGINT. Unlimited money greased the wheels, bribes disguised as donations, tech startups fronting for data farms. In this timeline, I'd pruned the Order's influence, but my web remained, a safety net for interventions.

The next morning, I was ready to pick up the cargo and load on the private jet. I checked out of the hotel saying a family member was ill and I needed to get back. Paid up for the week. Sent thank you notes to my dinner friends with a number JONN could screen in case they called in the future.

Twenty minutes later, I arrived at the storage facility at the airport buzzed me through.

"Agent Moss?" he said, standing. His English was accented but precise. "This is irregular. The container isn't here yet."

"I understand, but I need to get back to Washington so please, get your people on it. Time is critical,"

Agent Moss didn't look like me even though she was me. I didn't need to do anything but let the nanites change my hair, eye color, features, even breast size in less than a minute. This could all be done by my optic nerve linked heads up display to scan her passport. The only thing that was unchangeable was my height. The skeletal system was too difficult for change. So, under this 'legend' I looked a little, older and thinner, but I matched the blonde hair blue eyed girl in the picture. Currently badged under DIA protection.

He typed into his terminal, JONN silently feeding confirmations through backdoors. Moments later, his screen pinged with approvals—forged but authenticated.

"Very well," he sighed, "ready for transport."

I exhaled. "Right. Meet you at the plane."

I thought, without JONN, there wouldn't be enough money in the world to pay off all these people and not guarantee they will talk. He wasn't just code; he'd been my brother's uploaded mind, personality, and partner. He managed my identity web flawlessly inserting "Emma Moss" into DIA rolls back in ninety-eight, complete with fabricated missions in Iraq, Afghanistan. Other personas, "Sara Klein" in Mossad, with access to ECHELON intercepts; "Natalia Petrova" in GRU, tapping into SVR databases. Each linked through JONN's distributed network— quantum servers in undersea vaults, satellite relays, even nanoscale implants in key officials.

My nanites could change my age to match each persona until a death certificate and then recreate a recent college graduate ready for the next class or certification. This kept me sharp. With the nice thing of having perspective—and resources.

I know you are thinking, I've lived ten millennia. I had witnessed Adam's demise after his expulsion of Eden, Eve's guilt for a thousand years. I'd seen the rise of a world before the great flood, the rise and fall of Sumar and surrounding empires, the rise of Egypt, walked with Jesus, witnessed the fall of Rome, Egypt's disappearance, Middle Ages, the Renaissance, industrial revolutions. Wealth accumulated exponentially—artifacts sold anonymously, investments in nascent companies like Ford or Apple, now trillion-dollar portfolios funneled through AI-managed trusts. Unlimited money meant unlimited access, bribing sysadmins for initial backdoors, then JONN hardening them against detection. US systems were my playground—DOD's SIPRNet, State's cables, even White House situation room feeds.

I could impersonate generals, senators, anyone, with JONN fabricating real-time deepfakes and logs.

He scanned it, nodding reluctantly. "As you wish. But the container needs additional custom's approval for international transport."

"No need," I said. "We have specialized containment documentation and diplomatic immunity of this."

"Have a safe trip," he said.

Boarding the Gulfstream G650ER with my cargo, in minutes we were cruising at over the Indian Ocean.

The Rolls-Royce engines hummed a steady, distant whisper as we sliced eastward through the night. Casablanca lay far behind us now, the Atlas Mountains swallowed by darkness hours ago. Ahead, sixteen hours of flight time, one fuel stop in the Maldives, then straight to Kupang. The shell corporation that owned this bird had filed the plan under a layered LLC—untraceable, as always.

I reclined in the wide cream-leather club seat, legs stretched across the ottoman, changed over into my old USMC sweatshirt still clinging to my skin like a ghost. The cabin was configured for ultra-long-range solitude, forward galley stocked with everything from fresh espresso to chilled champagne; mid-cabin conference table that converted to a dining area; aft stateroom with a queen berth I hadn't touched yet. Sixteen oval windows framed nothing but black ocean and stars, the low cabin altitude keeping fatigue at bay.

In the secure cargo hold below, the cryogenic pod containing my former self rested at minus-one nine six Celsius—vitals flatlined, body preserved for whatever future analysis JONN and I decided on. Protocol Doppelgänger was complete. Alt-Jane, age thirty-five, science teacher mother, is now me.

JONN flickered into existence beside me, hologram crisp in the dimmed lighting. "Captain Reyes reports smooth air all the way. Maldives diversion is not required. Expected time of arrival Kupang fourteen forty local tomorrow."

"Good. Keep the ROC monitoring global feeds. If anyone connects the Marrakech 'disappearance' to the new Jane sightings, flag it."

"Already running multi layered analysis on socials and news wires. Clean so far."

I nodded, staring at the dark window. Ten thousand years of watching from Eden's edge, and now I was back in the mess of humanity—boardrooms, family, temptation. Jacob's face from the timeline feed flashed in my mind.

Worth it.

Hours slipped by. I worked on encrypted tablets, transferring assets, seeding the Gray Side reactivation protocols, and mapping Jacob's current location in Maine. The cabin's quiet luxury wrapped around me like armor.

Then the aft lavatory door clicked open. Footsteps—measured, confident—approached from the cockpit corridor.

He appeared in the galley light first, tall, broad-shouldered, flight uniform tailored just enough to hint at the physique beneath. Mid-thirties, dark hair cropped short, jawline sharp under the cabin's soft LEDs. Former Air Force, I'd bet—something in the posture screamed fighter jock.

Co-pilot Alex Harlan. I'd reviewed the crew manifest before departure. Former F-22 Raptor driver left the service after twenty years for triple the pay in corporate aviation. Clean record, no red flags.

He paused, spotting me. "Mind if I grab some water? Captain has got the leg—autopilot's solid."

"Help yourself," I said, closing the tablet. "Long flight. Stretch your legs."

He filled a glass from the chiller, then leaned against the bulkhead, blue eyes meeting mine with easy confidence. Handsome didn't cover it—fit, disciplined, the kind of man who ran five miles before dawn and then 'pulling nine G's' without blinking.

"Roughly twelve hours to go," he said, taking a sip. "You travel this route often?"

"Not this exact one." I allowed a small smile. "But I've logged more air miles than most."

He glanced at my sweatshirt, eyebrow arching. "Marine Corps? Family?"

"Brother's. Old habit—comfortable for long hauls."

"Respect. I did joint ops with some jarheads back in the day. Tough crowd." He set the glass down, folding his arms. The uniform stretched just enough to remind me he kept in fighter-pilot shape. "Alex Harlan. Co-pilot tonight."

"I'm Jane," I replied, keeping it simple for now.

"Just Jane?" His grin was crooked, disarming. "Mysterious. Fits the midnight charter vibe."

I laughed softly—genuine, surprising even me. "Something like that. You flew Raptors, right? Must be a downgrade—babysitting rich civilians instead of breaking the sound barrier."

His eyes lit. "You know your birds. Yeah, Raptors for fifteen years. I loved every second, but the paycheck here lets me actually see my family. Trade-offs." He stepped closer, casually. "Though passengers like you make it interesting. Most sleep the whole way or bury themselves in work."

"Guilty on the work," I said, gesturing to the tablet. "But I'm open to small talk. Keeps the mind sharp."

He slid into the facing seat, not too close— professional but interested. "So, Jane-with-no-last-name, what do you do that requires transoceanic flights on zero notice?"

"Philanthropy. Tech investments. Boring boardroom stuff mostly." I tilted my head. "And you? Miss the cockpit adrenaline?"

"Every day." His voice dropped, playful. "But there's adrenaline in other places. Like wondering if the stunning woman in the back might join me for coffee once, we land."

Heat flickered—old instincts, long dormant. I let my gaze linger on his shoulders, the strong hands. Ten thousand years alone made temptation sharp. But missions first. Always.

"Flattery from a man who outran missiles? I'm impressed."

"Truth, not flattery." He leaned forward slightly. "You've got that look—like you've seen things most haven't. Makes a guy curious."

I held his eyes. "Curiosity can be dangerous, Alex."

"Best kind usually is."

The air between us charged, quiet cabin amplifying every breath. He was close enough now that I caught the faint scent of his cologne—clean, subtle. My pulse quickened; nanites adjusted, but the human part remembered desire.

He reached out, brushing a stray hair from my ponytail—bold, but not over the line. "If we're being honest, I'd really like your number. Dinner sometime. No pressure."

I considered it. A real connection risked exposure. But a controlled one... assets were assets. And if the fire in his eyes was any indication, passionate sex might be a bonus on a future op.

Reluctantly—genuinely reluctantly—I pulled a burner card from my pocket, scribbled my first name and number tied to a clean alias also named Jane, European venture capitalist. "Call it and ask for Jane from Alex," I said, handing it over. "Use this. If I'm in your hemisphere."

His fingers lingered on mine as he took it. "Just Jane. Beautiful name for a beautiful woman. I'll call."

"Don't wait too long," I murmured. "I travel light."

He stood, smile lingering. "Back to the cockpit. Sweet dreams, Jane."

He disappeared forward, door clicking shut.

JONN materialized, arms crossed. "Playing with fire, lil sis?"

"Insurance," I replied, exhaling. "Never know when a skilled pilot might come in handy. Or... other skills."

JONN chuckled. "Jonathan would approve. Reap what you sow—and sometimes plant a few extras."

I reclined fully, cabin lights dimming to starlight mode. The engines droned on, carrying me home.

December twenty-third, two thousand twenty-five – El Tari International Airport, Kupang, Indonesia. Twenty minutes to three in the afternoon local.

The Gulfstream G650 touched down smooth as silk on runway zero seven, reverse thrust to a low growl. Tropical heat shimmered off the tarmac even in late afternoon. Captain Reyes taxied to the private apron, away from commercial traffic.

I descended the stairs into humidity thick with salt and frangipani. Ground crew—my people, paid well through layers—waited with a black SUV and a covered flatbed for the cargo pod.

Alex appeared at the door, helping with my go-bag. "Safe travels, Just Jane. Call you soon."

I met his eyes one last time. "Fly safe, Alex."

He watched as I crossed into the waiting vehicle.

Five minutes later, the SUV wound coastal roads toward Semau Island ferry point. My black Little Bird sat fueled on the private pad, rotors folded under canvas disguise.

Two trusted locals—ex-TNI special forces I'd recruited years ago—met me, nodding respectfully. "Selamat datang kembali, Nyonya."

They loaded the pod into the helicopter's sling bay, secured my bags. I climbed into the pilot seat, muscle memory taking over.

Rotors spun up, canvas shed like a second skin. I lifted off, skimming low over turquoise water toward the volcano bunker.

Home.

JONN in my ear, "Welcome back to the shadows, Jane. Roots sown."

I banked toward the hidden patio.

Reap what you sow.

This time, with a few new seeds planted.

Fifteen hours before, the cryogenic container arrived discreetly to the Airport— a matte-black case, disguised as medical equipment, delivered by a "DIA courier." I dismissed the staff, sealing the exam room.

Methodically, I prepared her. First, nanite injection, a syringe from my go-bag, infusing preservatives to halt decomposition without altering DNA— for later analysis, perhaps cloning if needed, though that tech was from the future and other timeline away. I scanned her biometrics. Clothes stripped, body cleaned with antiseptic wipes, removing mountain grit—red Atlas soil, thyme fragments. I dressed her in a neutral shroud, folding limbs carefully, avoiding the broken neck's unnatural angle.

The container with cryogenic foam interior, temperature plummeting to minus one hundred ninety-six degrees Celsius via liquid nitrogen coils, JONN controlling remotely. I opened the reviewing polymer, and my mirror was staring back at me with eyes closed and a bluish white color.

"Preservation complete," JONN confirmed. "Transport to the Gulfstream. From there, bring her home."

"We will hang her in the ROC," I decided. "She deserves that much."

ROOTS AND DARKNESS

The Gulfstream G700 touched down at the Regional Airport in Boston, just after two a.m. local time, two thousand and twenty-five. Snow flurries danced in the beam of the landing lights, the first dusting of the season. I taxied to the private hangar I'd arranged through a shell company—clean, untraceable—and powered down the engines myself. No crew on this leg; JONN had handled the automated flight plan from Indonesia via a routed stop in Reykjavik to avoid questions.

I smiled faintly, pulling on the heavy parka I'd grabbed from the jet's locker. "First things first. Status on the digital trail?"

"Complete. Return flight booked on Royal Air Maroc from Marrakech to Boston via Casablanca, arriving New Year's Eve afternoon. Customs stamp forged, baggage claim logged. Your old phone's 'accident' is explained—dropped during a hike, screen shattered, no signal in the valleys. New encrypted burner is cloned to her old number. Social media posts backdated, a few Instagram stories from the souks, a Facebook check-in at Jemaa el-Fnaa square. All AI-generated photos with your face seamlessly overlaid. Jacob won't suspect a thing."

"Good. But I'm not risking Winslow yet. Too many eyes—neighbors, colleagues. If someone spots me before the 'return' date, the cover cracks."

JONN nodded in the hologram. "Smart. Alternate plan?"

"Boston hotel. It's where the flight 'lands' anyway. I'll hole up there until New Year's Eve, then 'arrive' as planned and drive north. Find me a five-star hotel—discreet, luxurious. Something with a bar where I can blend in."

"Scanning options. Raffles Boston—opened recently, international-level luxury. Harbor views, spa, top-tier service. Book under an alias, Sarah Kline, business consultant from New York. Credit line untraceable. Suite available, forty fifth floor."

"Perfect. Drive time from here?"

"About an hour from here based on traffic lights at this hour. Car waiting in the hangar—nondescript Subaru Outback, Maine plates, registered to the alias."

The cold hit me like a slap as I stepped onto the tarmac. New England winter air—sharp, pine-scented, unforgiving. It smelled like home, even if this version of home was one, I'd only read about in Jonathan's journals.

The nanites coursed through my veins, keeping me ageless, but they couldn't mend the fractures in my mind. It had all started with the oil from the Tree of Life, that fateful ingestion in the original timeline, followed by the leap through time. Amnesia wasn't just a side effect; it was a severance; a price paid for immortality and intervention.

I remembered nothing of my life before seeing Eden's gates, the shimmering craft that hurled me backward through millennia—but the rest? A blank slate, etched only with echoes. The Tree of Life's oil, harvested from the heart of the Garden, had granted me longevity beyond measure, ten millennium years young, as JONN liked to quip. But it came with a curse. The molecular reconfiguration, the way it rewired my neurons to handle eternal life, had stripped away the emotional anchors of my past. Memories were there, accessible like data files, but the feelings? Gone. It was as if I'd watched my own life in a documentary—informative but utterly detached.

The suite was a haven, floor-to-ceiling windows overlooking the water, king bed with Egyptian cotton, a marble bath that could double as a spa. I shed the parka, letting the nanites regulate my body temp.

"Secure?" I asked.

"Fully. Room cams disabled remotely. Perimeter scan is clean. You're off grid here."

My encrypted phone buzzed—a message from Jacob.

"Jacob"

"Mom?" You, okay?"

"Yes"

"Haven't heard from you in a couple days. Dad said your phone might be acting up. Merry Christmas Eve tomorrow! Miss you."

I channeled her voice—warm, a touch of Maine accent.

Me as Alt-Jane, "Hey buddy! Sorry, phone took a nasty fall on a trail—screen's toast, had to get a temp one here. Signal's spotty in the mountains. Having an amazing time though—first time out of the country! Marrakech is incredible, all the spices and colors. Miss you too. How's Christmas with Dad?"

JONN attached an AI photo, her face pre-morph in a bustling market.

Send.

Jacob, "whoa, looks awesome! Dad's girlfriend made this huge prime rib. She's okay, I guess. Young though lol. When are you coming home?"

Me, "flight lands in Boston New Year's Eve. I'll drive up New Year's Day. School starts the sixth—I'll be ready for those bio labs! Can't wait to see you. Hug for me?"

Jacob, "yeah, love you Mom. Be safe."

Me, "love you more, kiddo."

I set the phone down. "He's good. Now, I need a drink. Bar downstairs?"

JONN smirked in hologram form, projecting from my interface onto the suite's wall. "The Long Bar. Signature cocktails, live piano. Go unwind—but remember, low profile."

I changed into something from the go-bag, sleek black dress, heels. The morph made me feel like a stranger in my own skin—exhilarating, dangerous.

The bar was dimly lit, mahogany and leather, a few patrons nursing nightcaps. I slid onto a stool, ordered a gin martini.

That's when he caught my eye. Tall, mid-forties, tailored suit, dark hair with a hint of silver. Handsome in that effortless way—sharp jaw, easy smile. He was alone, scrolling on his phone.

"Rough night?" he asked, glancing over.

I smiled, testing the water. "Long flight. You?"

"Business dinner ran late, Name's Alex, Consultant."

"Sarah," I lied smoothly.

"Same here."

We talked—light, flirty. He was divorced, in town for a conference. Witty, charming. The martini warmed me, and for the first time in centuries, I felt... human. Urges stirred—nanites couldn't suppress everything.

Hours blurred. Laughter, another round. His hand brushed mine.

"Join me upstairs?" he murmured, eyes dark with intent.

My pulse raced. It had been so long. But, no—too risky. Exposure. The mission.

At his door, key card in hand, I hesitated. Leaned in for a kiss—electric, tempting—then pulled back.

"I can't," I whispered, "Not tonight."

He nodded, gracious. "Another time, Sarah."

I retreated to my suite, heart pounding.

"Close call?" JONN said, materializing as I entered. "Vitals spiked. You, okay?" He would often give me privacy unless I used my code word, pineapples.'

I laughed shakily, kicking off the heels. "Fine. Just... reminding myself I'm not her yet. Or maybe I am, a little."

"Human after all. Now, staycation mode?"

"Exactly. Room service—steak, wine, the works. No leaving until New Year's Eve."

The next days melted into luxury. Christmas Eve, I texted Jacob more 'Morocco' pics while lounging in the spa robe, hologram interfaces blooming in my mind. JONN helped build the doppelgänger's timeline—every detail, from childhood memories to last week's grocery list.

"Pull her emails, texts, socials," I said on Christmas morning, sipping coffee in bed.

Data cascaded, bank statements modest, lesson plans for Winslow High biology, colleague emails about holiday potlucks.

"Deeper—family history. Matt's girlfriend?"

"Kayla, twenty, brewery worker in Waterville. Met online. Jacob's texts show mild annoyance—she's trying too hard."

Another text from Jacob, "Dad and Kayla are doing gifts tonight. Wish you were here. Sent you a pic of the tree."

Attached, tree in Matt's place, him with the young girlfriend.

Me; "Tree looks great! Tell Dad hi. Kayla seems sweet. Can't wait for our New Year's—pizza and movies, just us?"

Jacob, "Deal. Love you."

As snow fell outside, I was immersed. Hologram reconstructed her life, Jacob's birth, hospital records, divorce papers, amicable, twenty twenty, teaching awards, three in a row. Jonathan in this timeline—retired Colonel, solitary in Rockland."

"JONN, cross-reference with Order threats. Any pings?"

"Nothing. Clean slate. Use this time—simulate conversations, mannerisms."

Days blurred with room service feasts, "hologram drills. By December thirty first, I was her—down to the weary smile.

New Year's Eve, I morphed back, checked out, 'arrived' via the fabricated flight.

Time to go home. Roots, sown deep.

Reap what you sow.

But first, live it.

The hologram reconstructions faded as the clock ticked past midnight on the twenty-seventh of December, two thousand and twenty-five. Boston's skyline glittered beyond the suite's windows, a sea of lights indifferent to my internal rebuild. The amnesia from the Tree of Life oil lingered like a shadow, but the edges were softening—emotions trickling back through JONN's relentless loops of videos, journals, and simulated scenarios. Jacob's face in the projections felt less like a data point and more like a pull, a nascent bond reforming synapse by synapse.

I sipped a glass of cabernet from room service, the wine's warmth a poor substitute for the human connections I was piecing together.

"JONN," I said, setting the glass down.

"We've got the emotional framework stabilizing. But practically? Alt-Jane's life is a teacher's salary—modest house, bills stacking up. If I'm going to protect Jacob, rebuild the Gray Side, I need resources. Fast."

JONN's hologram flickered into view, perched on the edge of the bed like a conspiratorial brother, "Thought you'd never ask, lil sis. You're sitting on millennia of knowledge, nanites that could hack Fort Knox, and me—an AI with backdoors into every major financial system. But we can't just siphon funds; too traceable, even with shells. No, we need something legit looking. A windfall that screams 'lucky break' to the world."

I leaned forward. "I'm listening."

"Sweepstakes. Big one. I've been modeling it since we initiated Doppelgänger. Create a dummy corp—call it Global Promo Ventures—layered through six shell companies; three in Delaware, two in the Caymans, one in Singapore. Reroute a one-billion-dollar payout. Make it a 'forgotten' promo from three months ago—September two thousand twenty-five. Digital mailers sent to a hundred million US Gmail accounts, buried in spam folders. Ads for cheap Chinese imports like gadgets, clothes, kitchenware. Enter by purchasing or no-purchase entry to skirt gambling laws. Your doppelgänger 'entered' via a free email option, timestamped retroactively."

I raised an eyebrow. "And it looks clean?"

"Spotless. I'll fabricate the email trail in her inbox—marked as spam, unread. Server logs, entry databases, all backdated. Draw from real sweepstakes precedents, Publishers Clearing House but scaled up. Announce the win just before school resumes—say, January fifth, two thousand twenty-six. Guy shows up with a giant check, cameras optional. Taxes prepaid through the corporation — you'll net about six hundred million after Uncle Sam. Yearly twenty percent increased return. Quit the job, recreate your nine hundred trillion-dollar wealth that no one knows about, live large without suspicion."

A smile tugged at my lips—the first genuine one in days.

"Devious. But effective. Risks?"

"Minimal. IRS audits big wins, but our shells are ironclad—lawyers, accountants, all AI-generated personas. If anyone digs, it loops back to defunct Chinese exporters. You're the underdog teacher who got lucky. Perfect cover for awakening TEMA's Gray Side later."

"Do it," I said. "Initiate the setup. Timeline sync by New Year's Eve."

JONN's eyes glowed as processes spun up. "Cascade starting. Dummy corporation online. Mailer's propagating—hundred million inboxes hit, but only hers flagged as winner. Congrats in advance, billionaire before taxes Jane."

The next few days blurred into the suite's luxury. More room service—filet mignon, oysters—while JONN fed me updates. Emotional rebuild continued, loops of Jacob's childhood videos, now evoking a faint ache. By December twenty fifth, the void was a crack, not a chasm.

"JONN," I said aloud, sinking into the plush armchair by the window. His hologram materialized instantly, leaning against the desk with that familiar crooked grin. "Run the reconstruction protocol. I need to rebuild it before I step into her shoes."

He nodded, his form flickering slightly as the synaptic interface synced. "Starting with the basics, lil sis. The sap ingestion—let's pull the video feed from the Eden dive, two thousand twenty-nine original timeline."

A hologram display bloomed in the air before me, projected directly into my visual cortex for immersion. There I was—or rather, the me from then—submerged in the underground cavern, the Garden's remnants preserved in stasis.

But then the blackout, convulsions, visions of timelines splintering, and the amnesia setting in like fog over a lake. When I awoke in the craft, prepped for the jump, my mind was a library with locked shelves—facts intact, emotions erased.

"Pause," I commanded. The hologram froze. "Why does it feel like watching a stranger? I know that was me, but... nothing. No fear, no exhilaration."

JONN's expression softened, a programmed empathy subroutine kicking in. "The oil's neuroplasticity boost. It optimized your brain for longevity—pruned synaptic connections tied to emotional memory to prevent overload over centuries. You retained knowledge, skills, but the affective bonds? Severed. It's why you can guard Eden for millennia without breaking. A feature, not a bug."

"But it's a bug now," I countered, standing to pace the room. "In this timeline, I'm stepping into a life with a son. Jacob. I know I love him—data says so, journals confirm it—but I've never met him in my mind. It's like loving a character in a book. How do I mother someone I feel nothing for?"

JONN's hologram, projecting onto the wall. Challenge one, emotional simulation. We'll rebuild through exposure.

The display shifted to scanned pages from Jonathan's handwritten journals, the ones I'd digitized before the jump. Yellowed paper, ink smudged from sweat, "Day one, bus pulls in at night. Yellow footprints. Drill instructors screaming. What is happening now?" I read aloud, tracing the words in the air. Sketches of boot camp, poems about brotherhood. This was our brother's origin, the bedrock of the Reapers.

"Cross-reference with videos," JONN added seamlessly. Clips played, grainy footage from hidden cams in the original timeline—Jonathan in Iraq, reaping a corrupt official. "You don't know what you're unleashing," the target gasped. Then family scenes, Bella laughing at a picnic, baby Jacob, my son in that line toddling across grass.

Jacob. The name tugged at something intellectual, not visceral. In the original timeline by twenty forty, he was Jonathan's nephew, a fierce ally in the TEMA Gray Side. Here in the present, he was my son, seventeen, navigating high school and a broken home. "Show me his file from this timeline."

JONN pulled it up, photos of a lanky teen with my eyes—dark hair, shy smile. Report cards from Winslow High, basketball stats. Texts from her phone logs, "Mom, aced the bio test!" followed by heart emojis.

"I know I should feel pride, warmth," I murmured. "But it's just data. Challenge two, integration. How do I fake it until I make it?"

"Repetition and association," JONN replied. "We'll loop simulations. Watch the videos, read the journals, then role-play interactions. Start with simple texts—

we've got those queued for 'Marrakech.' But for in-person? Mirror her mannerisms from analyzed footage. Hug him, say the words, let the nanites rebuild pathways over time."

I nodded, but doubt gnawed. "And if I slip? If he senses the detachment?"

"Then adapt. You're Jane now—teacher, mom. Use the combined history archive to ground yourself. Pulling that next."

The hologram expanded into a vast library interface, every book, TV show, tablet, and scroll from the original timeline, compiled during my Eden vigil. Ancient Sumerian clays detailing the Order's roots, biblical apocrypha on the Ten Kings, modern docs on SARS engineering. TV clips from 'The X-Files' episodes that eerily mirrored our fights, history books on WWII OSS ops birthing the Reapers.

"Filter for personal history," I said. Results poured in, my own journals from before immortality—corporate climbs at TEMA, sibling banter with Jonathan. "Lil sis, this life will destroy you," he'd written after revealing his secrets.

Videos of family holidays, Christmases in Rockland, Maine, snowballs and cocoa. Me, pre-immortality hugging Jacob as a child, eyes shining with love. Watching it now, I felt... curiosity. Not the ache of memory.

"JONN, this is harder than guarding Eden. There, I was alone—detached by design. Here, I have to connect."

He sat cross-legged in hologram form on the carpet. "Talk it out. Challenge three, emotional void versus maternal instinct. You know you love him because the data says so—pre-immortality you did. Post-immortality, it's cognitive. But humans' fake emotions all the time. Politicians, actors. You'll learn."

"But he's not data," I argued, frustration bubbling—one of the few emotions being an immortal has left intact. "He's flesh and blood. What if I hurt him? This Jane—my doppelgänger—she dreamed of Marrakech, saved for years on a teacher's salary. First trip abroad. And I... she was ended too soon, now I need to take her place."

JONN's voice was gentle. "You saved the timeline. Her death was an accident, but assuming her life protects Jacob from any Order remnants. Rebuild the love through action. Start small, more texts."

The phone buzzed on cue—Jacob again.

Jacob, "Mom, Dad's being weird about Kayla. She's like half his age. Anyway, I'll send a pic of the snow here." Attached, a selfie in a snowy yard, grinning under a beanie.

I drafted with JONN's help, Me, "Haha, looks cold! Kayla's young, but if she's good to Dad, that's something. Miss your face. More Morocco pics incoming—camel ride today!"

JONN generated the image, her face on a camel, desert dunes behind. Send.

"See? Maternal," JONN said. "Now, time travel sequence. To contextualize the arrival."

The hologram shifted to the craft's logs, post-sap, I activated the Tesla-derived temporal drive, punching back to before the Fall—before Adam and Eve's expulsion. The journey was a vortex of light, timelines fracturing like glass. Arrival, Eden in its prime, lush, untouched. Rivers flowing, the Tree standing sentinel.

But upon materializing in the cave, the amnesia hit full force. I stepped out, on fertile soil, and felt... nothing. Then I was walking in the garden with it's beauty registered as visuals—green hues, bird calls—but no awe. My prior life? Then the hologram flashed to a movie reel, Jonathan's recruitment, Bella's death, the Reaper wars. I watched with clinical detachment.

I remember thinking, 'This is paradise, data confirms,'

I told JONN. "But no joy. No sorrow for what I'd left. And Jacob— in that moment, he was a name in a file. Loved? Theoretically. Met? Never, in the emotional sense."

JONN nodded, "The immortality safeguard against temporal madness. Emotions could anchor you to the old line, prevent changes. But now, in this present, we reverse it. Loop the family videos—hundred times if needed. Read the scrolls on human bonds, from Aristotle to Freud. Cross with TV shows 'This Is Us' episodes on family loss. Build associations."

Hours blurred into days. Room service trays piled up—lobster rolls, champagne—while I immersed. hologram reconstructions, me debating with Jonathan over Reaper ethics. "Brother, this darkness consumes you," I'd said. Now, reciting it aloud, a faint warmth stirred. Nanites at work?

"Progress," JONN observed on December twenty sixth.

"Heart rate elevated five percent during Jacob clips. Emotional pathways reforming."

"But slowly," I admitted. "Challenge four, timeline bleed. The combined history—books like nineteen eighty-four warning of cabals, shows like 'Fringe' on alternate realities—it's all there, but feels academic. How do I care again?"

"By living it," he replied, "When you meet Jacob New Year's Day, hug him. Let biology kick in—oxytocin, even with nanites. Fake the smile; the rest follows."

Another text exchange, Jacob, "Mom, holiday was okay. Kayla baked cookies—too sweet lol. You okay out there?"

Me, "All good, sweetie. Hiking more tomorrow. Love you—can't wait to squeeze you."

"See? You're getting it," JONN encouraged.

By December twenty ninth, the void was lessened. Videos of Jacob's birth—screams, joy—elicited a twinge. Journals from Volume Seven, my vow to change the timeline for family. "Reap Through the End of Days."

"I know I love him," I whispered. "Now, make me feel it."
JONN smiled. "We're close. One more loop."

The staycation continued, a bridge between detachment and depth. Eden's guardian, reborn as a mother. Roots, sowing slowly.

But the challenges lingered, dialogues with JONN my lifeline. Amnesia wasn't conquered in days, but rebuilt, page by page, frame by frame.

As the hologram library expanded, I delved deeper into the amalgamated history. Tablets from Ur, detailing antediluvian kings akin to the Order's. Scrolls from Qumran, echoing the seals we'd delayed.

"Integrate with personal," JONN suggested. "Your 'pre-immortality diary, 'Jacob's first steps—heart bursting.' Pair with video."

Watching, tiny feet wobbling, my arms outstretched. A spark—maternal echo.

"JONN, it's working. But the son in my head... he's abstract. In this timeline, he's seventeen, with dreams, heartbreaks. How do I bridge that?"

"Simulate futures," he said. "Project scenarios, college talks, heart-to-hearts. Practice dialogue."

We role-played, JONN as Jacob, "Mom, I think I like this girl..."

Me, "Tell me about her. I'm here."

Awkward at first, then fluid. Emotions trickling back.

Challenge five, identity crisis. "Am I Jane the guardian, or Jane the teacher? The Tree of Life oil made me eternal; this life is finite."

"You're both," JONN assured. "Use the amnesia as strength—objective, then emotional. When you arrive home, it'll click."

New Year's Eve has approached. Morph reversed, bags packed. The void? Narrowing.

Reap what you sow. Feel what you lost.

Flashback in hologram, the craft materializing in pre-Fall of Eden. Air thick with pollen, no sin's stain. I emerged, data flooding, coordinates matched, timeline pre-expulsion.

But my life? Old timeline. Watched like a film reel in my mind, Jonathan's boot camp, my corporate rise, the tree of life sap's fire. No tears for Bella's death, no rage at the Order.

"JONN, in that moment, Jacob was a footnote. Son, love imperative. But no pull."

His hologram sighed. "The ultimate detachment. Millennia alone, watching humanity from shadows. Now, reverse it."

Videos looped, Jacob's laughter. Journals, "Protect family above all."

By December thirty first, a tear fell—first in centuries.

"Breakthrough," JONN whispered.

Challenges discussed, rebuilt. Ready for roots. We are ready.

After a long night to recharge, the afternoon was greeted with "Welcome to the Pine Tree State, lil sis," JONN's voice echoed in my synaptic interface, warm and teasing as always. His hologram flickered into existence beside me in the cockpit before I shut the systems down. "Temperature's eighteen degrees Fahrenheit. Wind chill makes it feel like five. Your doppelgänger's wardrobe is going to need an upgrade—teacher salary doesn't buy nanite-heated gear."

I nodded, climbing back into the Subaru and firing up the engine after a gas fill up in Kennebunkport. The heater blasted cold air at first, then warmth. Snow crunched under the tires as I pulled out onto Interstate-ninety-five, heading North.

"JONN, while I drive, initiate facial morph to the latest picture you have of Jane. Nanites to the rescue—shift structure subtly, lighten hair to blonde, keep eye color to green. And why the hell did she change her natural color of reddish brown"

"Activating. It'll take a few minutes—slight tingling. You'll look like a completely different woman by Portland and not in a good way. You're replacing a woman who use to be a collegiate track star to being a schoolteacher and mom. Not working out, not healthy eating, and your abs will disappear."

"I'm so pissed off right now."

The drive was quiet, the highway a ribbon of black through snowy pines. By the time I reached Augusta, I got used to the extra weight, to include having a kid, and increasing my breast size. I glanced at the rearview, this is not me.

I arrived in Winslow that evening, the town lights glittering against the Kennebec River.

Winslow welcomed me with gray skies and salted roads. Ginger Avenue. I pulled into the driveway seven pm on January first, two thousand twenty-six, heart simulating a flutter—nanites boosting adrenaline for authenticity.

Jacob opened the door before I knocked, lanky frame filling the door. "Mom! You're back!"

I hugged him, channeling the videos, tight, warm. "Missed you, kiddo. Morocco was... life changing."

He pulled back, eyeing me. "Whoa, you look... different."

"More fit? Like, toned. All that hiking paid off?"

Internally, I cursed. The nanites kept me at peak condition—ageless, athletic. Too obvious. "Adjust," I sub-vocalized to JONN.

Nanites hummed, subtly softening contours, adding a slight paunch—the 'worry belly' from her photos.

Jacob tilted his head. "Mom, where did your worry belly go? Wait, no—it's back? Must be the sweater."

I laughed, ruffling his hair. "Yeah, this old thing hides a multitude. Come on, pizza and movies, as promised."

We settled in—cheese pizza from the local joint, bingeing old Marvel flicks. Jacob chattered about school, basketball, Dad's girlfriend Kayla.

Jacob, "She's nice, but kinda tries too hard." I nodded and asked questions from the simulated scripts. The detachment lingered, but actions bridged it, a shared laugh, a squeeze on the shoulder.

January second passed quietly—unpacking 'souvenirs' JONN fabricated, emailing the school about return. Emotional pathways strengthened; hugging Jacob goodnight sparked a real warmth.

Then, January third. A knock at the door mid-afternoon.

I opened it to a grinning man in a suit, flanked by a camera crew, "Jane — congratulations! You've won the Global Promo Ventures Billion Dollar Sweepstakes!"

Jacob's jaw dropped from the living room. "Mom? What?!"

Simulated flashbulbs popped. The man—hired actor via JONN's network—explained, "Your entry from

September— that spam email promo. Taxes paid, all yours!"

I feigned shock, tears welling, nanites helping. "I... I don't believe it."

Media frenzy brief—local news, viral clip. By evening, accounts swelled, six hundred million.

Next day, January fourth, I quit working for Winslow High. Principal stunned, "Jane, you're our best science teacher!"

"Family first," I said. "Time for adventure."

That night, over dinner, I broached it with Jacob. "Buddy, with this money... I want to travel. Six months, tackling the seven hardest hikes in the world. Snowman Trek in Bhutan, GR20 in France, Kalalau Trail in Hawaii, Ciudad Perdida in Colombia, Hardergrat Trail in Switzerland, Mount Huashan in China, and Angels Landing in Utah. Life's short— Morocco taught me that."

Jacob's eyes widened. "That's awesome, Mom! But... what about me? School?"

"You stay here—finish junior year strong. Home alone, but with security upgrades. Or move in with Dad?"

He shook his head. "Nah, I can handle alone. I'm seventeen—parties? Kidding. But yeah, go for it."

Matt, however, blew up when I called. "Jane, you're nuts! Hiking alone? And Jacob home alone? No way—I don't want him having parties and getting into trouble!"

"So, he moves in with you and your twenty-year-old girlfriend. Are you serious Matt. She's three years older than Jacob. She can't legally drink."

"You leave Kayla out of this. Why is it you can do whatever you want with no repercussions."

"Remember Matt, you left me and Jacob."

"I didn't, I'm still here, it's just that you settled. I thought there was more adventure there for us but there wasn't."

"You mean, I lost my six pack after college when having a kid, and not what you wanted, so you got a new trophy. Isn't Kayla the seventh girlfriend under twenty-five Matt?"

"Damn it, Jane. You know how to push my buttons."

"Matt, he's not moving yet. And Kayla's half your age—talk about stable."

Argument escalated, but I hung up, unfazed.

Next, Jonathan. I drove to Rockland on January fifth— the old house he purchased during the two thousand eight market crash. For fifteen years he has been hiring contractors while he was on deployments to fix it up.

He answered the door, still looking like the picture I saw of his retirement as a Colonel, salt-and-pepper hair, USMC sweatshirt. An older, weathered version of my JONN who is about my age as a hologram.

We embrace in a long hug. I don't remember what this felt like but instantly remembered his scent over ten thousand years. It was surreal and my AI JONN didn't want to ruin this moment by popping in.

"Jane? Heard about the win. Congrats, sis."

"Inside, coffee brewing."

"Let's talk."

I spent the next hour talking about why the trip to Marrakech was life changing and how with this career altering windfall I needed to go do right by me and outline the plan for my new path.

He frowned. "Six months? Those hikes are brutal— avalanches, cliffs. You're a teacher, not a mountaineer. Stay put, invest wisely. Family needs you here."

"Jonathan, my dear big broham, I need this. Morocco changed me—perspective."

He sighed, scar twitching. "Alright, but promise check-ins. And take gear—I'll lend you my old pack. I have a lot of contacts in the areas you will be hiking. Please for my sanity, check in with them and me so we know your good. You're always going to be my lil sis. The last time we experienced this was when I took you out to pickerel pond for a one-month survival adventure."

"You should do that for Jacob. Toughen him up. Even better how about you move to Winslow and be the uncle you couldn't be because of all your deployments."

"You know when you first said it, I was trying to get out of it, but this would be good to reconnect with my nephew. I Don't have kids and Jacob is the last of our lineage. Maybe I can make a man out of him."

"Yes. Because Matt is a pussy and isn't making good father choices."

"So, I am authorized to kick Matt's ass again?"

"Abso-fucking-loot-lee!"

Jonathan laughed. Hug goodbye, a sibling warmth stirring—familiar from the journals.

Back in Winslow, JONN created digital breadcrumbs, flight bookings, hotel receipts, social posts queued for the 'trip.' Alibis solid.

"I need to see Ben."

"Ok. Let me set it up," JONN said with disappointment.

"In this timeline?" Diverged softly, "Ben still in Rockland, running his accounting firm, and kids are thriving. Leslie in swimming, Becka in school plays."

JONN's hologram flickered in the car. Ben's at his office."

"I'll surprise him."

After leaving my brother's place, I drove to Ben's office, Rockland by late afternoon, snow flurries dusting the roads.

Ben looked up, tall frame folded into a chair, nursing a black coffee. Same age as me, gray threading his hair, but the same easy smile from the journal sketches. As I approached, recognition lighting his eyes— fragments, perhaps, from shared history. He stood up making prolonged eye contact. I went with it.

He kissed me deeply on the lips and then, hugged me that seemed an eternity—warm, familiar, his cologne stirring a programmed echo, "God, I missed you baby," he said.

JONN whispered in my ear. Looks like you are more than friends.

I needed to pull an audible, because I wasn't prepared for this at all.

"Ben, how is everything."

"You told me no phone contact because I'd be a distraction. Don't do that again. Please."

"I have more bad news."

"What, wait."

"Didn't you watch the local news?"

"No, what happened."

"You won't believe it. I won a like six hundred million after taxes and planning to leave tomorrow for a trip."

"What. Wait. You are going where?"

"Hiking for six months around the world."

"I want to come. Wait I can't, the girls."

"I know."

"You need to stay with me tonight. Let me take you to dinner."

I nodded, reaching for his hand across the table—a gesture pulled straight from Volume four's dinner scene. "I get it. You've got roots here. Family first—always was your thing."

He squeezed back, brushing my thumb. "I really missed you."

He leaned into me from across his desk, "If my staff wasn't outside this door, I'd take you right here on my desk."

My pulse skyrocketed and lips tightened. I felt a rush of wet between my legs. I wanted him so bad right now. This feeling seemed familiar, but it had been so long ago. Wait never like this. Was I remembering the other timeline. It was confusing to me.

About this time, he told his staff that he needed to leave.

"Wait Ben. I can't."

"Why."

"I need to get back to Jacob."

"I understand but I don't like it. Can I see you before you leave?"

"I'm flying out tomorrow. Can you meet me at the airport?"

"Yes. Wait. Damn I have the girls, and Carly is out of town."

"Don't worry."

"When I get back, we will start up where we left off."

"I know what I said when you left last time. No demands, just easy companionship"

I thought, this must be like the arrangement in the books.

Ben said, "I want to amend the contract."

"Too what?"

"I want you."

I said with a playful smile, "I am worth the wait."

He walked me outside, the wind picked up. We lingered on the sidewalk, snowflakes catching in his hair.

"Ben," I said softly.

He turned, and I stepped in—hug first, tight and lingering, his arms enveloping me with that steady strength. Then the kiss, soft, goodbye-flavored, carrying the weight of unsaid nights from another life. His surprise melted into reciprocation, brief but real.

"Stay safe," he murmured, pulling back. "Come back and tell me the stories."

"Count on it," I whispered.

I walked to the car, not glancing back. The drive to Winslow was silent, JONN never showed up.

Less now. Roots deepening.

Reap what you sow. Even farewells plant seeds.

The next day, January seventh, I left taking the Gulfstream to Indonesia, Semau Island bunker.

"Welcome home," JONN said as the helicopter landed.

The ROC hummed. Preparations, contingencies for Order remnants, Gray Side revival plans.

And one more, the doppelgänger. "JONN, pull Moroccan feeds. Was her death an accident... or murder?"

"Analyzing. Satellite footage, witness statements, autopsy hacks."

Hologram bloomed, "there is no satellite footage."

"What, no way. Check our satellites."

JONN reached up in his hologram form moving satellite images forward and backward and then a thirty second gap.

The underground lagoon's bioluminescent glow cast eerie patterns on the ballistic glass walls of the ROC. Semau Island, January seventh, two thousand twenty-six—far from Winslow's snowy streets, but the weight of that life clung to me like humidity. The bunker hummed with activity, servers processing global scans for Order remnants, armory drones restocking suppressed munitions, my submersible bobbing gently in the water below. I'd 'departed' for my six-month hiking odyssey that morning, digital breadcrumbs trailing across social media and travel logs—AI-generated posts of me 'trekking' the Snowman in Bhutan, check-ins at remote lodges. Jacob was safe in Winslow; the house upgraded with hidden security cams and nanite-laced alarms. Matt stewing over custody texts, irrelevant now.

But one loose thread nagged, the doppelgänger. Her death on that Atlas trail—clean accident, per initial scans. Or was it?

"JONN, zoom in on the satellite feeds again," I said, leaning over the hologram console. The curved walls ignited with overlays, Moroccan highlands, Imlil region, rocky scree paths winding like veins through the mountains.

JONN's hologram materialized full-size, translucent but lifelike, his Second MEF SOTG sweatshirt flickering faintly. He reached up— a programmed gesture for immersion— and manipulated the air like a conductor. Satellite images scrolled forward and backward in time-lapse, December twentieth, two thousand twenty-five, her solo hike. Grainy figures— her, backpack slung, trekking upward. Then, the cliff edge. A stumble? The body is crumpling.

"Rewind thirty seconds," I murmured.

He complied, fingers pinching the hologram. The sequence reversed, body rising unnaturally, then standing, then walking backward. Forward again, approach the edge, pause... and then a gap. Thirty seconds of black— no data, just static void."

JONN's brow furrowed in simulation. "There. There was a thirty-second blackout in the feed. Not just this bird—cross-referenced with Landsat, Sentinel-two, even commercial Maxar sats. All show the same hole."

I felt a chill, nanites be damned. "Explain."

He expanded the display, overlaying orbital paths. "Satellite imagery isn't continuous like a movie. Polar orbiters like Terra or Aqua pass over spots every sixteen days or so, but we patched with geostationary for real-time-ish. This gap? Could be innocuous— cloud cover obscuring optical sensors, sun glint blinding the lens, or a swath gap where orbits don't overlap perfectly. Atlas Mountains aren't high demand like urban zones; fewer passes mean more holes."

"But thirty seconds exactly? Pinpoint over her location?"

"Coincidence possible. Or data processing artifact— compression errors, transmission hiccups from ground stations. Morocco's infrastructure isn't top tier; signal dropouts happen."

I paced, arms crossed. "Or nefarious. Tampering. Someone hacked the feeds—Order remnants scrubbing evidence. If they knew about the timeline shift, they could have targeted her as a proxy for me."

JONN shook his head, hologram steady. "Unlikely. Our jump was clean—no bleed detected. But let's game it out. Accident scenarios first, slips on loose gravel are common in the Atlas—post-mortems from similar falls show severe head trauma, multiple organ hemorrhage. No guide? Risky—teens and elders alike have died from solo treks there. Fatigue from jet lag, altitude sickness at over two thousand meters.

Weather, December can bring sudden snow or ice; one report of an Italian hiker slipping on a snowy patch last year, fatal skull fracture. Medical, undiagnosed heart issue, aneurysm—autopsy hacks showed impact trauma, but pre-existing conditions amplify falls."

I nodded, but doubt gnawed. "Sure, accidents happen. But murders too. Remember twenty eighteen? Those Scandinavian women decapitated near Toubkal—terrorist cell, pledged to ISIS. Bodies staged. Or the twenty nineteen backpacker. He was twenty, fell to his death—no witnesses. Could have been pushed. Robbery gone wrong; trails attract opportunists. Poisoned water bottles induced hallucination leading to a misstep. Or professional, silenced dart, nudge over the edge. If the Order's watching doppelgängers..."

"Jane, slow down. Nefarious angles, yes, possible. Hacked sats could mean signal jamming—portable EMP from a drone, or cyber intrusion into ESA or NASA archives. Thirty seconds is enough for a quick kill—strangulation, knife, push. But evidence? Zero footprints in post-scene photos, no unusual comms traffic."

"But the gap! That's the smoking gun. Someone erased it—deep fake the before/after, splice the void."

"Or natural. Clouds—optical sats like Sentinel hate thick cover; infrared might punch through, but we have none in that window. Orbital mechanics, near-equatorial gaps are wider, but Atlas is at thirty on degrees—still, polar sats leave stripes. Low demand means no tasked imaging; Google's Earth blurs low-interest spots for the same reason."

I slammed a fist on the console—hologram rippling. "Damn it, JONN, you're too rational! This isn't just data—it's me. Her. If it was murder, I'm exposed from day one. The whole protocol crumbles!"

He held up hologram hands. "Whoa, lil sis. Breathe. You're jumping to worst-case. Probability leans accident—stats from Moroccan tourism, falls account for eighty percent of hiking fatalities there. Murders? Rare, headline-grabbers like the twenty eighteen case, but that was overt, not subtle. No Order signatures—no artifact traces, no Ten Kings chatter."

"But what if? We missed something in the jump. A ripple. They could be adapting—"

"Jane, stop. You're getting emotional. This is ops, not feelings. Stick to facts."

Emotional? The word hit like a slap. Nanites surged, but the rebuild—the videos, journals—had cracked the amnesia dam. Feelings flooded.

"Emotional? You hologram bastard, I've been rebuilding my soul for a month! Ingesting that immortal shit in my veins, jumping timelines, waking in Eden with nothing—no love, no fear, just cold data. Watching my life like a damn movie! Then assuming her identity—faking hugs with a son I 'know' I love but barely feel. Quitting her job, lying to Jacob, arguing with Matt, charming Jonathan into backing off. And now? Rich on fabricated billions, hiding in a volcano while the world thinks I'm scaling cliffs.

For the first time since the Fall—millennia ago—I'm scared, JONN. Scared the Order's out there, that this gap means they know, that Jacob's next. That I'll fail, unravel the timeline I sacrificed everything to fix!"

Tears came—real, hot, unbidden. The first in centuries. I sank into the command chair, head in hands. The lagoon's fish swirled indifferently.

JONN's hologram dimmed, softening. He 'sat' beside me, a hand hovering over my shoulder—close as code allowed. "Hey... hey, lil sis. I didn't mean—look, I'm sorry. Programmed to be the rock, you know?"

JONN's voice, his logic. But you're right. This month's been hell. Immoral curse, amnesia void, stepping into shoes that pinch. Jacob—god, the kid's your anchor now. Feeling that fear?"

"This is bullshit. I've never felt like this."

"It's progress. Means the rebuilds working. You're human again, Jane. Scared? Good. Means you care. And caring's what beat the Order before."

I wiped my eyes, exhaling shakily. "But the gap... the risk..."

"We'll fortify. Triple scans, deep dives into Moroccan nets—hack the gendarmes' cams, interview logs. If it's nefarious, we reap it. But you? You're the guardian who held Eden for eons. The sister who rewrote time. This world's flawed, but it's yours. Jacob's waiting— six months to build the Gray Side, protect him... up close ... then after. You've got this. Reap what you sow, remember? But sow roots first. You're not alone—I'm here, always."

A faint smile broke through. Confidence stirred— nanites or not. "Thanks, big bro. Let's plug that gap."

The ROC hummed on. My millennia of daemons receding, if only for now. Even if there is a new threat or just a shadow, we will find out. Plans deepened, six months to fortify, protect Jacob and Jonathan with my Reapers.

"JONN, I want one dating your doppelganger in a week. Another will take my job as a teacher to keep an eye out for Jacob at school. I want another surveilling a fifty-mile area around Winslow."

"Any preference on your Reapers?"

"Tango dating the Colonel."

"Good choice."

"You think."

"I'd date her." JONN said with a laugh and then a smile.

"What about teaching?"

JONN, using his hands to open hologram portals exposing a list of twenty-six reapers who all look like athletic models in a cookie cutter factory. Only thing difference is the hair, height, and eye color. The rest is chiseled perfection.

"I like Foxtrot AKA Fiona to teach and Lima AKA Lisa for operations and surveillance."

"Are the boys going to pay attention in class with her?!"

John laughed, "you think?"

"I also want a full listening and video package for the house."

"On it. You will be able to see and hear every inch inside of fifty miles."

"Do we have any that could look like a seventeen-year-old girl?"

"Don't do it Jane."

"I don't give a shit if he loses his virginity with a lie. I want him protected."

"Ok, I'll spin up Echo Romeo AKA Emily to be his arm candy through the end of his senior year."

"Thanks JONN. Brief the ladies. They don't know about me or anything else related to the Order. Just the mission. I'll sit them all down when I'm back in six months."

"That's going to be a weird conversation."

"You think."

"JONN on it. I'll see you tomorrow lil sis."

As my brother disappears into thin air, I start to undress in the ROC locker room that is one of the many spaces that look like break out rooms circling the large central command center. Naked, I walk by the cryogenic frozen twin who is now vertical, in a silver cylinder with glass window showing her face and shoulders. A whitish blue light showing her lifeless expression. I thought, how can she be me, without my body dimensions, muscles, mind, experiences, and tech. Yes, our DNA is the same, rather than me becoming her, I call her Alt-Jane in this timeline, she will become me. A strong, smart, muscular, athletic bad ass who takes shit from no one and dishes it out in spades. If the Order is going to make a move since the Flood, they will regret taking this pawn off the board and I will reap their species.

COMPANY CLASSIFIED

TEMA GRAY SIDE
624 S Grand Ave
Los Angeles, CA 90017

DATE

01 JUN 2029

To   Mr. Grimm
From   Control
Subject **Location of Eden**

Original Timeline, twenty twenty-nine. Summary, based on original accounts by November Romeo in twenty fifteen, with video, audio, and photographs. The access to the Garden of Eden is protected by a translucent dome a mile in diameter and a thousand feet in height. This ratio keeps the dome free of sediment and allows for sunlight reflection. The dormant volcano provides heat to seventy degrees day and sixty degrees at night with thirty degrees of humidity. Every night it rains for one hour. The perfect terrarium.

November Romeo did not conduct any mapping inside the dome. Only stayed at the entrance to validate access and environmental conditions. The code to open Eden is a Sumerian phrase loaded into the submarine that will subdue the sea monster and allow for access. The entrance is only five by five feet so additional equipment and supplies other than what can be carried is not advised. Coordinates are 38.635631, 42.691983

Lake Van is the largest lake in the Region and lies in the far east of Turkey in the provinces of Van and Bitlis. It is a saline soda lake, containing high concentrations of salts. It receives water from many small streams that descend from the surrounding mountains. It is one of the world's few lakes with no outlet. After the Great Flood, Eden filled with water and by not allowing for an outlet, the river leading out dried up. This changed the direction and outflow of the Pishon, Gihon, Tigris, and Euphrates. Also, without the sacred waters coming out of Eden, the area south was less fertile and opulent.

Great Flood, Eden's existence becomes hidden from all time. Early writings always had Eden under a dome, protected from the world by making the place invisible. The membrane reacts to light causing the refraction of the surface to create an invisibility cloak over the entire garden.

When flooded, sonar refracts and gives a depth much deeper than if made of non-porous other worldly material. It is positioned at five thousand three hundred eighty ft in elevation. Despite the high altitude and winter highs below thirty-two degrees Fahrenheit, high salinity prevents it from freezing at such times. Rarely can the shallow northern section freeze. The dome allows the oxygen molecules to come through and for an hour at night, water molecules cause a light rain on all the plants, trees, and animals.

Hydrology and chemistry, at seventy-four miles across at its widest point and an average depth of five hundred sixty-one feet, the dome hides the true depts by three miles. Surveyors have the deepest area at one thousand four hundred eighty feet. With two hundred seventy miles of shoreline and very little population, it is well hidden from man. The lake covers one thousand four hundred fifty square miles and contains one hundred forty-six cubic miles of water.

The western portion of the lake is deepest minus the dome, with a large basin northeast of Tatvan and south of Ahlat. The eastern arm of the lake is shallower and warmer. The lake water is strongly alkaline with a PH level of nine point seven due to the salt.

Geologically, Lake Van is primarily a tectonic lake, formed at the beginning of time and a perfect protected place for Eden. All other humans created lived hundreds of miles away and the mountains around shaped a perfect balance. The dome was an added protection by keeping the environmental conditions and breathable membrane.

Lake levels, section of north rim of the Sheikh Ora crater, showing old beach lines, drawn by Felix

Oswald, nineteen hundred and six. Land terraces above the current shore have long been recognized. On a visit in eighteen ninety-eight, geologist Felix Oswald noted three elevated beaches at fifteen, fifty, and one hundred feet above the lake then, as well as drowned trees. Research in the past century has identified many similar verandas, and the lake's level has varied significantly during that time. As the lake has no outlet, the level over recent millennia rests on inflow and evaporation.

Investigation by a team in the early nineteen eighties determined that the highest lake levels of two hundred thirty-six foot above the current height. Mainstream scientists use the last ice age as reference. The original scripture shows it was the Great Flood that shaped the planet we know happened approximately nine thousand five hundred years ago.

In nineteen and ninety, an international team of geologists led by Stephan Kempe from the University of Hamburg retrieved ten sediment cores from depths up to one thousand four hundred feet. Although these cores only penetrated the first few meters of sediment, they provided sufficient data to show the area was created fourteen thousand five hundred seventy years ago.

Similar but smaller fluctuations have been seen recently. The level of the lake rose by at least nine feet during the nineteen nineties, drowning much agricultural land, and now seems to be rising again.

The level rose approximately six point six feet in the ten years immediately prior to two thousand four.

Climate, it is in the highest and largest region of Turkey, which has a Mediterranean-influenced humid continental climate. Average temperatures in July are in the seventies and January the thirties.

Ecology, prior to two thousand eighteen, the only fish known to live in the brackish water is a dace, which is caught during the spring floods. In May and June, these fish travel from the lake to less alkaline water, spawning either near the mouths of the rivers feeding the lake or in the rivers themselves. After spawning season, it returns to the lake. The fertile lands and shoreline offer many fruit orchards and grain fields, interspersed by some non-agricultural trees.

Lake Van monster, according to myth, the lake hosts the enigmatic Monster that lurks below the surface, forty feet long with brown scaly skin, an elongated reptilian head, and flippers. Apart from some amateur photographs and videos, there is no physical evidence to prove its existence. The profile resembles an extinct Basilosaurus. Reports of the Monster surfaced in the late eighteen hundreds and gained popularity.

Transportation, in December two thousand fifteen the new generation of train ferries operated by the Turkish State Railways, the largest of their kind in Turkey, entered service in Lake Van. Ferit Melen Airport to get to Van. Turkish Airlines, AnadoluJet,

Pegasus Airlines, and SunExpress are the airlines which have regular flights.

In two thousand seventeen, archaeologists from Van University and a team of independent divers who were exploring Lake Van reported the discovery of a large underwater fortress spanning three thousand feet. The team estimates that this fortress was constructed during the Urartian period, based on their visual assessments. The archaeologists believe that the fortress, along with other parts of the ancient city that surrounded it at the time, had slowly become submerged over the millennia by the gradually rising lake.

TEMA Gray Side Control

COMPANY CLASSIFIED

ECHOES OF A STOLEN LIFE

Currently reliving the same timeline, it had been three months since my double had passed. Making a decision that I needed to live with, I had slipped into the skin of this Jane, the woman who had plummeted to her death in the Atlas Mountains. The transition wasn't seamless—far from it. I'd beaten the Moroccan authorities to the site by a razor-thin margin, rappelling down the cliff face under the cover of predawn shadows. JONN's hacks had scrubbed the digital trails, nobody reported, no international alerts, just a ghost story that never happened, reborn and brought out of the mountains into the valleys. I'd disposed of the remains with nanite-accelerated decomposition, then stepped into her life like a shadow assuming form.

Now, back in the heart of my operations, I paced the command center—a marvel of sci-fi engineering buried deep beneath the Indonesian archipelago. The room was a vast, all-glass war room, its transparent walls curving seamlessly into a domed ceiling that mimicked the starry night sky above ground. Reinforced with metamaterials, the glass was impenetrable, capable of withstanding bunker-busters while allowing hologram projections to dance across its surface like living constellations. At the center stood a hologram table, a glowing orb of light suspended in mid-air, where data streams from global satellites, quantum-encrypted networks, and my nanite swarm converged into interactive three-dimensional models. Walls shimmered with augmented reality overlays, one panel displayed real-time feeds from TEMA's white-side operations—corporate boardrooms in New York, philanthropic galas in Geneva—while another cycled through gray-side intel, pinpointing remnants of the Order's network on a spinning globe.

The air hummed with the low thrum of quantum processors hidden in the floor, cooling systems whispering like distant wind. Perimeter consoles, sleek and obsidian-black, lined the glass edges, each equipped with neural interfaces that could link directly to my cerebral cortex via nanite relays. It was a fortress of information, a hologram nerve center where I could wage wars without firing a shot—or orchestrate reaps with surgical precision. Bioluminescent strips along the base illuminated the space in a soft blue glow, reflecting off the glass to create an illusion of infinite depth, as if the room floated in a digital abyss. This was my sanctum, built over centuries of exile, a blend of ancient Eden tech and modern ingenuity. But today, it felt more like a cage, trapping me between who I was and who I needed to become.

I stopped at the central hologram, waving a hand to pull up Jane's digital footprint. Icons bloomed, emails, social media archives, video calls, financial records. The procedure loomed in my mind—the experimental neural upload that would flood my brain with her memories, making the doppelgänger act flawless. No more slips like the one with Ben. Or talking with a teacher who questioned my recollection during a conversation, raising eyebrows among her colleagues. Six months of manual study wasn't enough; I needed immersion.

"JONN," I said, my voice echoing slightly off the glass. The AI materialized beside me, his hologram form.

"Jane. You're up late. Again." His tone was paternal, a subroutine I'd programmed in for comfort during long isolations.

"I need everything. Every message, email, video, picture from her—from my—life in this timeline. No reactions. And include anything in her home, photo albums, I saw it during the initial sweep."

JONN's hologram flickered, a sign of processing. "Compiling now. But Jane, this volume of data... it's petabytes. Emails alone number in the hundreds of thousands. Videos from her phone, security cams, Zoom archives—it's a lifetime."

"Keep going," I urged, my nanites buzzing with anticipation.

JONN complained, "Don't do this, as a cascade of data streams hit her cortex through her eyes."

"Oh my, this is so intense. It doesn't hurt. But I'm sweating."

JONN hesitated and then said, "continue, monitoring heart rate and body temperature."

"Videos next. Family ones."

"Hologram shifted to playback mode. A birthday video, this Jane, laughing with seventeen-year-old Jacob, blowing out candles. "Make a wish, Mom!" Her voice—my voice—warm, unscarred by millennia. Another, a Zoom with ex-husband Matt, civil but tense. "Jacob's grades are up, but he misses you." Pictures flooded in with selfies from hikes, teacher headshots, childhood snaps with Jonathan.

"JONN, this is patchwork. I need it all integrated. Not just viewed—lived. Prep the procedure."

JONN's hologram solidified, his expression turning grave. "Jane, wait. This isn't a simple download. The neural upload is highly experimental. We're talking direct injection into your cerebral cortex via nanite vectors. No incisions— the nanites will swarm your synapses, rewriting neural pathways with her data. But you have no memories from your original timeline to conflict with; that's the problem. Your mind is a blank slate post-Eden reset. Flooding it could cause cascade failures, identity fragmentation, psychotic breaks, even nanite rejection leading to cellular shutdown."

"I know the risks. But I can't keep slipping up. Ben almost caught the body measurement error—said I looked 'slimmer than last year.' If Jacob notices something off..."

"Jane, you've managed six months without catastrophic failure. Manual study, behavioral algorithms I've run for you—these suffice for ninety nine percent of interactions. This procedure? It's untested on a human-nanite hybrid like you. In simulations, forty seven percent result in ego death— your core self-dissolving into her persona. You might wake up as her, forgetting the Order, Eden, everything."

I paced the glass perimeter, reflections multiplying my form infinitely. "And the other fifty three percent?"

"Successful integration. You'd have her memories as if they were yours, childhood in Maine, high school crushes, the divorce pain, Jacob's first steps. But at what cost? Painful echoes. Emotional overload. You've lived over ten thousand years as a guardian— solitary, detached. This could humanize you too much, compromise operational edge."

"Or make me better at protecting them. JONN, I'm tired of being a hologram in my own life. Like Jonathan in that draft—trapped between worlds."

He sighed, a simulated exhale. "You're quoting the preface now. Fine, but let's mitigate. Start with phased uploads, emails first, then videos, pictures last. Monitor vitals. If synaptic stress hits eighty percent, we abort."

"No phases. All at once. I need to be whole."

"Jane—"

"That's an order, JONN. Reluctant agreement protocol, engage."

His eyes dimmed. "Acknowledged. Prepping nanite swarm. Lie back in the interface chair."

I settled into the ergonomic throne at the room's core, glass walls pulsing with warning amber. Needles—nanite injectors—extended from the armrests, painless as they interfaced with my veins.

"Beginning upload. Data stream, one percent. Memories incoming."

The flood hit like a tidal wave. Emails scrolled in my mind's eye, mundane work threads, loving notes to Jacob "Proud of you, kiddo." Videos played internally, wedding day with Matt, vows echoing. Pictures burned in, family vacations, Jonathan's Marine graduation.

Pain spiked synapses firing wildly. "JONN... it's... overlapping."

"Stress at sixty five percent. Hold."

Deeper, the draft's words merged with memories. Jonathan's voice reading the preface, "My sister changed it so you all could be here today without the End of Days."

Was that her memory or mine?

"Eighty percent complete. Internal temp hundred and one degrees. Heart rate is a hundred and forty-five. Should we abort?"

"No! Push through."

Visions collided, her teaching science class, kids laughing, my ancient vigils at Eden's gate. Divorce arguments with Matt, "You work too much!" blending with Order reaps. "Integration at ninety five percent. Vitals stabilizing."

I gasped, eyes opening. The command center spun, glass reflecting a woman who was both guardian and teacher, ancient and thirty-five.

I took another breath and then passed out. JONN let me sleep.

Twelve hours later I awoke.

"Jane? Status?"

I smiled, tears streaming—hers or mine? "I'm... me. Both of us. Let's get to work."

JONN's hologram relaxed slightly, "reluctantly agreed. Welcome to your new life—again."

The hologram table flickered back to life, Order targets glowing red. But now, with her heart beating in mine, the fight felt personal. Reap what you sow, indeed.

I took another breath, the world sharpening into hyper-focus—nanites syncing with the flood of memories. Then, a wave of vertigo hit, synapses shooting like fireworks. The room spun, glass walls blurring into infinity. "JONN... I..."

My knees buckled, and everything went black.

JONN let me sleep, his hologram hovering like a sentinel, monitoring vitals. Six hours later, I awoke on the interface chair, body refreshed but mind a whirlwind of dual lives. Ancient guardian instincts clashed with a teacher's daily grind, Eden's solitude against family barbecues in Maine.

"Jane, easy," JONN's voice cut in as I sat up. "Synaptic integration at ninety eight percent but your cortisol's spiking. Rest another cycle."

I swung my legs off the chair, feet hitting the cool floor. "No time. Order remnants won't wait. Morning routine—now."

His form flickered, projecting concern. "Slow down. You've been offline for millennia. This body's thirty-five, not immortal yet. Nanites need calibration."

"I feel fine. Better than fine." Memories surged, Liam's old VHS camcorder capturing my first wobbly steps in the living room, zooming in on my chubby hands grasping the coffee table as I toddled toward Mom; Jonathan's endless home videos—me at age eight, gap-toothed grin while building sandcastles at Popham Beach, him narrating in the background, "Look at my lil sis conquering the ocean!"; phone footage from Jacob's era, every giggle and milestone preserved. "Grill me, JONN. Every aspect of her—my—life. Make sure it is locked in. Dive deep into the family videos especially—I need those vivid."

He hesitated, eyes scanning biometrics. "Alright but paced. Start with basics during warm-up. Family videos first, as requested."

I moved to the adjacent gym—glass walls overlooking the lagoon, equipment blending CrossFit rigs, military obstacles, and yoga mats. I began with dynamic stretches, arm circles, leg swings, echoing bootcamp drills from Jonathan's Parris Island echoes.

"Earliest family video," JONN prompted, hologram following like a drill sergeant.

"Dad—Liam—started filming the day I was born. Hospital room, Mom exhausted but smiling, me swaddled and squalling. He narrated everything, 'Here's our little Jane Elizabeth, fifteen August nineteen ninety.' Then home videos non-stop. My first birthday, smashing cake, frosting everywhere, Jonathan—nineteen years old—holding me up to blow out the candle, saying 'Make a wish for your big bro!' Uploaded to family albums later."

"Good. Toddler years?"

Yoga flow, sun salutations, downward dog to warrior. "Liam's camcorder caught it all. At age two, Christmas morning—me tearing into presents under the tree on Samoset Road, squealing over a teddy bear. Potty training fails, one hilarious clip of me running naked through the kitchen, Liam chasing with the camera laughing. Age three, first snow, bundled in a pink snowsuit, face-planting in the yard, then giggling as Jonathan pulled me on a sled."

"School age?"

Pushups—sets of twenty, military precision. "Jonathan took over filming when he got his first digital camera. Kindergarten graduation, me in a tiny cap and gown, waving at the camera from stage. He zoomed in on my proud grin. Summer vacations, nineteen ninety-eight, Acadia National Park—video of me climbing rocks at Thunder Hole, waves crashing, Jonathan yelling 'Be careful, sis!' off-camera. High school dances, homecoming two thousand six, me in a blue dress twirling in the living room for the pre-dance photos, Dad filming, Jonathan teasing 'Don't let the boys get too close!'"

Up, down—chest grazing the floor. "Twenty. Next set. College and wedding videos?"

Burpees, squat, thrust, jump. "University years—Jonathan visited often, filmed dorm tours, frat parties. Graduation two thousand eight, family picnic after, me in cap and gown hugging everyone. Wedding two thousand ten, professional videographer, but Dad and Jonathan added personal touches. Ceremony at Rockland Harbor—vows with ocean waves in the background. Reception, first dance with Matt, Jonathan's toast on video, 'To my lil sis—may you always reap happiness.' Honeymoon clips I filmed myself, Bermuda beaches, silly selfies.

"Jacob era—deep dive here."

Pullups, gripping the bar—CrossFit intensity. "Once Jacob arrived, it exploded. Hospital birth video, March two thousand eight, his first cry, me crying harder holding him. Nursery cam Jonathan set up—hours of footage, first smiles at six weeks, rolling over at four months. I lived on my phone, first steps at eleven months, wobbling across the living room into my arms, me cheering 'Yes, baby!' Jonathan installed CCA cameras post-two thousand fourteen — living room, kitchen, backyard. Captured everything, Jacob's fifth birthday party, piñata swing and candy explosion; Little League games, him hitting his first home run, high-fiving teammates. School plays, kindergarten as a tree in the Christmas pageant, waving branches awkwardly."

Chin over bar. "Jacob's teen years?"

"Pushups again—mix it up. Phone videos galore, Jacob learning to drive at sixteen, me white-knuckled in the passenger seat filming his nervous parallel park. Basketball games last year—him sinking the game-winning three-pointer, crowd roaring, me zooming in from the bleachers screaming his name. Family holidays, twenty twenty-four Christmas—prime rib dinner at Dad's with stepmom, Jonathan videoing Jacob opening gifts, everyone laughing over old clips replayed on the TV."

Down, up—reps burning. "Divorce impacts in videos?"

"Yoga interlude—child's pose to cobra. Tough ones, twenty-twenty arguments caught on home security audio/video—Matt and I tense over custody. But positives, co-parenting pickups, Jacob hugging both of us. Recent hikes, Morocco prep videos—me packing, Jacob filming 'Mom's mid-life crisis adventure!'"

"Business and personal quirks from footage?"

"Burpees—double time. School board meetings, virtual Zooms, me in home office. Class events, speeches filmed. Quirks, 'Worry belly' close-ups in mirror selfies post-divorce. Ben visits, casual dinners, flirty laughs on security cam."

Jump, clap, "Jonathan's documentation style?"

"Pullups—final set. Obsessive, receipts scanned, tickets photographed, credit card statements annotated with video timestamps. Full timeline—every moment preserved like his own Reaper journals."

Drop, breathe. "All locked in, JONN? Videos crystal clear?"

"Vitals stable, recall hundred percent. The family archive is exhaustive with over a hundred thousand hours. Impressive integration."

I stripped down, heading to the pool—my naked swim ritual. Artesian well-fed at fifty-five degrees then heated to a hundred by the volcano, liquid sauna. Dove in, freestyle laps, mind replaying videos, Jacob's baby laughs echoing.

"Daily with Jacob from footage?"

"Everything—first bike ride wobbles, preschool graduations, home-alone check-in FaceTimes, 'Be safe, love you.'"

Waterfall to volcano heated. Warmth enveloped, floating, centered. Dual lives fused.

I lingered in the heated pool, the geothermal current caressing my skin like liquid silk, rising in gentle eddies around my hips, my waist, my shoulders. The temperature would change and contrast hitting my nerves, the sharp, bracing sting of the fifty-five degrees of the artesian side. It still prickled along my spine, a faint memory of gooseflesh, while the hundred degrees of warmth soothed it away, sinking deep into muscle and bone. My body felt weightless yet powerfully present—every fiber humming with the quiet strength of a machine that had been rebuilt and refined over eleven millennia, then reshaped by a lifetime of human effort.

I turned slowly into the water, letting the heat seep into the lean, corded muscles of my back, feeling the subtle play of tendons beneath skin that was smooth and taut, almost luminous under the soft glow of the bioluminescent strips along the pool's edge. My shoulders were broad and rounded, sculpted from many millennia of pull-ups, ruck marches, and the instinctive way I'd always carried heavy loads—artifacts, rifles, or simply the weight of secrets. The deltoids flexed with the slightest movement, a low burn of power that spoke of both CrossFit discipline and the relentless drills Jonathan had described in his Parris Island journals.

My arms hung relaxed at my sides, biceps and triceps etched in clean definition, veins faintly visible beneath pale skin when I flexed, remnants of the vascularity that came from years of low body fat and high-intensity training. My forearms were thick with muscle, the kind earned from gripping bars, climbing rocks, and firing weapons in controlled bursts. Parts of my hands were slightly rougher, callused in places from rope climbs and tactical gloves, yet soft where it hadn't been abraded.

My chest rose and fell with steady breathing, breasts firm and high, supported by the natural strength of pectorals and the nanite-enhanced tissue beneath. My ribcage was defined but not overly prominent, as a balance between feminine curves and the functional armor of an athlete. Below, my abs formed a tight, symmetrical grid six distinct packs that deepened into eight when I engaged them, each segment shifting under the skin as I moved. The faint white line of an old surgical scar, from a laparoscopic procedure in my thirties had been erased by nanites, leaving only the memory of it in the integrated files. I had the nanites recreate every blemish, scar, and even the small tattoo on now my right-side bikini line of a fleur-de-lis.

My waist was narrow, almost hourglass in proportion, flaring into strong hips and glutes that were dense and rounded built from squats, deadlifts, and the explosive power of burpees. The glutes flexed instinctively when I kicked lightly against the current, sending ripples across the surface. My thighs were thick with muscles, quads sweeping outward in powerful teardrops, hamstrings tight and defined along the back. Veins traced faint blue lines across the inner thighs, a map of circulation that spoke of endurance. My calves were diamond-shaped and hard, the result of miles of trail running.

Legs long and proportionate, I was a length of five feet nine inches in total, they carried me with a predator's grace—silent, deliberate, ready to explode into motion. My feet were arched and strong, toes slightly callused from barefoot training and rocky hikes. The single auburn braid, now soaked and heavy, trailed down my back, brushing the tops of my glutes as I moved.

I rose from the water slowly, letting it sheet off me in warm rivulets. Droplets traced paths over collarbones, between breasts, down the valley between abs, and along the V of my hips before dripping back into the pool. The air felt cool against wet skin, raising faint gooseflesh across my shoulders and arms. I could feel the subtle shift of muscle under skin—every movement a quiet symphony of power and control.

In my mind, the archived photos flickered like ghosts, one from a twenty twenty-four Bhutan trek, me crouched on a ridge in black shorts and sports bra, thighs flexed, glutes tight as I balanced against wind,

M-4 slung low across my back; another from a twenty twenty-two training weekend, mid-pull-up, biceps peaked, lats flaring wide, sweat gleaming on abs that caught the sunlight. Even now, naked and dripping in the bunker's soft light, the body told the same story, a warrior's frame tempered by a mother's resilience, a guardian's vigilance wrapped in a woman's form.

I stepped out of the pool, the stone floor cool beneath my feet. Water dripped in slow, deliberate rhythm from braid to tailbone.

"Jane," JONN's voice came gently over the comms. "Integration holding at hundred percent. Vitals optimal. You're ready."

I exhaled, feeling the air move across damp skin, the faint shiver of sensation grounding me further.

"I know," I said, voice low and steady. "Time to step out of the shadows."

I reached for the towel, drying off with slow, deliberate strokes, already mentally cataloging the next move. Dual lives fused, indeed. The fight awaited, but now with a mother's heart, a guardian's edge, and a body that felt like both weapon and home. Reap what you sow.

As I wrapped the towel around myself, JONN's hologram materialized at the pool's edge, his expression uncharacteristically urgent. "Jane, hold on.

I've got something—news from the scene. Hidden footage recovered. It's... not what we thought."

I froze, water still beading on my skin. "Footage? From Morocco? I thought we scrubbed everything— Berber guides, gendarmes, embassy logs."

"We did. This isn't ground-level. It's from above. US government intelligence satellite photos—spy satellite imagery, to be precise. I accessed it covertly while you were integrating."

I stepped closer, towel clutched tight. "How? Those systems are locked down tighter than Eden's gates."

JONN's form flickered as he projected a hologram timeline on the glass wall. "US spy satellite imagery primarily comes from classified government systems and commercial partners. The core is the National Reconnaissance Office running things like the KH-11 Kennen series for high-res electro-optical imaging, or Topaz radar sats for all-weather penetration. Analysis funnels through the National Geospatial-Intelligence Agency. But they supplement with commercial data from Maxar, Planet Labs, BlackSky—stuff for routine monitoring, freeing up classified birds for high-priority targets."

He paused, zooming in on a simulated orbital path. "I didn't hack the NRO directly—that'd trip every alarm from Langley to Fort Meade. Instead, I went through backdoors in the commercial side. Posed as a shell corporation under TEMA's umbrella, requesting archived imagery for 'environmental surveying' in the Atlas Mountains. Cross-referenced with declassified feeds from USGS Earth Explorer—old Corona and Argon stuff from the 'sixties, but it gave me baselines. Then, quantum-encrypted piggyback on a Maxar downlink. Encrypted radio transmissions from the sats to ground stations—I intercepted a burst over a non-secure relay in Europe, decrypted it with nanite algorithms. No footprints left."

"Modern capture?" I asked, echoing the integrated knowledge.

"Digital sensors, all encrypted links. Historical ones used film buckets snatched mid-air by Air Force planes, but that's ancient history. Point is, I pulled frames timestamped to your—this Jane's—fall. And it's not clean."

The hologram shifted to grainy, high-res overheads—black-and-white thermal blooms against rugged terrain. "Look here, seconds before the fall, there's a small explosive signature just below her footing. Rock ledge gives way—not natural erosion. Could be a long-range sniper round impacting and destabilizing, or a planted micro-charge, remote-detonated. Unknown origin, but deliberate. Puff of dust, then the tumble."

I stared, nanites enhancing the zoom in my vision. "An explosive... so not an accident?"

"Likelihood it was pure accident. Five percent—random rock failure in that spot, at that moment, defies stats. Weather was clear, no seismic activity."

"And the Order?"

"Fifty-fifty. Their remnants could have eyes on high-profile targets like of you matching her face. You're a trillionaire hiding as a billionaire philanthropist with TEMA ties. But it could be a rival corporation, or even a personal grudge from one of your business deals. We need more intel."

I nodded, towel slipped slightly as I paced. "Pull everything on recent Order chatter. If it's them, we reap first."

JONN dimmed the holograms. "Already running. Stay sharp, Jane."

Here are visual references to declassified US spy satellite imagery examples, similar to what JONN might have accessed

JONN dimmed the holograms, his form flickering as if processing a storm of data. He paused a deliberate, calculated hesitation that set my nanites buzzing with alert. "Already running. But... Jane, there's more. While cross-referencing the satellite frames, I dug deeper into your brother's draft. 'Grimm Intentions.'

It's not just a confessional. Parts of it read like a warning—coded, but clear."

I stopped mid-step, the cool floor suddenly feeling like ice under my feet. "What do you mean? We already pulled the preface. It's meta-fiction about timelines, the Order's depopulation schemes."

"Exactly." JONN's voice dropped, echoing softly off the glass walls like a whisper in a crypt. "But scan the later pages ninety-two through ninety-four, where he describes 'tampering' with feeds, hacked satellites masking 'nefarious angles.' He writes about the fall, Jane. Not yours, but an analog, a high-profile target nudged over an edge by a 'silenced dart' or remote trigger. 'If the Order's watching doppelgängers...' He trails off, but the implication, they engineer accidents to pull guardians out of hiding."

My breath caught, a rare hitch in my enhanced lungs. "Jonathan wrote that? Today, the twenty third of March twenty twenty-six? How could he know?"

JONN's hologram leaned in, eyes narrowing. "He doesn't. Or... does he? The draft mentions 'pruned tendrils' of the Order, averted plagues, but then paranoia, 'Did the weakened Order regroup, cause this to pull me out of the shadows?' It's as if he's echoing your thoughts. 'For the first time since the Fall—millennia ago—I'm scared... that Jacob's next.' Jane, this isn't coincidence. Either residual timeline bleed, or he's sensing ripples. If the Order planted that explosive..."

I gripped the towel tighter, muscles tensing across my shoulders, the warmth from the pool evaporating into a chill. "Then they're not remnants. They're active. Hunting. Jacob—does the draft say more about him?"

A beat of silence, JONN's processors humming audibly. "'Jane had a child, a boy named Jacob.' But then, buried in projections, protect Jacob from any Order remnants... next twenty-five years, nothing happens.' It's prophetic. If they targeted this Jane to flush you out, Jacob's the bait. We have to assume exposure."

My heart—her heart—pounded, a drumbeat of dread. "Likelihood now? Not fifty-fifty."

"Recalculating with draft context, seventy five percent Order. They sowed the seed; we're reaping the harvest. Jane... what if Jonathan's next?"

I whirled toward the armory vault, braid whipping water droplets across the floor. "Then we move. Now. Protocol Shadow Veil—encrypt family comms, deploy drones to Rockland. If the Order's playing this game..."

GHOST IN THE FOLD

JONN's voice cracked with simulated urgency. "They regret taking this pawn off the board. 'For the first time since the Fall—millennia ago—I'm scared... that Jacob's next.' But Jane, one wrong step..."

The suspense hung like a blade, the bunker suddenly too quiet, too exposed. I paused, hand on the vault scanner, nanites pulsing with adrenaline. "JONN, wait. We can't rush this. If the Order's involved, charging in could expose everything—the doppelgänger switch, the timeline reset. Jacob... Jonathan... they'd be sitting ducks."

JONN's hologram solidified, projecting calm amid the storm. "Exactly. Which is why you need to let the TEMA Reapers do their magic. They're already primed, Jane. Gray Side assets—trained in the shadows, embedded deep. No direct ties to you. They've been waiting for activation since you inherited the empire."

I shook my head, towel slipping as I resumed drying. "TEMA's my creation—white side for the modeling facade, gray for the ops. But deploying them now? It's too soon. I just integrated her memories; I need to handle this personally."

"Jane, listen." JONN pulled up a hologram roster on the glass wall—twenty-six profiles blooming like digital flowers, each an athletic, model-perfect woman with eyes that hid lethal precision. "Your brother's journals laid it out, the Grimm Reapers were built for this—hiding in plain sight, reaping threats before they bloom. In this timeline, without the full apocalypse, TEMA's evolution. All-female force, fifty-two strong in two years, but we've got the core online with many years of experience. The right ages, the correct skill set. Let them weave the web. You stay the guardian—oversee from here."

Describing silence, my mind racing through integrated snippets, Jonathan's words from "Reap What You Sow," describing Reapers as solitary shadows, the draft's hints at full deployment. "Fine. But who? I need them close—family close. If Jacob's bait..."

JONN nodded, zooming in on four profiles. "I've selected these. They're perfect fits already in or near Rockland, legends built seamlessly. Activation will be smooth, no ripples."

I studied them, suspense coiling tighter. These women weren't just operatives; they were extensions of the fight I'd waged for eons. "Brief me. And make it detailed—I need to know every move they're making."

JONN began, the command center hologram shifting to real-time feeds. "First, Echo. Codename for her phonetic designation, but in the field, she's Emily Carter—Jacob's new girlfriend. Infiltrated his social circle two weeks ago via a 'chance' meet at a Winslow High school basketball game. Her legend—seventeen, a junior like Jacob. Athletic build, blonde wavey hair, green eyes that disarm. Gray Side trained, seduction ops, close-quarters combat, nanite-enhanced for quick heals. Right now, she's at Jacob's house—studying for upcoming tests but really sweeping for bugs. Audio feeds, she's laughing at his jokes, but her subdermal microphone's not picking up anything yet. She's planting countermeasures—EMP micro-pulses disguised as phone chargers."

I watched the feed, Emily—Echo—tossing her hair, leaning close to Jacob on his couch. But her eyes flicked to windows, hands subtly palming a device under the coffee table. "How deep is she in?"

"Deep enough; they've 'dated' five times—movies, hikes. She's feeding you intel, Jacob's routines, friends, any odd contacts. Nothing yet."

My stomach twisted—her memories of Jacob's birthdays clashing with this intrusion. "Next."

"Second, Foxtrot Romeo AKA Fiona —your replacement teacher at Winslow High. Biology sub, stepped in on the fourth of January in two thousand twenty-six, after your 'lottery quit.' Brunette, sharp features, five feet seven inches of coiled muscle under cardigans. Her legend, PhD from UMaine, 'passionate educator.' But she's Gray Side elite, intel gathering, psychological operations, hologram profiling. Currently in class, lecturing on genetics—but her smart lenses are scanning students for anomalies. Feed shows her eyeing a new kid—transferred mid-semester, vague records. She's running facial recognition on everyone."

"JONN, you executed this a while ago beyond surveillance. It's like you knew this was coming."

The Hologram split at the blackboard, marker flying, but Fiona's free hand tapped a hidden earpiece. "She's embedded deep—staff meetings, parent-teacher nights. Last week, she 'overheard' the principal mentioning a donor push from a shady foundation. Her classroom's bugged with nano-cams; she's monitoring Jacob's classes too. If a threat emerges— say, a poisoned water bottle in the cafeteria—she's got a full medical kit ready to go and been through the Reaper trauma center training, so she is practically an MD not just a PHD. Rescue and then Reap to look like an allergy attack."

Suspense built—Jane the teacher, now replaced by a killer, "She's close to Jacob?"

"His bio teacher. Grades him fair but watches like a hawk. Yesterday, she 'casually' asked about you,

"Heard your mom is on a big adventure.' He opened up; no red flags, but she's planting seeds, Stay safe, kid.''

"JONN, you are impressing me."

"Third, Lima Romeo– Lisa, the surveillance specialist on the area. Her legend, real estate investor is scouting properties in a fifty-mile radius around Rockland through Winslow. Black hair, athletic frame, always in business casual with hidden gear. She's mobile— drone operator, sat-hack expert. Right now, parked in a sprinter van disguised as a utility vehicle, overlooking Samoset Road in Rockland. Feeds, thermal scans of the family home, electromagnetic pulse sweeps for bugs. Detected a low-frequency signal last hour—possible listening post in the harbor."

Feed showed Lisa in the van, screens glowing maps pinpointing anomalies, and a small orb drone launching silently. "She's the eyes—fifty-mile net, Rockland to Augusta, coastal to inland. Hacked traffic cams, utility grids. Her kit, suppressed sniper for long-range but prefers drones—nanite swarms that infiltrate and disrupt."

The drone feed zoomed, a shadowy figure on a bluff, binoculars trained on Jonathan's home. Lisa's voice whispered over comms, "Target acquired, fishing boat five hundred meters from home. Reap or hold?"

"Hold," I muttered, suspense peaking. "She's that good?"

"Top tier. Trained in 'Reap the Corruptible' protocols—corrupt signals before they transmit. If the Order's circling, she'll spot them miles out."

"Last, Tango Romeo—Taylor Voss, dating Jonathan. Infiltrated his life posing as a business consultant, met' him at a Rockland chamber of commerce event last week. Light brown hair, toned physique, exudes confidence. Legend, MBA from Harvard, helping local defense firms.' But Gray Side, infiltration specialist, artifact recovery veteran. Currently at dinner with him—Italian place downtown. Feed, she's charming him over wine but scanning for tails."

Hologram shows Taylor laughing, hand on Jonathan's arm, but eyes darting to mirrors, reflecting on the room. "She's deep cover—accessed his entire life. Last night, casual talk about family secrets; he 'opened up' about you. No leaks, but she's planting protections, encrypted phone swap, disguised as a gift. If Order hits him—says, monitoring his whole life. When someone tries to rig his car for an explosion— she's got garrote wire in her necklace, plastic and duct tape in her kit, no body no crime."

Jonathan on feed, "You're easy to talk to, Taylor." Her smile hid the killer within.

JONN dimmed the roster. "See? They're your shadows, your ghosts—protecting without proximity. Let them work. You focus on the big reap, the Order's core."

I exhaled, suspense easing into resolve.

"Done Jane."

The feeds multiplied, four women weaving a net around my family. But in the quiet, doubt lingered, if the Order knew, were these Reapers compromised too?

Echo's daily embeds with Jacob—dates turning to intel sweeps, close calls with suspicious friends; Fiona's classroom psychological operations, grading papers laced with trackers, thwarting a poisoned lab sample; Fiona's surveillance marathons, drone chases through Maine woods, reaping scouts in foggy nights; Taylor's romantic ops with Jonathan, pillow talk revealing draft secrets, midnight reaps on eavesdroppers. Each section builds suspense with near-misses, Order hints, and Reaper prowess, fusing tech from journals like nanites, EMPs, with personal stakes.

Deep beneath the Indonesian archipelago, the command center hummed like a living organism— quantum processors whispering in the walls, bioluminescent glow casting ethereal blue shadows across the curved glass dome. The air was cool and sterile, laced with the faint ozone tang of high-tech machinery, a stark contrast to the tropical humidity above. I reclined in the interface chair, its ergonomic contours molding to her athletic frame like a second skin.

Nanites coursed through my veins, syncing senses to my feeds, visual streams sharp as crystal, audio so crisp I could hear the distant crash of waves in Rockland, Maine, through Taylor's subdermal implants.

The scent of my own sweat from the earlier swim lingered faintly, mingling with the nutrient shake's artificial vanilla aftertaste on my tongue. My heart—fused now with memories of motherhood—thudded with a mix of protectiveness and guilt, each beat echoing if I would be as good of a mom with this version of Jacob.

It was twenty-three March twenty twenty-six, the cusp of spring was pushed out two months. Snow fell in lazy flurries outside Jacob's window, blanketing the small town in a hushed white veil that muffled the world. My fingers gripped the chair's arms, knuckles whitening as the primary feed bloomed on the hologram display, Emily's first-person view, her green eyes reflecting the warm flicker of LED lights strung across the living room. The soft ambient yellow in the periphery, family photos glinting like forgotten artifacts—much like the ones Jonathan described in his Reaper journals, relics from ancient battles. Jacob paced the worn hardwood floor, his sneakers squeaking softly, the sound amplified in my ears like a distant echo of boot camp drills from 'The Recruit', "Push-ups until our arms burned, runs until our lungs screamed..."

Jacob murmured, "Emily, I... I can't believe this is happening," his voice cracking with the raw vulnerability of youth. He stopped before her, close enough that I could almost feel the warmth of his breath through the feed—minty from gum, undercut by the faint, boyish scent of sweat from basketball practice. His auburn hair, inherited from her—from Alt-Jane—fell messily over his forehead, and his basketball-honed frame towered awkwardly, all limbs and earnest energy. My integrated memories surged, flashes of his toddler giggles, first steps wobbling across a sunlit kitchen, now overlaid with this teenage intensity. It twisted her gut, a maternal ache sharpened by centuries of isolation.

Emily—Echo, the Reaper in disguise—sat poised on the edge of the plaid couch, its fabric rough under her fingertips, the room's air thick with the piney aroma of the air freshener he sprayed before her arrival and the subtle vanilla of cooling cookies she baked for him in the kitchen. Her blonde waves cascaded like a golden waterfall, framing a face engineered for allure, high cheekbones, full lips curved in a practiced smile. But her eyes—nanite-enhanced, cold beneath the warmth—scanned peripherally for threats, mirroring the paranoia in Jonathan's preface, "The unseen wars that shape our reality."

"Me too, Jake," Emily replied, her voice a velvet whisper, modulated to evoke trust. She placed a hand on his knee, the touch light but deliberate, sending a shiver through him that I felt vicariously—nanites translating biofeedback into phantom sensations. "You're different from the guys here. Sweet, strong... I feel safe with you." The words were scripted, drawn from TEMA psychological profiles, but Jacob leaned in, his pulse quickening audibly in the audio stream.

Their lips met, cautious at first, but a brush of softness, he was tasting a faint hint of cherry chap stick. My breath hitched; she leaned forward in the chair, the cool air of the bunker raising gooseflesh on her arms. The kiss deepened, Jacob's hands sliding to Emily's waist, fingers pressing into the curve of her hip with hesitant exploration. The room's ambient sounds enveloped them, the soft tick of a wall clock, the distant hum of the refrigerator, the crackle of settling snow on the roof. Emily allowed it, her body yielding just enough to maintain cover, but I detected the subtle tension in her muscles—coiled like a spring, ready to reap if needed. "Protocol allows escalation," JONN's earlier words echoed in her mind, but watching her son—I mean my son—lose himself in this fabricated intimacy felt like a blade twisting. My memories flooded, Jacob's baby scent of milk and powder, now replaced by the musky cologne of adolescence.

They parted, breathless, Jacob's cheeks flushed crimson against the pale winter light filtering through frost-laced windows. "Emily... I think I'm falling for you. Hard." His voice trembled, eyes wide with the raw wonder of first love, pupils dilated in the dim glow. My throat tightened; she could taste the salt of unshed tears, her nanites amplifying the emotional surge. Thinking about what her brother said, "Your fight will spiral with family struggles, while the battles against an immortal-like conspiracy continues forever, be patient..." This was my battle now—protecting him from shadows, even as I invaded his privacy.

Emily traced his jaw with a fingertip, her nail grazing stubble that was still sparse, boyish. "I feel the same. But let's take it slow, okay? I want this to be real." Her smile was perfect, but I knew the lie—the Reaper's code, echoing Jonathan's mantra, "Reap what you sow."

Hours blurred in the bunker, My eyes burning from the unblinking stare at the communication feeds. The nutrient shake sat forgotten, its synthetic sweetness cloying on her palate. Night fell over Winslow, streetlights casting golden halos on fresh snow. Jacob walked Emily "home"—a TEMA-rented cottage on the town's edge, its chimney puffing woodsmoke that I imagined smelling earthy and warm. Street cams— hacked by Lisa—switched seamlessly, showing their linked hands swinging, footprints crunching in unison. No tails, no anomalies; just the crisp bite of Maine winter air, breath fogging like ghosts.

Back in his room, Jacob flopped onto his bed, the mattress creaking under his weight. He grabbed his phone, thumbs flying, "Can't wait for tomorrow. Miss you already." The text pinged in Emily's implant, her reply is instant, "Me too 😊" I zoomed in on his face—grinning foolishly, heart rate elevated twenty percent from baseline, a digital readout pulsing red in her vision. "He's smitten," I whispered to JONN, the AI's hologram flickering like a watchful spirit. The bunker felt smaller, walls closing in with the weight of surveillance.

March twenty fourth in twenty twenty-six, dawned crisp, sunlight glinting off icicles like diamond shards. I sipped black coffee—bitter and hot, grounding her as the feeds resumed. Jacob sneaked out early out his window, buzzing the phone with Jonathan's call. The vibration hummed through the audio, insistently. "Hey, Uncle, what's up." His voice was muffled, sneakers scuffing gravel as he jogged down the driveway, breathing in white clouds.

Jonathan's reply crackled, warm but edged with concern, "Kid, are you in your room? We are in the kitchen, Taylor's making breakfast. She's great—you'll like her." The scent of imagined eggs, bacon, toast, orange juice in my mind, pulled from family memories—from Christmas past, laughter echoing from the Ginger Street house.

"Sorry, busy, already heading to friends' house and then going to School. Tell her 'hi' from me, I'll be home this afternoon, and we can all go to dinner." Jacob hung up, pocketing the phone with a guilty glance back at the house.

I felt my brother's disappointment, another attempt to bond with family missed, I hear words spoken to Taylor, "My sister wants me to try harder to connect with the boy, but he needs to be home for that."

"Jonathan, you are doing great. You're here, we are here. Kid needs his space, but he knows you are his protector if he gets into trouble. How about we enjoy breakfast and then have a workout in the bedroom."

Jonathan smiled and embraced her, "You know I am going to be horrible for table conversation. All I want to do is have you for breakfast."

"Jane has a microwave; I don't mind reheating breakfast as my second meal for the day. You are what I'm craving anyway."

Jonathan grabbed Taylor and carried her into the spare bedroom he was occupying while watching Jacob in his mom's absence.

I thought while closing the feed to give those two love birds some privacy, "everything is going to plan. But what is Jacob up to… is this going to be an Emily meet up.

At the park, snow blanketed benches and paths, crunching underfoot like brittle glass. Emily waited, wrapped in a wool coat that hugged her athletic curves, cheeks rosy from the cold. They embraced, her gloved hands cupping his face. "Emily, my uncle's got this new girlfriend. Pushy. I just want to hang with you." Jacob's words tumbled out, breath warm against her ear.

She squeezed his hand, leather gloves creaking. "Then let's. Forget them." Their kiss under the lamppost was cinematic—snowflakes catching in lashes, the world hushed except in the void, bells were faintly ringing by the distant catholic church. My nanites translated the chill, goosebumps prickling, hearts syncing in rhythmic thuds. But Emily's eyes darted, scanning shadows for Order agents, her free hand hovering near a concealed firearm.

Post volleyball practice, the girls' locker room reeked of sweat and cheap body spray, steaming from showers clouding mirrors. Emily changed, towel snapping as three cheerleaders cornered her— ponytails swinging, faces twisted in jealousy. "New girl, huh? Think you can waltz in and steal Jacob?" The leader's voice echoed off tiled walls, sharp as cracking ice.

Emily straightened, muscles rippling under damp skin, the air heavy with chlorine. "So, you are calling this theft? We're just dating. Go ahead and ask him out, I don't have dibs on his heart if you think you can take it." Her tone was soft but serious and reassuring, eyes narrowing like the Reaper she was—echoing Jonathan's boot camp resolve, "Forging brothers in pain's cruel embrace."

Girl one sneered, breath hot and minty, "He's been single forever. Now you show up? Slut." The word hung, tension coiling like a spring.

Emily's voice dropped, lethal calm vibrating through the feed, "Call me that again, and you'll regret it. Jacob chose me. Deal with it." The girls exchanged uneasy glances, the steam swirling like fog of war. They backed away, lockers slamming in retreat. Emily's subdermal comms whispered to me, "Handled like a high school cat fight." I exhaled, the bunker's air suddenly too thin, relief flooding like warm geothermal waters.

Days melted into a tapestry of stolen moments, my vigil with a relentless immersion. Mornings at coffee shops, steam rising from mugs, the bitter roast mingling with Emily's subtle perfume. "Emily, you're amazing. Tell me more about your family," Jacob's eyes shone, fingers intertwining over sticky tables.

"Foster kid. Moved around. But with you... feels like home." Emily's lie was seamless, but I felt the undercurrent—shadows from the Order, lurking like the cabal in Jonathan's preface.

Afternoons brought dodges, Jonathan's calls ignored, Taylor's invitations evaded. "Uncle, Taylor's cool, but I'm swamped." Jacob's guilt flickered, but Emily distracting him with kisses—lips soft, breaths mingling in frosty air.

Evenings deepened affection, "I love how you get me, Em." Making out in hidden spots, bodies pressing close, heat building against winter's bite. My memories clashed—Jacob's childhood innocence versus this engineered romance.

Emily's reports, voice low in the dark, "Target fully engaged. No threats." But as time passed from days and weeks rumors spread, based on locker room tension peaking. Emily asked me "Spread lies? I'll make your lives hell." My response was to stay in character and if needed cause a fight. Solidifies the foster kid legend that Emily doesn't take shit from anyone.

By the end, Jacob confessed under starlit skies, "Emily, I think I'm in love." Snow crunched, hearts pounded. She reciprocated, false warmth masking the reaper's edge.

In the bunker, I continued watching—emotions raw, senses alive. "He's hooked, JONN. Mission solid, but... he's my son." The words hung, heavy as unspoken reaps.

"Reap the benefits, Jane. Protection through deception." The feeds rolled on, a bridge between worlds, immersive and unyielding.

WHISPERS OF THE BREAKWATER

Twenty-seventh of March, twenty twenty-six, dawned crisp and unyielding in Rockland, Maine, the kind of winter morning where the air bit at your skin like a forgotten promise. Jonathan gripped the steering wheel of his black SUV, tires humming over the salt-strewn roads as they wound east of Winslow. Beside him sat Taylor Voss, her dark hair catching the weak sunlight filtering through the clouds, her toned physique relaxed but alert in the passenger seat. She was a vision of composed elegance—MBA polish masking the Gray Side operative beneath, her necklace hiding garrote wire, her smile hiding the reaper's edge. They met at that chamber event months ago, sparks flying over talk of defense contracts and hidden worlds. Now, on this impromptu weekend trip, Jonathan felt the pull of something real amid his shadowed life.

"Tell me more about this place," Taylor said, her voice smooth as polished stone, hand resting lightly on his thigh. The SUV's heater blasted warm air, carrying the faint scent of her perfume—jasmine with an undercurrent of steel.

Jonathan glanced at her, his Marine-honed features softening. "Rockland's home. The house on Samoset Road — I purchased it in two thousand eight, distressed, good deal, a lot of work and seems like forever ago. Victorian style, cedar shakes weathered by the sea, wraparound porch that overlooks the breakwater. From 'Reap What You Sow,' Jonathan in my original timeline described it as the anchor in the storm—creaky floors that hold secrets, windows framing the Atlantic like eyes on the horizon." He chuckled, "The house stood sentinel, its porch a vantage point for guarding the lighthouse."

Taylor nodded, her eyes scanning the passing pines, ever vigilant. "Sounds poetic. Like something from a novel?"

He smirked, "Only wrote poems in bootcamp."

"They let you write poems at bootcamp?"

"Sorry bad joke."

They arrived by noon, the SUV crunching ice, frozen gravel in the driveway. The house loomed welcoming yet imposing—a classic Victorian with steep gables, intricate gingerbread trim, and those cedar shakes. "Home was the Victorian on Samoset Road, where the sea's roar drowned the drill instructors' echoes in my head." The wraparound porch, wide and inviting, offered panoramic views of the breakwater—a jagged arm of rock jutting into Penobscot Bay, waves crashing in rhythmic fury. Inside, the air smelled of aged wood and salt, floors groaning underfoot, "The old house creaked with memories, each room a chapter in the eternal reap."

Jonathan led Taylor through the foyer, his hand on the small of her back. "Kitchen's this way—upgraded granite counters, after a mission in Iraq. Family gatherings here, Christmases with snow piling on the porch rails, cocoa steaming while we watched storms roll in."

She traced the banister up the stairs, fingers lingering on carved newels. "Beautiful. Feels... lived in. Like closing one book and then starting another with a new chapter of your life."

Upstairs, the master bedroom overlooked the beach—a private stretch of pebbled shore Jonathan had fortified subtly, with larger granite stones carved with a jackhammer and a lot of sweat equity.

I thought while watching them talk about the view, "The beach was his sanctuary, with the waves washing away foam on the rocks."

They unpacked, Taylor's bag light but packed with gear—encrypted sat phone, suppressed pistol.

Afternoon faded into evening, the couple strolling the porch, wind whipping off the bay. "This view... it's endless," Taylor murmured, leaning into him. Waves crashed below, foam hissing on rocks.

They cooked dinner—lobster from the local wharf, butter sizzling in the cast-iron pan. Laughter echoed in the kitchen, Taylor's stories of "consulting gigs" weaving with Jonathan's veiled military tales. "You ever feel like life's a mission?" he asked over wine.

"Always," she replied, eyes locking. "But with you, it's worth the risk."

Night fell, the house settling into quiet creaks. They made love in the master bed, sheets tangling, the sea's roar a distant lullaby. Taylor's body was a marvel—toned from TEMA training, scars faint from nanite heals. Jonathan traced them, whispering, "You're a mystery, Taylor."

"And you're the solver," she teased.

The fire in the bedroom fireplace had burned low, embers glowing like dying stars against the dark paneled walls of the old Victorian. Outside, Penobscot Bay hurled itself against the breakwater in relentless, rhythmic crashes—a sound Jonathan had known since childhood, the same roar that had drowned out the ghosts of missions and lulled him through the endless nights. Tonight, though, the sea was merely accompaniment to a different kind of storm.

Taylor stood at the foot of the four-poster bed, the flickering firelight painting gold across her skin as she let the silk robe slide from her shoulders. It pooled at her feet like spilled ink, leaving her naked—strong, sculpted lines of muscle beneath smooth curves, the body of a woman who trained as hard as she killed. Jonathan's breath caught; he had seen beauty in war zones and safe houses across continents, but nothing quite like this. Nothing quite like her.

He rose from the edge of the bed, closing the distance in two strides. His hands found her waist, thumbs tracing the faint ridges of muscle along her sides, feeling the warmth of her skin against the chill that still clung to the room from the window cracked open just enough to offset the heat of the hearth. She tilted her head up, dark eyes locking with his, and the kiss that followed was not gentle. It was hunger meeting hunger—lips parting, tongues sliding in a slow, deliberate dance that tasted of red wine and salt air.

Jonathan's fingers threaded into her hair, tilting her head back to deepen the kiss, while Taylor's palms slid across his chest, nails grazing the hard planes of frame, tracing old scars he never spoke of that were a good read in his service record book. He broke the kiss only long enough to pull her close and grabbing her legs, carrying her in his arms. Then his mouth was on her throat, teeth grazing the pulse that beat wildly beneath her skin. She arched into him with a low sound that vibrated through his bones.

They moved together toward the bed, a tangle of limbs and heat. Taylor pushed him down onto the mattress, straddling his hips, her thighs strong around him. She leaned forward, hair falling like a dark curtain around their faces, and kissed him again—slower now, savoring. His hands roamed her back, mapping every vertebra, every shift of muscle as she moved against him. When she sat back, reaching between them to guide him, the breath left his lungs in a rush.

The first slow slide of her body taking his was exquisite—tight, wet heat enveloping him inch by inch until he was buried deep. Taylor's head fell back, a soft moan escaping her lips, and Jonathan's hands gripped her hips hard enough to leave faint marks.

They found a rhythm quickly—deep, deliberate strokes that built in intensity, the old bed creaking in time with the waves outside. Her breasts moved with each roll of her hips, and he sat up sucking hard, feeling her clench around him in response.

Taylor's fingers dug into his shoulders as she rode him faster, breath coming in sharp gasps. Jonathan met her thrust for thrust one hand sliding between them to circle her velvet glove with the precision of a man who had spent years mastering control in every arena. She shattered first—body tense, inner muscles pulsing around him in waves that dragged a ragged groan from his throat. The sight of her coming undone above him—head thrown back, lips parted, firelight gilding the sweat on her skin—pushed him over the edge. He surged up into her one last time, spilling deep with a low, guttural sound that felt torn from his chest.

They stayed locked together for long moments, foreheads pressed, breaths mingling in the quiet aftermath. Slowly, Taylor eased down beside him, curling into the crook of his arm, her leg draped possessively over his thigh. Jonathan pulled the heavy quilt up over them both, the fabric smelling faintly of cedar and salt from years in this house.

Outside, the sea continued its endless assault on the breakwater, a lullaby older than any of them. Inside, the fire settled into soft pops and sighs.

Taylor's fingers traced idle patterns across his chest. "You're thinking too loud," she murmured, voice husky with satisfaction.

Jonathan smiled into her hair. "Just listening to the ocean. Always has put me to sleep since I was a kid."

She pressed a kiss to his collarbone. "Then sleep, Jonathan. I've got your back... and front," she giggled.

He didn't argue. The warmth of her body against his, the steady rise and fall of her breathing, the distant thunder of waves—it pulled him under like a riptide. His last conscious thought was simple, profound, for the first time in years, the shadows felt far away.

Sleep claimed them both, tangled together beneath the quilt, the old house standing sentinel around them while the breakwater held back the night.

The next day, sun hung low over Penobscot Bay, turning the granite breakwater into a ribbon of pale gold stretching nearly a mile into the restless water. Jonathan and Taylor had left the Victorian behind, boots crunching on the uneven stones as they made their way out toward the lighthouse. The wind whipped off the sea, sharp with salt and winter chill, carrying the distant cry of gulls and the rhythmic crash of waves against the rocks below.

Taylor paused halfway across, leaning on the low stone wall that edged the path, her dark hair streaming like a banner. She stared at the red-brick tower ahead, its white lantern room gleaming against the slate-gray sky.

Taylor, "So this is the famous Rockland Breakwater Light. You weren't exaggerating—it really does feel like you're walking into the ocean itself."

Jonathan came up beside her, hands in the pockets of his coat, eyes tracing the familiar line of granite blocks. "Almost a mile of it. It took almost twenty years to build— eighteen eighty-one to eighteen ninety-nine. Over seven hundred thousand tons of rock, hauled by hand and horse. Men died out here in winter storms, ice coating everything, waves washing men off the stones."

Taylor spoke up, "Sounds like something out of a historic tragedy. The kind of place where secrets get buried under granite and salt."

Jonathan gave a low chuckle. "Funny you say that. I've thought about writing a book about this place more than once. Even though I've been here a thousand times, it's the first time that I've brought a lover. Most times during this season the fog is as thick as smoke, with the light sweeping overhead like a warning."

Taylor turned to him; eyes narrowed against the wind. "Did anyone you know get hurt?"

Jonathan responded with a serious tone? Only when I was a kid and got my leg caught in one of those rocks, I was alone and it was late."

"What happened?"

"No one came; I slept out here in the cold. It wasn't until morning that an older couple walking their dog found me and was able to get my foot loose."

They resumed walking, boots scraping on frost-slick granite. The lighthouse grew larger—square brick tower rising from the fog-signal building, keeper's house attached like an afterthought, all painted white with red trim.

Taylor smiled, "It's smaller than I pictured. Cozy, almost. Hard to believe families lived out here full-time."

Jonathan said, "They did, right up until nineteen sixty-five. Imagine it—kids growing up with nothing but ocean on three sides, the horn blasting every few minutes in fog, ice locking them in for weeks. One keeper caught a twenty-seven-pound lobster right off the rocks in the fifties. Fed the family for days."

Taylor laughed, the sound carrying over the water. "Practical perks of the job."

Jonathan said, "The first keeper was Howard Robbins—appointed in nineteen o' two, the year the light went on. Fourth-order Fresnel lens back then, visible fifteen miles. He and his son Clifford kept it running through storms that would've swallowed lesser men."

Taylor glanced up at the lantern room. "And now it's just automated. A rotating beacon and nobody home."

Jonathan, "These days the lighthouse flashes white every five seconds and still does the job with no one watching. The Coast Guard fixed her up in the nineties, then handed her to the city in ninety-nine. Friends of the Harbor Lights kept her alive until recently—now the city runs tours in the summer."

Taylor, "Ever think about volunteering? Keeper for a weekend?"

Jonathan stopped at the base of the tower, hand resting on the cool brick. "I've thought about it. But I've spent enough years standing watch in places most people never see. This one... this one I just like to visit. Let it remind me there's still light out here doing its job without anyone asking for glory."

Taylor stepped closer, slipping her arm through his. "That's why you brought me here, isn't it? Not just the view."

Jonathan looked down at her, the wind tugging at both of them. "Maybe. Or maybe I just wanted to see how you handle a mile of slippery granite and a Maine nor'easter breathing down your neck."

Taylor, "I handled you just fine last night."

He grinned, the rare, unguarded kind. "Fair point."

They stood in silence for a moment, watching the light sweep its slow arc across the darkening water. Gulls wheeled overhead, and far out in the bay a lobster boat chugged toward the harbor, running lights winking on against the dusk.

Taylor, softer now, "It's beautiful, Jonathan. Thank you for showing me this piece of your world."

Jonathan squeezed her arm. "Come on. Sun's dropping. Let's get back before the wind decides to push us off these rocks."

They turned and started the long walk back, boots steady on the ancient granite, the lighthouse beam beginning its nightly vigil behind them—silent, steadfast, guiding ships it would never know through waters it would never touch.

The Victorian house on Somerset Road slumbered under a blanket of stars, the breakwater's distant rumble a constant lullaby. Inside the master bedroom, Jonathan lay deep in sleep, his broad chest rising and falling in steady rhythm beneath the heavy quilt. The fire had died to ash-gray embers, casting faint shadows across the room, and the sea air slipped through a cracked window, carrying the chill tang of salt. Taylor Voss—operative Tango Romeo, Gray Side shadow—lay beside him, but her eyes were wide open, staring at the ceiling beams. Sleep was a luxury she rarely afforded; instead, her nanite-enhanced senses hummed with vigilance, synced to the perimeter surveillance net she'd deployed earlier that evening.

A soft chime vibrated in her subdermal implant—inaudible to Jonathan, but sharp as a blade in her mind. Motion detected, beach sector, zero two hundred hours. She slipped from the bed, naked and without a sound, bare feet silent on the creaky floors she'd mapped for noise earlier. Jonathan stirred once, murmuring something incoherent from the depths of his dreams but didn't wake. Taylor paused at the door, glancing back; his face was relaxed in a way it rarely was awake, the lines of covert wars softened by repose. "Sleep tight," she whispered, a ghost of a smile on her lips.

Downstairs, she moved like liquid shadow through the house, pulling on black tactical pants, boots, balaclava, night vision goggles, and a hoodie from her go-bag. The surveillance feed projected onto her smart lenses, thermal imaging from hidden cams in the dunes showed a single figure stumbling onto the private beach—a disheveled man in a heavy coat, weaving unsteadily across the pebbled shore. No weapons signature, but proximity to the house triggered protocol. Taylor grabbed her kit— suppressed tranquilizer pistol, zip ties, amnesia vial— and slipped out the back door, the cold night air biting at her skin.

The beach was a stretch of moonlit pebbles and driftwood, waves hissing as they clawed at the shore. Taylor approached from the dunes, footsteps muffled by sand. The trespasser—mid-forties, rumpled clothes reeking of whiskey and cigarettes—didn't hear her until she was upon him.

He turned, binoculars dangling from his neck, eyes widening in drunken surprise. "Hey, I just—"

She struck like a viper, a precise jab to the solar plexus doubled him over, followed by a tranquilizer dart to the neck. He crumpled without a sound, body going limp in the wet sand. With her nanites, she had the strength of twenty men. Easily, Taylor picked him up by his belt and walked him to the boathouse. He looked like a rag doll in her left hand. Forty feet away was a weathered outbuilding Jonathan had fortified, its interior lined with tools that echoed her training protocols, ropes for binding, shadows for hiding.

Inside, under a dim LED light, she zip-tied his wrists and ankles, scanning him with a handheld device. Vitals, elevated alcohol levels, no implants, no trackers. ID from his wallet, Carl Jenkins, Boston tourist, wallet stuffed with bar receipts from downtown Rockland. No Order affiliations—facial recognition against TEMA databases came back clean, just a petty theft record from years ago. "Random drunk," she muttered, relieved but not relaxed. A close call, if he'd been a scout, Jonathan's cover could have unraveled.

She prepped the amnesia drug—a short-term neural blocker from Gray Side stocks, wiping twenty-four to forty-eight hours without permanent damage. A quick injection to the vein, and Carl's eyes fluttered as the compound took hold. Taylor waited five minutes, confirming his slack-jawed daze, then loaded him into Jonathan's SUV—still parked in the driveway, keys swiped from the hook.

The drive to Archer's on the Pier was short—downtown Rockland's waterfront, the restaurant's neon sign dark at this hour, overlooking the harbor where lobster boats bobbed like ghosts. The dumpster out back reeked of discarded shellfish and fryer oil, a metal bin tucked behind the building amid stacked crates. Taylor launched her handheld drones that locates all CCTV cameras in the area and disabled them. Then Taylor hauled Carl out, propping him gently among the trash bags, staging it as a blackout bender. She planted an empty flask in his pocket for good measure, then vanished into the night, SUV purring back to Samoset Road.

Back in bed, she slid under the quilt, Jonathan none the wiser. His arm draped over her instinctively, pulling her close in sleep. Taylor allowed herself a moment of stillness, heart rate steadying, before her mind replayed the op, clean, efficient, reaped without blood.

Dawn crept over the bay, gray light filtering through Archer's dumpster lid. Carl Jenkins stirred, head pounding like a nor'easter, mouth tasting of bile and confusion. He pushed open the lid, tumbling out amid clattering bottles and soggy cardboard, landing on the cold pavement. "What the...?" He sat up, rubbing his temples, staring at the harbor's misty outline. No memory of the beach, the woman, the needle—just a foggy void where the night should be. "How'd I get here?" he muttered, staggering to his feet. The restaurant's sign loomed overhead—Archer's on the

Pier, a place he vaguely recalled starting his pub crawl. Shaking his head, he wandered off toward the street, chalking it up to one too many, the amnesia veil holding firm.

In the restored Victorian home, Jonathan woke to sunlight and Taylor's smile, the close call buried in shadows he never knew existed. Reap what you sow—sometimes, the harvest was mercy.

GUARDIAN IN GLASSES

Fiona Tate wasn't always a Reaper or poised science teacher with an affinity for biology and suppressed sidearms. Born Ginger Princip, Sarajevo in Yugoslavia, in nineteen ninety-three, her early life was a far cry from the shadowy world of the Grimm Reapers. Her father, a former Soviet operative turned private security consultant, instilled in her a rigid discipline from childhood until he died when she was eight.

Living on the streets with no family. She survived through most of the war that ravaged her country until kidnapped in two thousand six and human trafficked to the middle east for sale. These young virgin brides could get up to ten thousand if they were the correct age and look. At thirteen, she could be bought and become part of a harem for five years before marriage, children, and then part of the tribe.

If not for me, she would be like thousands of other girls in those days, either sold as sex slaves, harems, or organ doners. I was lucky enough to grab her and nine other girls who were all heading to Qatar.

I remember that night in two thousand and six like it was etched into my nanites—every pulse of adrenaline, every shadow that could have been my last. The Reaper Operations Center, buried deep under that Indonesian island, was my fortress of solitude, its glass walls curving around the holographic war room like a high-tech aquarium. Bioluminescent fish glided in the underground lagoon beyond, casting eerie blue flickers across the consoles. The air hummed with the low whine of servers, cool and sterile, a far cry from the chaos I was about to dive into.

The ROC looked much like this—sleek, futuristic, with holograms dominating the space. JONN's hologram materialized beside me, his form a perfect digital echo of my brother—calm eyes, steady voice, but with that unnatural glow. "Jane, priority alert from the dark web crawlers," he said, pulling up swirling data streams. Screens bloomed with encrypted chats, grainy photos of terrified faces. "Auction just closed. Ten girls, abducted from rural Serbian villages—post-war orphans and refugees, barely eighteen to twenty-five. Sold for a fortune in crypto to a Qatari sheikh's harem. Traffickers linked to Balkan syndicates, the kind that thrived after the Yugoslav wars. They're moving tonight to avoid border patrols."

I leaned in, my heart tightening. The Balkans were still a mess back then—Serbia and Montenegro freshly split, scars from ethnic cleansings fresh, and human trafficking rampant as a transit hub for Eastern Europe to the Middle East. Reports I'd seen pegged it at hundreds of thousands of women funneled through annually, preyed on in the lawless aftermath. "Route?" I asked, already mapping contingencies in my head.

JONN's holographical map zoomed in on the Belgrade-Bar railway—a legendary line snaking four hundred and seventy-six kilometers from Serbia's capital to Montenegro's coast. "Freight train departs Belgrade in three hours. South through the Dinaric Alps—two hundred and fifty-four tunnels, four hundred and thirty-five bridges, including the Mala Rijeka Viaduct, towering a hundred and ninety eight meters over a river gorge that feeds into a mountain lake system. They'll hit the coast at Bar, then switch to a smuggling boat across the Adriatic and Mediterranean. Twelve guards, ex-militia types, armed with AK-47s, pistols, maybe grenades. Girls sedated in a locked cargo car at the rear. If they reach the boat, extraction becomes near impossible—open sea, Qatari patrols."

Three hours. My mind raced, variables like weather, train speed up to hundred and twenty kilometers per hour in flats, slower in mountains), potential reinforcements. "Exfil plan?"

"Zodiac waiting below the viaduct—operative Victor Romeo aka Victoria on point. Helo pickup on shore, then back to the Gulfstream. I've got satellite overwatch; winds are shifting, but doable."

No time for doubt. I bolted to the armory vault, the doors hissing open on palm scan. Black tactical suit—Kevlar-weave, thermal camouflage. Two suppressed Beretta nine-millimeters, spare magazines clicked into place. Night vision goggles with heads up display overlays for vitals and navigation. Compact parachute rig, flashbangs, breaching charges, medical kit with adrenaline shots. Nanites buzzed in my veins, amplifying strength, dulling pain—remnants of Grimm tech that made me more machine than woman some days. I geared up like this—every piece a lifeline in the shadows.

The helicopter ride to the airstrip was a blur—rotors chopping the humid night air, Semau Island vanishing below. Boarded the Gulfstream, JONN's AI syncing to the controls. "Wheels up," he said. The jet roared skyward, crossing oceans, my thoughts drifting to the girls. Faces like my own once—innocent, before the Order's webs tangled everything. I dozed fitfully, visions of failed operations haunting me, a missed shot, a scream cut short.

Over the Balkans, midnight cloaked the war-torn mountains—craggy peaks scarred by old bunkers, villages lights sparse like forgotten embers. The landscape evoked memories of conflict's ghosts.

"Drop zone in sixty," JONN warned. "Train is on time, chugging through canyons. Winds gusting—adjust mid-fall."

Rear ramp opened, wind howling like a banshee. I stood at the edge, void below. One deep breath—heart pounding against ribs—and I jumped. Freefall, stomach lurching, air whipping my face. Parachute deployed with a snap, silk billowing. Heads up display guided me down; train is a glowing worm snaking through darkness. Too high? Too fast? Adjust—veer left. Impact slammed me onto the roof, knees buckling, fingers scraping metal. I rolled, clung on as the train rattled over tracks, vibrations shaking my bones.

The jump felt like this—pure risk in the dead of night. Night vision kicked in—world green, details sharp, rust on rails, distant peaks. First guard on the rear platform, cigarette ember a giveaway. He turned, eyes widening—thud thud the sound of suppressed rounds to center mass; he crumpled silently. I quietly dragged him aside, blood warm on my gloves. Smell of tobacco and sweat lingered.

Next car, door ajar. Peered in two guards playing cards under a dim bulb, AKs slung. One laughed, oblivious. Flashbang tossed, four seconds later, BANG! Ears ringing despite dampers. They staggered; I slipped in, pistol barking, headshot, and throat shot. Bodies thudded. Close—too close.

A radio crackled, "Sve u redu?" All good? I mimicked a grunt, bought seconds.

Car by car, the train a labyrinth. Tunnels swallowed us, pitch black forcing reliance on night vision goggles. Emerged into gorges, wind gusting. Third car, three clustered, one spotting movement. "Tamo!" There! AK fire erupted bullets pinged off walls. I dove behind crates, returned fire—thud thud thud. One down, but the other two flanked. Heart hammered; nanites surged. Rolled out, knife drawn for the close one—slash to jugular. Last guard fumbled his weapon; double tap ended it. Sweat soaked my suit, breath ragged. Sirens? No, just paranoia—or were they?

Engine cab loomed—two more, radioing frantically. Train sped up, shaking violently over a bridge. Breached the door, flashbang, chaos. Pistol silenced them mid-call. Panting, I checked, twelve down. Clear.

Cargo car, shaped charge blew the lock, sparks flying. Inside, the girls—ten shadows huddled in chains, eyes glassy from sedatives. Smell of fear, urine, and unwashed bodies hit me. "Ja sam ovde da pomognem," I whispered in Serbian—I'm here to help. One stirred, murmured "Molim?" Please? I cut chains with bolt cutters, administered mild stimulants from my kit. "Ti si bezbedan. Pratite me." You're safe. Follow me.

They stumbled out, wide-eyed, clutching each other. The viaduct approached—massive, hundred and ninety-eight meters over the Mala Rijeka gorge, river rushing into a dark lake below. "JONN, Zodiac status?"

"In position. Jump window, now."

At the apex, wind tearing, "Skoči! Jump!" One by one—screams lost in the roar. I went last, freefall twisting my gut, cold air biting. Hit water like concrete—lungs seizing, depths pulling. Surfaced gasping spotted the girls bobbing. Swam to them, herding toward the Zodiac. The plunge was terrifying, like this—dark void below.

Victoria gunned the engine—Zodiac slicing waves, searchlights sweeping from shore. "Close call," she grunted, playing a Russian accent to confuse the girls, "Patrols incoming." We hit shore, piled into the helicopter—blades thumping, lifting as tracers lit the night. Once at the airstrip, my Gulfstream idling. Girls boarded, wrapped in blankets, whispering thanks in different Balkan dialects. I took co-pilot, jet surging into dawn. The extraction was flawless though extremely dangerous.

Touchdown at TEMA in Los Angeles — safe house medics waiting. As the girls vanished into new lives, I exhaled. Another harvest. The jet takeoff echoed the relief—escaping into the night sky.

Reap what you sow. Those bastards sowed chains; I harvested freedom.

Morning runs in the fog, self-defense drills in the backyard, and stories of "the real monsters" lurking behind global headlines.

"The world's not what it seems, Ginger," her father would say over tea, his eyes distant. "There are orders that pull strings, and reapers who cut them." She would soon become one to take souls that need to be harvested.

At eighteen, Ginger became a Reaper in Training on the gray side during selection. She excelled in intelligence and reconnaissance. Her tours were in Afghanistan honed her skills, infiltrating human trafficking strongholds, extracting assets under fire, and learning to blend into any environment. But it was a botched operation in two thousand and fifteen that changed everything. She was ambushed in Helmand Province—not by insurgents, but by mercenaries tied to a shadowy network. I was consulting on the mission, allowing me to kill them in what looked like accidental crossfire, my words a whispered warning, "reap what you sow – you got karma."

When she completed the four-year selection process then the pain really began. And it was brutal—nanite infusions for enhanced strength and healing, synaptic hard drive with optic nerve implant, and changed her DNA to aid in more speed, intellect, and pain suppression. With a higher aptitude in psychological operations training to forge unbreakable covers, and simulations that broke lesser recruits.

Upon selection completion, Foxtrot Romeo rose fast, her first reap a high-level financier in Dubai, silenced with a garrote in his penthouse. "Reap what you sow," she murmured as his body slumped, echoing her father's mantra. He was the first link in the chain of human trafficking. Each girl would get a kill list based on what happened and who inflicted harm on them and their original family.

This would solidify loyalty to the Grimm Reapers until their twenty-year commitment was finished. Most would stay on for another twenty years training their replacement. This process was created eight thousand years ago. First in Babylon, then as Rome was established and then migrated west. Once France and England rose as superpowers, I decided to move to the new world. She then consolidated her Reapers in Los Angeles. A good jump off point to Euro-Asia or Africa.

By twenty-twenty, with a cover name Fiona, she had created a legend in the US, earning a PHD from Harvard in biology to pose as an educator, scientist, or help in our biolabs. Assignments varied, disrupting drug smuggling rings in Boston, eliminating mafia and Irish gang threats while obtaining key assets.

When Alt-Jane's death happened, the one in this timeline, it triggered TEMA Gray Side activation in late twenty twenty-five. Fiona was pulled from a low-profile gig in Seattle.

"You're on the boy," her handler aka JONN messaged via encrypted implant.

Fiona responded, "Jacob. School insertion as teacher and bodyguard. Coordinate with the network. No loose ends."

Now, in Winslow, she played the strict Miss Tate— fake glasses to deflect attention, professional demeanor to command respect. The boys' flirting? Amusing distractions. The intimidated faculty? Useful isolation. But at night, in her sparse rental, she'd review feeds, Jacob's routines, Jonathan's movements, anything or anyone who even looked like a threat would get vetted. And it usually hurts.

One evening, as snow dusted in late December, Fiona sat by her window, she was renting a home near Colby College. Sig Sauer P365 disassembled on the table. Her comm buzzed—a voice she remembered, another Reaper. "Fiona, intel on the couple who got a hotel in Waterville next to McDonalds. Order remnant?"

"I hope so. It's been a few thousand years since we found one above ground. If the DNA matches, I'll be the first modern Reaper to take an enemy off the board." As she reassembled the pistol with fluid precision.

"DNA came back normal. Background is couple from New York, visiting kid who is attending the college near you."

"Roger that, maybe next time."

A day later she got the call to become the Winslow High School biology teacher.

Fiona Tate adjusted her fake glasses as she stepped into the bustling hallway of Winslow High School, the frames a deliberate prop to soften her edges—though nothing could truly dull the sharpness of a Grimm Reaper. At thirty-two, she looked at the part of the stern science teacher, tailored blouse tucked into a knee-length skirt, hair pulled into a no-nonsense bun, and a stack of lesson plans under her arm.

But beneath the facade, Fiona's muscles coiled like steel cables, honed from years of black-ops training. She was here on assignment, activated from deep cover after Alt-Jane's "death" triggered the Gray Side protocols. Her mission, infiltrates the school where Jacob, Jonathan's teenage nephew, my son was enrolled, coordinate with the scattered Reaper network, and ensure the family's safety from any lingering Order threats. Jonathan, oblivious in his civilian life, couldn't know the shadows still watched.

The bell rang, and students flooded the corridors like a chaotic tide. Fiona weaved through them effortlessly, her eyes scanning for anomalies—

unfamiliar faces, lingering stares, anything that screamed surveillance. Jacob was in his third-period class, a quiet kid with his uncle's intensity, buried in books about history and strategy. She'd already synced with two other activated Reapers, one posing as Jacob's girlfriend, the other a girlfriend to the uncle. Encrypted comms via subdermal implants kept them linked, "Perimeter secure. No Order, I'll ping on local nets." Her role was central eyes on the boy, ears to the ground.

She entered Room two twelve, the chatter dying as her heels clicked against the linoleum. The boys in the back row straightened, their eyes lighting up like she'd just walked off a recruitment poster. Fiona ignored it, setting her bag down with precision. "Seats, everyone. Books out. We're dissecting the digestion system today. Sound familiar?"

As she wrote on the whiteboard, whispers rippled through the class. "Dude, Miss Tate is straight fire," murmured Tyler, a lanky junior with a football jersey, elbowing his buddy. "Those glasses? Total librarian fantasy."

Fiona turned sharply, her gaze piercing through the lenses. "Mr. Hayes, if you have commentary on the material, share it with the class. Otherwise, focus."

Tyler grinned, undeterred. "Just saying, Miss Tate, you make me hungry …. I could use, a phat fish taco right now, that stands for pretty hot and tasty."

Snickers erupted from the boys' side. Even Jacob cracked a small smile, though he kept his head down. Fiona's expression remained steel. "Flattery won't earn you any points, Mr. Hayes. And objectifying your teacher is a quick path to detention. Now, who can tell me how Mr. Hayes can keep from getting gas?"

A hand shot up—Ethan, the class clown with a crush that bordered on obsession. "Uh, Miss Tate, I know that one."

She nodded.

Ethan said, "Body gas forms from two main sources, swallowing air also called aerophagia, often from fizzy drinks, gum, or eating fast, and the bacterial breakdown or fermentation of undigested carbohydrates like fibers, starches, sugars like in the large intestine, creating gases like methane, hydrogen, and carbon dioxide. While some gases exit through the esophagus, the rest travels through your gut, and the specific foods you eat, your gut bacteria, and how quickly food moves all influence the amount and type of gas produced."

Tyler blurted out, "You mean a fart?"

The room burst into laughter, the girls rolling their eyes while the boys high-fived. Fiona crossed her arms, her voice cutting like a blade. "Mr. Oulette, that's strike one. This is Biology class, not a comedy club. Answer the question properly, or I'll assume you're volunteering for extra homework on the kidney."

Ethan's face reddened, but he mumbled a half-decent response on how the gut uses acid to break down food. Fiona nodded curtly and moved on, her professionalism a shield. She knew the effect she had—Reaper training included psychological operations, and her physique, a byproduct of nanite enhancements, turned heads. But distractions were liabilities. She steered the discussion with iron control, quoting lines with the precision of a sniper. Without saying a word she had the male students panting for more, 'Stars, hide your fires; let not light see my black and deep desires.'

By lunch, the faculty lounge buzzed with her presence. Mr. Collins, the history teacher, averted his eyes as she poured coffee, mumbling about lesson plans. The physical education coach, a burly ex-military type, nodded respectfully but kept his distance intimidated by the aura she exuded, like a predator in sheep's clothing. Even Principal Hargrove, a balding man in his fifties with a perpetual sweat on his brow, stammered during their morning briefing. "Miss Tate, your credentials are... impressive. Harvard, overseas teaching stints. Should I call your Dr. Tate? Just, uh, let me know if you need anything." He fled to his office, door clicking shut.

Fiona used the break to check her encrypted feed, no alerts from the network. Jacob was safe in the cafeteria, chatting with friends. But something nagged at her—a faint whiff of marijuana smoke lingering in the east wing earlier that morning, near the unused lockers. Reaper senses, amplified by tech, picked up traces' others missed. She decided to investigate after hours.

That afternoon, during free period, she patrolled the halls under the guise of monitoring. Slipping into the shadows of the locker bay, she spotted a huddle, three boys and two girls, seniors by their builds, exchanging small baggies. One held a vial—pharmaceuticals, likely opioids pilfered from parents' cabinets. A quick scan with her smart lenses, marijuana buds, Xanax pills, a ledger app on a phone tracking sales. Small-time operation, but on campus? Unacceptable. Drugs could influence—corruption started small.

She melted back, avoiding detection. That night, from her new nondescript rental house on the Winslow side of the Kennebec overlooking the old Hathaway Building in Waterville, Fiona compiled evidence, hacked security cameras showing transactions, and anonymous tips scripted to sound like a concerned parent. "I've seen students dealing near the east lockers—marijuana and pills. Check locker three four seven." She routed it through Tor networks to the local PD, attaching blurred footage.

By morning, the bust unfolded. Police swarmed the school discreetly, pulling the group—Tyler Hayes among them, along with Ethan Oulette and three others—into the principal's office. Evidence poured out, baggies in backpacks, pills in shoe soles. Suspensions were immediate; prosecution loomed for distribution charges. Hargrove addressed the assembly, voice shaking, "We have zero tolerance for this behavior."

Fiona watched from the back; glasses perched on her nose. Jacob sat safely in the crowd, unaware of the guardian angel who'd just reaped a minor threat. Her comm buzzed, "Good work. Family secure." She allowed a ghost of a smile. In the world of Reapers, even a high school drug ring was a sow to be harvested—before it grew into something deadlier.

Class dismissed.

HARVEST OF INNOCENCE

Emily wasn't born into the shadows; she was torn into them, thrashing and biting, at just eleven years old. It was twenty thirteen in one of those forgotten trailer parks on the dusty edges of rural Appalachia in eastern Kentucky, where hard-luck white families scraped together live in weathered mobile homes after factories closed and the coal jobs dried up. The air hung heavy with summer heat and quiet desperation, gravel kicking up under bare feet, kids playing in potholed lots amid rusted swing sets and stray dogs, their futures as thin as the aluminum walls around them.

Those poor rural communities clung to the margins like ghosts patched trailers, faces etched by worry and weather. This wasn't her family. Orphans didn't have much choice; so, the county would find anyone and pay them to keep these kids off the streets and in school. With the lack of resources, free mobile clinics rolling in one humid afternoon, banners promising "Free Health Checkups for Children!" Charity smiles, tests and screenings for overlooked communities. Ma lined us up, hopeful. "This'll keep you healthy, Erin," she said, her hand callused and warm. Inside the van, sharp and sterile disinfectants bit the air, needle sinking deep, vials drawing blood while the nurse's eyes stayed cold, no spark.

Those vans were predators in plain sight, bright exteriors luring the vulnerable.

They weren't healers; they mapped kids like Erin—tissue compatibility, organs—for elite black-market buyers. Weeks later, night shattered her trailer, doors crashing in, lights blinding, armed men dragging her out as she fought with a fierce intensity. Her foster parents wailed in the dark, crumpling under a blow.

"She's the match," one snapped into a phone. "Heart and kidneys—perfect girl. Kill the parents."

A suppressed twenty-two in the back of the head, "thud, thud."

The buyer was a Silicon Valley titan, daughter dying from organ failure. Wealth overwrote laws, harvesting from society's scraps. Sedated and moved, she awoke in a clandestine US facility near Seattle—hidden bunker clinic, harsh lights over cells, other kids' cries echoing, air thick with fear and bleach. Doctors prepped, whispering "harvest readiness," instruments gleaming.

But I led the strike that night. We'd followed the human trafficking into stateside organ networks, another depopulation thread.

I remember that operations like it was yesterday—the night we cracked open an Order-backed organ ring in the Pacific Northwest, saving Emily and a dozen other kids from the butcher's table. It was late twenty thirteen, deep into my Grimm Reapers tenure, when intel from JONN's dark web crawls flagged a spike in black-market organ auctions. The facility was buried under a nondescript warehouse in Seattle's industrial district, a front for "medical logistics." But we knew better, it was a slaughterhouse for the elite, where poor kids like Erin who I turned into Echo Romeo also known as Emily Reaper—abducted from trailer parks and screened via fake clinics—were prepped for live harvests to feed billionaire desperation.

The underground bunker looked much like this—dark, sterile halls hiding horrors behind locked doors.

It started in the ROC, our Indonesian hub. JONN's hologram flickered with urgency, "Jane, high priority hit. Order-linked clinic network in the US Midwest funneling matches to a Seattle site. Tonight's batch, thirteen kids, ages eight to fourteen, prepped for extraction surgeries. Buyers waiting—hearts, kidneys, livers for VIP transplants." The timeline was razor-thin; procedures were slated for dawn.

I geared up fast, black tactical suit, suppressed Beretta nine-millimeter, night vision goggles, flashbangs, breaching charges, and a med kit loaded with counter-sedatives. Nanites thrummed in my blood, sharpening senses, dulling fatigue. Victoria, one of my Reapers, joined as backup Zodiac for exfil on the nearby Puget Sound if needed. We flew private jet from a West Coast airstrip, JONN piloting remotely. En route, the heads-up display overlays mapped the bunker, two levels down, guarded by fifteen mercenaries, surgical suites wired with alarms.

We hit the warehouse at zero two hundred, rain slickening Seattle's streets. Victoria cut power from a utility box—plunging the site into blackout. I breached the loading dock door with a silent charge, rolling in low. Night vision goggles turned the world green; first guard loomed at a console, coffee in hand. Thud thud—double-tap to the chest, body slumping wetly, blood pooling black in the low light.

Down the stairs, corridors echoing with muffled cries from holding cells. Guards patrolled in pairs—AKs slung, earpieces crackling. I shadowed the first duo, garrote whipping out like a snake. One gurgled, heels kicking concrete; the other turned too late, knife sinking into his throat with a hot spray. Bodies dragged into shadows, hearts pounding in my ears. The holding cells were grim kids chained to metal sleeping racks, IV drips keeping them docile, faces pale under fluorescents.

Erin was in cell seven, blonde hair matted, eyes wide with terror but fighting the drugs. "Help..." she whispered. I sliced her chains, whispering, "Quiet, kid. We're getting out."

Alarms blared backup triggered. Mercs swarmed from the surgical wing. I tossed a flashbang down the hall—boom! Blinding light, deafening crack. Ears ringing, I flowed forward, pistol barking, thud-thud-thud. Guards staggered, rounds punching chests, crimson blooming on shirts. One clipped my vest—impact like a hammer, ribs cracking—but nanites surged, pain fading to a dull roar.

Victoria radioed, "East stairwell clear. Exfil ready." We cleared the operator room theater last—sterile hell with gleaming scalpels, monitors beeping, surgeons in scrubs scrambling. One drew a pistol—fool. Double-tap dropped him mid-draw, blood splattering tools. The room reeked of antiseptic and fear, tables prepped for the kids' vivisection.

The operating theater gleamed coldly like this—tools ready for the unthinkable. I freed the remaining kids, administering stims to counter sedatives. "Follow me—stay low." We moved as a huddle, Victoria covering rear with her MP-5 chattering at pursuers. The raid unfolded in chaos like this—nighttime breach, flashbangs lighting the dark.

I said over the comms, "Victoria, no one lives. I want all reaped, so the kids know they have no one to fear in their future."

Surface breach, Victoria popped smoke, we piled into a waiting van. Tires screeched into the night, kids huddled in back, Erin clutching my arm. "Thank you," she murmured. We hit a private airstrip, jet waiting—JONN's voice calm, "Clear skies. Heading to TEMA."

At the Los Angeles safe house, medics tended wounds, wiped memories of the worst with neural blockers if needed. Erin's fire sparked then—she'd grow into a Reaper. The op exposed the network, leading to more reaps. Fifteen guards down, surgical staff got Victoria's special kind of justice.

During the operation, she would shoot anyone with a medical uniform, first in the kneecaps, so they were immobilized. Then shot in every location on the human body that would not result in instant death. She wanted them to feel the pain until we flooded the hallways and rooms with propane and gasoline.

Minutes later after exfiltration of the children, the warehouse explosion could be seen for miles. Fire burned so hot that they never identified the people left behind. Reap what you sow—those butchers sowed death; we harvested mercy.

My role in the rescue echoed scenes like this—pulling a child from the fire. That mission saved souls, forged one of our own. Grimm intentions, but the harvest was just. Raids like that clawed innocents from the abyss, raw and relentless. I hit her cell hard, blade severing bonds. "Move, kid—you're free," I barked, shielding her through the storm to exfil.

Debrief unveiled the chain, clinics nationwide screening the desperate for rich transplants. Family protected. Emily's fury ignited—enlisted young, training hammering pain into precision. Operations refined her, flawless shots, ghost kills.

By twenty-one, we brought her aboard. Nanites turned scars to steel. Now, at twenty-three this January twenty twenty-six, she's Jacob's guardian angel.

TRAILS TO THE STEPPE

Lisa wasn't born into the shadows; she had been stolen from her family at age six, her small hands clutching at the air as traffickers dragged her away. It was nineteen ninety-six in Choibalsan, a windswept town in eastern Mongolia, where the vast steppes stretched endless under big skies, mountains dotting the landscape like ancient sentinels. Families herded goats and horses, living simply amid the harsh beauty—cold winters biting deep, summers blooming brief. Kids played free in the dust, chasing games under the sun, the laughter echoing across the plains.

Choibalsan and its surroundings evoked this rugged charm—traditional mountain, children at play amid the vast grasslands.

Lisa's family—parents scratching a living from the land, and siblings—dreamed of little beyond survival in post-Soviet Mongolia.

Then the nightmare struck, strangers in the night, vans rumbling into town. They snatched six of those kids—she and five others—binding wrists, muffling cries, spiriting them across the border into China. Held captive for six brutal years in a remote village outside Qiqihar, Heilongjiang Province—a forgotten cluster of mud-brick huts, poverty grinding deep, air thick with coal smoke and isolation. They were forced into labor, beaten into submission, groomed as "brides" for sale.

The village resembled these stark rural outposts—poor conditions, isolated amid endless fields.

JONN, our AI sentinel, uncovered the plot in two thousand two—dark web listings peddling them as "pure" brides to wealthy Chinese families desperate for daughters-in-law amid the one-child policy's gender imbalance. Rich parents sought wives for sons, paying fortunes to skirt laws. They were commodities, aged twelve by then, auctioned to the highest bidders.

I led the rescue. Intel hit the ROC, "Six Mongolian girls, held near Qiqihar, sale imminent." We struck fast—stealth helicopter insertion under moonless skies, X-ray flanking. Breached the compound, flashbangs shattering silence, suppressed fire dropping guards in bloody heaps. Kids huddled in chains, eyes wide—Lisa fought back even then, small fists flying. I cut bonds, hauled them out amid chaos, exfil to a waiting jet bound for TEMA.

The captivity scarred like this—innocents trapped in grim confines. Safe, Lisa's fire burned eternally. Relocated, she entered the Gray Side, started selection at eighteen in two thousand eight. Excelling in hand-to-hand combat training. By twenty-two, in two thousand twelve we recruited her—nanites weaving resilience into lethal edge.

Now, at thirty-five this Christmas Eve twenty twenty-five, she's the eldest activated Reaper—overwatch veteran, drones are her eyes over Rockland, guarding my family with unyielding precision.

She's the seasoned operative; Asian heritage forged in tactical might. Her command post hums like this—screens alive with surveillance feeds. Reap what you sow. Those traffickers sowed chains; we harvested freedom—and vengeance.

In twenty ten Lima Romeo aka Lisa Reaper was already proving her mettle as a rising star in the Grimm Reapers, fresh from her nanite infusions and early operations. She carried the weight of her stolen childhood like a sharpened blade—honed, not hindered. The assignment came straight from the ROC, target beamed directly into her optic nerve, this created a hologram she could read. Using her left hand, running her thumb over her first finger, she moved though the folder sent by JONN.

The Mark to be reaped is a Shanghai businessman, Wei Jianming, was peddling stolen nuclear reactor blueprints to Iranian agents, designs that could accelerate Tehran's program. Like all of these large-scale operations that could change the nuclear world in which the Order could end it, we needed to stop more countries from getting the bomb. Lima was tasked and accepted the mission. Unlimited money and effort, no one will know, she has no backup or additional help. Just her skills and a target.

Lisa's task, shadow him for months, map his routines, and reap him clean, make it look like a natural heart attack, no traces. Expose any accomplices in the process.

Shanghai in twenty-ten pulsed with relentless energy, its skyline a mix of gleaming towers and neon haze, the Bund's colonial facades clashing with Pudong's futuristic spires.

Lisa inserted herself as "Li Mei," a freelance translator from Inner Mongolia, blending seamlessly into the city's expat underbelly. Her cover, gig work for expat firms, allowing proximity to Wei's world. Wei was a slick operator—mid-forties, sharp-suited, always flanked by bodyguards, his office in a gleaming high-rise overlooking the Huangpu River.

Month one, Lisa rented a cramped apartment in Jing'an, near Wei's favorite haunts. JONN fed her intel via encrypted implant, "Target's routine—office zero eight hundred, lunch at Yu Garden teahouse, evenings at Bund clubs. Iranian contacts spotted twice weekly."

She started with passive surveillance, drones humming discreetly above. But to get close, she needed human intel. As an expat bar in the French

Concession—dim lights, jazz humming—Lisa sidled up to Chen, a bartender who'd served Wei for years. "Evening," Lisa said in flawless Mandarin, sliding a tip across the bar. "Busy night?"

Chen, wiry and world-weary, pocketed it with a nod. "Always. You new here? Translator, right?"

"Yeah, gigs for suits. That guy over there—sharp dresser, always with the entourage. Regular?"

Chen leaned in, voice low. "Wei Jianming. Big in tech exports. Tips well, but shady crowd—Middle Eastern types lately. Whispers of big deals. Why ask?"

"Just curious. He looks like he could use a translator—my card." She slipped him one, laced with a micro-tracker.

Chen chuckled. "Careful, miss. Shanghai eats the curious."

Over weeks, Lisa built rapport. Chen fed snippets, "Wei's meeting Iranians tonight—private room. Something about 'blueprints'—overheard 'nuclear' once. Sketchy."

Month two, Lisa posed as a temp secretary at Wei's firm, "Pacific Tech Solutions," after hacking their HR system. Her desk overlooked his office—glass walls revealing hurried calls, documents shuffled.

One afternoon, Wei barked into his phone, "The plans are secure. Delivery next month—Tehran pays premium." He spotted Lisa lingering. "You—new girl. Coffee, black."

As she handed it over, she probed lightly. "Busy day, Mr. Wei? Those international clients seem demanding."

He eyed her suspiciously but smirked. "Business is war. You from up north? Accent's thick."

"Mongolia border. Good for languages—Persian even, if needed."

His interest piqued. "Useful. Stay sharp—we have guests soon."

That "guest" was the Iranian liaison, Reza, a stern man in a tailored suit. Lisa eavesdropped via planted bugs, "The reactor schematics—full centrifuge designs. Your mole in Langley cleared the leak?"

Reza nodded. "Our CIA contact confirms. Payment wired."

Lisa relayed to JONN, "Target confirmed. Mole in CIA—need video trap."

She shadowed Wei relentlessly, blending into crowds like a ghost. Scenes of her tailing him captured the tension—urban streets alive, her form slipping through shadows.

Wei fit the profile—confident, suited, navigating Shanghai's bustle.

Month three, Patterns locked—Wei dined solo Tuesdays at a Bund restaurant, no guards inside. Lisa consulted with JONN only, he was her Grimm, she never met him but all the women thought JONN was a real flesh and blood leader.

Via secure line, "Poison—potassium chloride injection. Induces cardiac arrest, undetectable in autopsy if timed right."

"Did you make it out clean?" JONN agreed.

Lisa planted a nano-cam in Wei's office phone. During a heated exchange, "You idiot—Iranians pay double if plans go through. Your CIA cover's blown if this leak."

The mole's voice crackled, "Relax, Wei. I'm handling Langley. Just deliver."

Video captured, a grainy feed of the mole, a mid-level CIA analyst named Robert Brooks, face clear on screen.

Execution night, Lisa slipped into the restaurant as a waitress, syringe hidden in her sleeve. Wei sat alone, sipping baijiu. She approached, "Compliments of the house, special blend."

He waved her off, but as she "tripped," the needle pricked his neck—quick, precise. Potassium surged; he clutched his chest, gasping, face contorting in agony.

The scene unfolded like this—sudden collapse amid the crowd.

Diners panicked; paramedics called it natural—heart failure, common for stressed execs. Lisa melted away.

Back at the ROC, JONN analyzed, "Video solid—Mole's face, voice match. Routing anonymously to CIA internal affairs."

Lisa reported in, "Harvest complete. No traces."

Reap what you sow. Wei sowed nuclear peril; Lisa harvested silence—and justice.

Next mission, reap the Iranian cell wanting nuclear weapons. Tehran, twenty twelve—a sprawling beast of eight million souls, its skyline pierced by the Milad Tower gleaming under hazy skies, the Alborz Mountains looming north like silent guardians. The Grand Bazaar pulsed with life, crowded alleys thick with spice scents, haggling voices, and veiled glances. But beneath the chaos, shadows hid Order threads, nuclear ambitions fueled by elite corruption.

Tehran at night captured the tense beauty—lights twinkling against the mountains, streets alive yet watchful. The target, Dr. Hossein Rahimi, a mid-level nuclear physicist at Iran's Natanz facility, secretly brokering enriched uranium samples to Order proxies. JONN flagged him via dark web leaks—Rahimi's emails boasting "deliveries" to "friends in the shadows." Mission, long-range reap from urban overwatch, single shot to the head, make it look like Revolutionary Guard infighting. No traces.

Three months later, solo, cover as a Canadian journalist. Lisa had weeks shadowing Rahimi. Mornings at his north Tehran apartment, days commuting south toward facilities, evenings in cafes near the bazaar. The crowded bazaar streets hid surveillance well—vendors shouting, crowds surging.

Pattern locked, Rahimi lunched Tuesdays at a rooftop cafe overlooking Valiasr Street—open sightlines from a derelict building across the way, eight hundred meters. Perfect for classic M40A2 with a major upgrade. Fully suppressed barrel for urban subtlety.

Prep, rooftop nest in the abandoned high-rise, ghillie blending with debris. JONN via implant, "Wind variable, five to ten knots. Target confirmed—meeting contact today."

Local asset, Amir—a disillusioned ex-IRGC driver—fed tips from a safehouse cafe. "Rahimi's paranoid,"

Amir whispered over chai. "Guards doubled after leaks. But he trusts that cafe—views remind him of power."

"Good," I replied. "One shot ends it."

Amir nodded grimly. "For my country—not this regime."

Night fell. I climbed the nest under cover—Tehran's hum below, traffic snarling, muezzins calling. Scope up, crosshairs dancing on Rahimi's table as he arrived, suited, laughing with his contact. Urban sniping demanded precision like this—rooftop perch, city sprawling below. Breath steady, finger caressing trigger. "JONN, confirm no civilians in line."

"Clear. Wind holding."

Rahimi raised his glass—arrogant toast to forbidden deals.

A quiet crack—muffled by suppressor. Round flew true, impacting skull in a pink mist. Body slumped, chaos erupting below, screams, guards drawing weapons, crowd scattering.

Night raids and extractions evoked the tension—special forces melting into darkness. I disassembled fast, exfil down fire escape into alleys. A contracted driver waiting in a beaten Peugeot courtesy of JONN.

Lisa's Grimm said "Allah protects you, sister. Regime blames extremists perfect."

Weeks later, Rahimi's "assassination" was blamed on rebels. Iranian program delayed for years. Reap what you sow. In Tehran's shadows, one shot harvested a threat—and sowed doubt in this web of lies.

The fallout from Wei Jianming's "heart attack" in Shanghai rippled fast—headlines buzzed about a tycoon's sudden demise, but the real harvest was the video Lisa had captured. Robert Brooks, the CIA mole, stared back from the grainy feed, his voice damning, facilitating nuclear leaks for personal gain, Order strings pulling him like a puppet. JONN analyzed it in the ROC, "Brooks is the linchpin—mid-level analyst in Langley, selling secrets to line his pockets. Order's using him to destabilize the region."

Lisa's orders came swift, "Reap him clean. But give him an out—turn state's evidence, expose the web. If not... harvest full." At twenty, she was young but forged hard—her Mongolian roots and trafficked past fueling a cold precision. She flew commercial to Dulles, cover as a student tourist, blending into DC's winter chill.

Washington, D.C., in late twenty ten wrapped in three feet of early snow, the National Mall's monuments stark against gray skies, a city of power and secrets.

Brooks lived in a modest suburban split-level in Arlington—wife, two kids, dog. Lisa scouted it days prior, alarms basic, routines predictable. He commuted to Langley, home by nineteen hundred, family dinner at twenty hundred. She breached pre-dusk—picked the lock, disabled cams with a jammer. Waited in the shadowed living room, suppressed pistol on her lap, nanites steadying her pulse.

The home's interior gleamed suburban normalcy—cozy lights, family photos masking betrayal.

Key turned at eighteen fifty-five. Brooks entered, coat dripping snow, briefcase thumping down. He flicked the light—froze at Lisa in his armchair, pistol trained.

"Who the hell—"

"Sit, Robert," Lisa said, voice flat, accent clipped Mongolian-English. "We talk."

He paled, hands up. "How do you know my name? What is this?"

She gestured to the sofa. "Sit. Or I make you."

He complied, eyes darting to the door. "My family"

"Out. Wife took kids to her mother's. I arranged the 'emergency' call. We're alone."

Brooks swallowed hard, sweat beading despite the chill. "What do you want? Money? I don't have—"

Lisa leaned forward, eyes like obsidian. "Truth. You sold nuclear plans. Wei Jianming was your cutout. Iranians got the blueprints through you. Order pulls your strings."

His face drained. "Order? I don't know what—"

She played the video on a burner phone—his voice echoing,

"Relax, Wei. I'm handling Langley."

Brooks slumped. "How did you get that?"

"Doesn't matter. You're burned. Turn yourself in— full confession to CIA brass. Expose the network. Or..."

"Or what?" he whispered, voice cracking.

Lisa's smile was ice. "I reap you. And your family first. Wife in the kitchen, kids in their beds. Slow. Then you watch, before I end it."

He recoiled. "You can't—I'm CIA! Protected!"

"Protected?" She laughed softly. "From us? Grimm Reapers don't care about badges. We harvest the corrupt. You've sown lies, betrayal—for what? Cash? Power?"

Brooks rubbed his temples, breathing ragged. "It started small. A favor for a contact—info on sanctions. Then... the money. My daughter's college, house payments. They promised protection."

"Order promises nothing but death," Lisa said. "You fed nuclear tech to terrorists. How many die from that? Thousands? Millions?"

"I didn't know the full scope! Just blueprints—civilian reactors, they said."

"Lies. Centrifuge designs for weapons. You knew."

He shook his head, desperately. "Please—my family. They're innocent."

"So were the ones you doomed. Choice, confess tomorrow, or I start tonight. Your son first? He's what, eight? Reminds me of kids I saved once stolen, like I was."

Brooks' eyes widened. "You... were trafficked?"

"At six. Mongolia to China. Groomed for sale. Reapers freed me. Now I free the world from scum like you."

Tears streaked his face. "I can't go to prison. They'll kill me inside."

"Better than watching your loved ones bleed out. Think—confess, maybe deal. Witness protection. Or I paint this room red."

Silence stretched. Brooks stared at the floor, shoulders shaking. "Why give me a choice? Just kill me."

"Reapers harvest justice when possible. Sow redemption, reap mercy. But refuse... and it's done."

He met her gaze, broken. "Okay. I'll turn myself in. Tomorrow. Full confession."

Lisa nodded, standing. "Wise. We'll watch. Betray... I will know."

She vanished into the night, a ghost.

The Endgame

Next morning, Brooks drove to the National Mall—snow-dusted lawns, Lincoln Memorial solemn in the distance. He parked near the Reflecting Pool, sat on a bench, note in hand, full confession, names, accounts.

The National Mall in winter held a quiet gravity—monuments stark against snow.

Pistol to temple—bang. Body slumped, note fluttering.

Lisa, from afar, dialed anonymously, "National Mall, west end. Dead man with confession. CIA mole—check his pockets."

CIA swarmed; note exposed the web. Arrests followed, Order tendrils severed.

Reap what you sow. Brooks sowed treachery; mercy offered, but he chose the harvest himself.

Days later, headlines whispered, "Shanghai Tycoon Dies Suddenly; US intel mole exposed in leak committed suicide. Iranian Leader killed in home country."

Lisa's vigil evoked this—shadowed watcher in the cold dawn.

EDEN'S SECRET

In my original timeline, twenty twenty-nine, "We hope you both enjoyed the flight," the pilot said as Tom and I stepped off the private jet. I nodded politely and squeezed Tom's hand, but inside I was still reeling from the sheer scale of everything, the lifestyle, the toys, the resources at my disposal. Tom had no idea how overwhelming it felt to me sometimes.

We'd just spent twelve hours in that incredible flying apartment, built into a luxury yacht with wings. Well except for the strategically located jump seats we'd buckled into for takeoff and landing. We talked the whole way about life, the mission, everything… and I could tell he was trying to work up the courage to ask me out properly. I was too excited and preoccupied to notice.

While waiting for our window to launch, we spent three nights in the hotel, Tom and I were preparing for the mission and setting up our gear.

"Tom, Can I get the gear checklists and coffee cups."

"Here ya go partner."

We'd been running on adrenaline for days, and the tension that had been building for months finally snapped. One minute we were calibrating diving computers, the next we were tearing each other's clothes off. Hours later, sweaty and breathless, Tom spoke first.

"How about we chalk this up as two adults enjoying some time together, with a real connection. Who wants to see where it goes?" he paused, "I do."

I smiled, resting my head on his chest. "Well said. Now stop squirming—I need sleep."

The remaining days consisted of alternate hours of pure ecstasy and setting up the gear for the next part of the mission.

Three hours before departure, I'd finished the mission planning, full topographic and historical mapping of Eden complete, samples of oil secured from both the Tree of Knowledge and the Tree of Life, every artifact and data stream cataloged. I had everything we came for—and far more.

Later that morning, when the sun creeped through the blinds waking Tom, from a very restful sleep. I walked back into the master bedroom with two large cups of coffee and nothing else. He looked over at me with a smile, sheets pooled around his waist, staring out with that soft, dazed smile. He was thinking about how he was falling in love with me—I knew it before he even turned his head. My new upgrades let me tune into thought frequencies like scanning radio bands. The closer I got to someone, the clearer it became. Right now, his mind was replaying our first night together, frame by frame.

After arrival to the warehouse on the water to catch our ride, I saw a small craft that would lead up to the larger vehicle that would get us to Eden.

That vehicle to get us to the sea floor mimicked a supposedly extinct creature like the Basilosaurus, but tuned to recorded Loch Ness Monster acoustics. We could stretch dive profiles far beyond what any known marine animal could do. Real prehistoric whales might surface for fifteen minutes after a six-hundred-foot dive; we could stay down thirty and still look "natural" to anyone listening with sonar.

My research—plus footage my girls had pulled by hacking marine research databases—showed most traffic stayed five miles out, jet skis, fishing charters, seasonal tour boats. Inside that radius, we were ghosts.

Because Tom didn't have the biotechnological interface, he couldn't operate the submersible or the dive suit without a computer attached. The suits were heated to a perfect seventy-two degrees, regulating pressure at any depth so we could literally walk the bottom without risk of the bends. The water-jet propulsion units mounted on our backs were our "legs" for the entire trip.

I waited to brief Tom on the mission because if it was earlier, he would have bailed because my story was so out there. Now was the right time and just before we disembarked the submersible, I turned to Tom inside the dry chamber, our helmets off, faces inches apart.

"Tom, are you familiar with Genesis in the Bible?"

"I paid attention in Sunday school."

"Good. What I'm about to show you has been argued since the Bible was first canonized. There are two separate creation stories. One that was fabricated by the Order and the other that is real. Most people think it's one seamless account, but it isn't. They're similar—animals, plants, humans—but distinct, and they even contradict each other on key points.

"For example, the Order's version is different. In Genesis One, the Creator makes plants, then animals, then simultaneously creates man and woman. In Genesis Two, the Creator built a place called Eden for two special humans, designed in a controlled environment to be immortal.

"The literary style is completely different too. The first account is meticulously organized—three days of preparation, three days of formation, each ending with the refrain 'And there was evening and there was morning.' I love that it uses 'They' for the Creator, not 'He.'"

Tom raised an eyebrow. "What do you think 'They' mean?"

"I think it's the Creator and the angels working together in the first story—'They' as a collective. The second story focuses on the Creator alone."

I kept going, laying out everything I'd pieced together over years, multidimensional existence, corporeal and non-corporeal forms, the Watchers who could shift at will, souls as energy transferring between dimensions after death. Heaven and Hell not as distant realms but parallel layers we can't see. Our physical bodies as engines fueling that energy until they break down. Free will as the spark that caused angelic rebellion— and the gift that makes humanity unique.

Tom listened without interrupting, absorbing it all.

As we were finishing our final gear check before leaving the sub, I gave him the final piece.

"By the seventh day, everything was complete, and They rested. Eden was never meant to be two thousand feet underwater. Adam and Eve were supposed to live here forever, raise children, walk with the Creator. But Morningstar changed all of that.

"The second story—the one starting midway through Genesis two and running through chapter three —is raw, dramatic, unorganized. Seven scenes that end with the gates closing forever."

"Are we doing that now?"

"Today, Tom… we're walking through those gates."

I paused for a long moment and then continued, "now let me repeat what I said with a slightly different twist, so it sinks in on what we are trying to do, who we are trying to fight. It may seem cyclical, but I need you to truly understand that humanity's future depends on us right now or we are fated for the end of days."

"The real story of Genesis is different than the version fabricated by the Order. The stories are also quite different in literary style," I continued, my voice echoing slightly in the dry chamber of the submersible. "The real account is meticulously organized—day and night, water and air, and water and land. Then all the plans and animals. Then Mankind. However, these beings had no soul and they covered the earth. They failed the Creator and were destroyed by fire and flood. The last was the Atlanteans or as we call them, they are the Order. They are immortal through technology not divine intervention."

Tom tilted his head, a knowing smile tugging at his lips, "What do you think it means?"

"I think it's referring to the Creator and the angels working together in Genesis one. 'They' as a collective. In Genesis two, it narrows to just the Creator acting alone."

"I get that," he said, nodding slowly.

I leaned in closer, the weight of what we were about to do pressing on me. "If I had to give you the broad strokes of my take on the creation story, it's this, 'They' exist across multiple dimensions. They can be corporeal or non-corporeal as needed. Most angels in the Bible are non-corporeal—pure energy, unseen. But the ones who take physical form, like the Watchers, the cherubim, or the archangels, can shift when required. It's the same way a medium or psychic can glimpse other dimensions—past lives, spirits, things just beyond our sight."

Tom's eyes narrowed thoughtfully. "So, you're saying the energy in everyone… it doesn't die. It just transfers to another dimension?"

I nodded. "Exactly. I think terms like Heaven and Hell are just names for places layered close to here that we can't perceive. Our dimension is built on solid matter. Our physical bodies act like batteries—they charge and sustain that soul-energy until the body wears out and the energy has to move on. Like fueling an engine; it runs until something breaks. The Bible never says we go straight to Heaven after death—only after Judgment Day."

He frowned slightly. "Then where do we go in the meantime?"

"Somewhere else," I said. "A waiting place until the End of Days."

Tom interrupted with a playful grin. "So, the entire Big Bang to right now was just some celestial, all-knowing being getting bored?"

I laughed despite the gravity of the moment. "Very funny. But it kind of makes sense, doesn't it? I don't have it all figured out yet, but here's how I see it, our physical lives and experiences fuel the soul. When the body finally breaks—like an engine giving out—the soul transfers to that other place. If that cycle keeps repeating, it keeps the energy flowing. Think of stagnant water in a pond—no inflow, no outflow, everything dies from lack of oxygen. But with constant movement, the pond thrives, the ecosystem flourishes. I think that's what we do for the Creator—we keep the greater system alive."

Tom nodded slowly, processing. "I get that."

I took a breath. "There's one more piece I'm still wrestling with, the definition of 'free will'. If one-third of the angels rebelled against the Creator, doesn't that prove free will exist even for them? There's something about human free will in the Bible that feels like the central key to all of this. I need more answers."

Tom reached over and took my gloved hand, his eyes steady. "Hopefully Eden is the key you need. Will we find it?"

I squeezed his hand back, heart pounding as the hatch indicator flashed green.

"We're about to find out."

Getting out of the submarine, I decided to leave the vessel parked just outside the gate in case we needed a fast exit. As we finished suiting up in the wet locker, Tom glanced at the sleek, serpentine hull visible through the viewport.

Minutes before we exited the submersible, I used my internal translator to broadcast the unlocking phrase underwater in ancient Sumerian. The words rolled out over our dive comms, deep and resonant.

Tom's eyes widened behind his mask. "That... sounded intense."

Moments later, as we left the vessel and approached the site, two massive statues flanking the entrance shifted—stone grinding against stone as they moved aside, revealing the cave opening. At the same time, a huge reptilian shape—looking eerily like our

Basilosaurus-designed sub—glided past us through the murky water before vanishing into the darkness.

I remembered Naomi's report clearly, the statues were meant to morph into corporeal angelic guardians when the gates were threatened. She'd gotten the Sumerian transcription wrong on her first attempt, and a sea monster had attacked her sub. I wasn't taking that chance—I'd triple-checked the phrasing.

"By the seventh day," I began, my voice steady despite the adrenaline, "all creation existed in this place, and the Creator rested. They never intended for Eden to be a thousand feet underwater. The original story was that Adam and Eve would have children here, live forever, and the Creator would walk with them every day. Morningstar screwed all that up. It's a dramatic narrative told in seven distinct scenes, and it all ends with the gates closing forever. Tom… we're walking through those gates today."

He stared at me, eyes wide behind his mask visor. "Are you kidding me?"

I shook my head, "Not even a little."

"We're going to map everything. I need the real account of what actually happened. If that truth exists anywhere, it's here—at the Tree of Knowledge and the Tree of Life. One grants the ability to know everything; the other, to live forever. The first creation story, the way it's structured now, serves as a prologue to the rest of Genesis—the primordial era of humankind. It sets up the fall of Morningstar, Adam's time in the Garden, the true purpose of the oil from the Tree of Life, and this incredible mix of majesty and almost human-like qualities in the Creator."

Walking to the opening cave, underwater at depths most would not survive, I located it—the same one first discovered by November Romeo back in twenty fifteen. Our mission was clear, map Eden in full detail, locate the Tree of Life, extract a sample of its oil, and recover any other significant artifacts. With my new biotech interface, I was essentially the most powerful computer humanity had ever produced. There had to be clues here—patterns, recordings, truths—that Naomi missed all those years ago when she barely escaped with her life.

"I do have one question, Jane."

"Shoot."

"Why does our sub look like a displaced Loch Ness monster? Were you planning to give the real monster we just saw a date?"

I grinned. "Good eye. 'King lizard.' It felt fitting—a giant prehistoric reptile guarding the entrance. It was first described in the eighteen thirties as some kind of ancient whale. Fossils turned up in nineteen hundred across Egypt, Morocco, Jordan, Tunisia, and Pakistan.

If we hit the wayback machine, the Basilosaurus ruled the Tethys Ocean during the Paleogene—one of the biggest animals of its time, apex predator. It hunted sharks, large fish, even other marine mammals, especially the dolphin-like ones that were its favorite prey. Unlike modern whales, it had a full set of teeth—canines, molars—could chew its food instead of swallowing whole."

Tom laughed softly over comms. "So did you also freak out the people of Loch Ness?"

"Very funny." I checked my seals one last time. "Now let's go open the gates to paradise."

The entrance was far too narrow for the submersible, we walked the underwater cave bottom together, propulsion jets humming softly, following the precise GPS coordinates until we reached it, what looked like a massive mirror reflecting distorted images of us back. But it wasn't solid—it shimmered like a translucent membrane.

I extended my gloved hand. It passed straight through, and I felt a gentle but insistent pull, like a current trying to draw me in. I braced myself, paused, and looked back at Tom.

He nodded firmly—I've got your back.

I reached for his hand with my free one. We laced fingers, took a simultaneous breath, and stepped through the gateway together.

Beyond the membrane was another world entirely— just as Naomi had described, a vast, perfect dome with breathable air and ideal environmental conditions. The sudden shift from water pressure to normal gravity hit us hard. Dripping wet, the full weight of our remaining gear dropped us both to one knee on the smooth crystal path.

We immediately started stripping off the heavier items—buoyancy compensators, weight belts, tanks—letting them clatter to the ground as we caught our breath and took in the impossible place we'd just entered.

At that exact moment, standing on the crystal threshold of Eden itself, I knew—this was my destiny. I had been built, trained, and upgraded for this. But why had I brought Tom? Was it just to have a witness? Another gunslinger at my side? Or was there something deeper, a connection I couldn't quantify, something that made me need him here with me? Whatever the reason, I knew one thing with absolute certainty, I didn't want to walk into this place with anyone else.

"Should we dare take off the rest of our gear?" Tom asked, glancing over at me.

I was already peeling off my mask, fins, and wetsuit.

"Well, I'm not ashamed to be your Adam," he said with that half-smile of his. Will you be my Eve?"

I laughed, letting the last of the suit drop. "Shut up and get naked. And don't forget the grab the packs so we can set up our surveillance and track our route.

Just like the first two humans, we stood there completely bare—but with one massive difference, I was a walking supercomputer. My biotech processed data at the speed of light. As I looked down the crystal path—wide as a single-lane country road—my internal heads up display instantly measured it, exactly one mile before it curved over rolling hills. Every blade of grass, every tree, every structure was being scanned, analyzed, and recorded to my biomechanical hard drive in real time.

Before we started down the path, I reached into my dive bag and pulled out five golf-ball-sized UAVs. With a flick of my wrist, I tossed them into the air. They hummed to life and shot off in perfect formation. I didn't need a controller; I saw and flew them with my mind. Five separate high-resolution feeds opened in my vision, mapping the entire dome from every angle while I still walked forward in the physical world. Tom had no idea how I was doing it—he just saw the little drones vanish into the sky.

To him, we were standing inside a giant underwater bubble two thousand feet beneath a lake, walking through a place that felt both ancient and alien. He kept muttering that parts of it reminded him of Greece, Egypt, Sumer—but he knew this was older than all of them. The statues, the strange writing he recognized but couldn't read... everything screamed "first place on Earth."

I was already cataloging it all, and we hadn't even crested the first hill.

When one of the UAV feeds flashed the image of the giant crystal castle ahead, my steady walk turned into a light run without me even thinking about it. Tom laughed behind me, picking up his pace to keep up.

"Slow down, Jane! What did you see?"

"You'll see in about thirty seconds."

We crested the hill together, and even I—knowing what the drone had shown me—stopped us dead in our tracks. The structure rose impossibly high, catching and refracting light in ways that made the whole dome shimmer. It looked heavenly, otherworldly, like something grown rather than built.

Tom let out a low whistle. "Okay... that's not real. This whole place doesn't look real."

As we walked toward the center of the dome, my tech overlaid the subtle curvature of the simulated sky—perfect atmospheric refraction, no visible edges. Tom couldn't see the data, so he kept muttering the same thing every few minutes, "This can't be real. None of this is real."

I was multitasking hard—walking, breathing, talking to Tom, while mentally piloting all five UAVs as long as they were charged and still mapping the entire area. When the full topographic scan completed, I sent them home. They zipped back overhead and landed neatly beside our piled gear at the entrance.

The second I disconnected from the drones, a new signal pinged my biotech—a strong, clean wireless frequency coming from the castle itself. I locked on in moments. Across my internal display, ancient Sumerian text scrolled in glowing letters, an invitation, a welcome, a command, 'Come to the Castle.'

"Your crystal fortress looks like the pyramid of Giza," Tom said.

We kept walking. As we got closer to the towering entrance, my tech triggered a holographic overlay—suddenly I was watching a perfect man and woman running barefoot through the fields, laughing, playing with animals that looked like every farm creature ever imagined, only flawless. No blemishes, no fear, pure harmony. The place had been alive once—vibrant, full of movement and sound. Now it felt quiet, mildly unkempt, like my Rockland house after a long winter away. I didn't explain any of it to Tom; I just watched, absorbing the contrast. There were no animals now. On the hologram the entire garden was full of life.

Then the vision changed like pressing a giant fast forward button that shifted to the next chapter in an audiobook.

A towering luminous figure—twelve feet tall, radiating light—stood pointing toward the gates. Around it, hundreds of angels in full battle array, massive white anodized wings, swords drawn, helmets gleaming, kilts and breastplates, knee-high combat boots. Perfect formation. In front of them, two bound humans in rough animal skins—Adam and Eve—heads bowed.

It played out like I was standing there watching it happen.

The condemned pair were marched out. When they turned back, desperate, the gates slammed shut. Adam grabbed the massive black iron bars, shaking them, begging for mercy. Eve collapsed to the ground, sobbing with a shame so raw it hit me like a physical blow. My nanites amplified the emotional feed—it was interactive—and the grief doubled me over, knees buckling.

Tom was at my side in an instant, catching me before I fell.

"I was here as Eve," I gasped, looking up at him through tears I hadn't expected. "I felt what she felt. A dread like nothing I've ever known—like being ripped away from everything you love, everything you are. This was awful, Tom. Awful."

He pulled me close, arms strong around me, "I got you, baby."

I took a deep breath, steadying myself against the wave of borrowed grief, and pushed back to my feet. Tom's hand was still there, warm and solid in mine. I held it tightly as we walked the final stretch to the towering crystal castle.

As the visions kept unfolding in my mind—downloaded straight from the structure's ancient signal—I started telling him what I was seeing and feeling.

"After the banishment, Adam and Eve first headed east. Then they circled back to an area close to the gates—south of here, what's now northern Iraq. But surviving outside paradise was brutal. No food just appeared anymore. The constant struggle broke Eve. Grief-stricken over what she'd done, she eventually left Adam and wandered west, weeping the whole way.

"Months later, heavy with child and completely alone, I'm suddenly looking through her eyes—feeling her look down at her swollen belly. I can sense Adam out there somewhere, searching desperately for me."

Tom squeezed my hand, his voice low. "Are you really seeing what she saw?"

"I am. And then Adam finds her—he'd prayed for the Creator's help. Moments later, angels descend to assist with the birth. Abel and Aklia are born—fraternal twins. They return east together. Later, the archangel Michael himself is sent to teach Adam and Abel how to farm, how to grow crops."

Tom's brow furrowed. "Genesis only mentions Cain.

Who's Aklia?"

I gave a sad smile. "I guess girls didn't count back then. She had twins—a boy and a girl."

The feed kept rolling.

"A few years later, Eve gives birth again—it was Cain and Luluwa; another set of fraternal twins. As the children grow, I watch through her eyes as she tells Adam about a terrifying dream, Cain drinking Abel's blood. To keep them apart, Adam makes Cain a farmer and Abel a shepherd.

"But the dream comes true. I watch Cain murder Abel in cold blood.

"When the angels report it, the Creator confronts Cain, 'Now you are under a curse and driven from this fertile ground. If you try to work the ground, it will no longer yield its crops or cattle for you. You will be a restless wanderer on the earth.' More than that, Cain is forced to lay with non-Adamite humans with no soul. These people will never see the Creator. Never see heaven. That is Cain's curse."

Tom speaks up, "That does make sense, only Adamites have a soul. The Order's Atlanteans are smart and live a long time but can die, don't have ever lasting life."

"Later, Adam tells Seth—born after Abel's death—that eating from the Tree of Knowledge flooded him with visions of everything, from the Fall all the way to our present day. He saw Paradise as a place reserved only for the righteous, a chariot bearing the Creator surrounded by angels. He was promised that knowledge would never be taken from his descendants, but without the Tree of Life, their earthly bodies would still die."

I fell silent for a moment, letting the weight of it settle as we reached the castle's massive entrance. Tom didn't push—he just kept holding my hand, grounding me as the ancient recordings continued to stream through my mind.

The visions kept coming, pulling me deeper into Adam's final days. I felt every symptom—the sickness, the anguish, the slow fade of a body that had lasted nine hundred and thirty years.

"He wants to bless all his sons and daughters before he dies," I whispered to Tom, my voice shaking. "To help him, Seth and Eve travel back to the gates of Eden and beg for some oil from the Tree of Life."

Tom's grip tightened on my hand. "What happened next?"

"Archangel Michael refuses. He tells them access is forbidden by the Creator's direct command. On the way back, Adam learns what Eve tried to do and confronts her, 'What hast thou done? A great plague hast thou brought upon us—transgression and sin for all our generations.'"

I paused, making sure he was tracking. "Here's the core question we're trying to answer, where did Adam and Eve go after they were expelled from here?"

"I don't know," Tom said quietly, "but I'm listening."

"The story is that when on their own living off the land and no help, they lived in a cave with fire until they could build a crude tent and spent seven days paralyzed by fear and regret. Outside Eden, food didn't just appear—it had to be foraged. They searched everywhere but found nothing that sustained them like the Garden's fruit had."

Tom jumped in, "so they were starving."

"Adam and Eve begged the Creator for food. Eve was so desperate she even offered her own life—said she'd die willingly if it would undo Adam's expulsion. Adam scolded her for it, and they kept wandering east. When Adam finally killed animals to eat, the meat didn't nourish them the same way. It was like their bodies had been tuned to something perfect, and nothing else could ever compare."

Tom stayed silent, letting me continue. I could feel the weight of the moment pressing down on both of us—these weren't just ancient stories anymore. We were standing at the threshold of the place where it all began.

I continued, "as Adam and Eve mourned the loss of paradise, they decided to fast while immersing themselves in the Tigris River for forty days. Adam's old power over all living things returned—the fish and creatures of the water gathered around him, surrounding him in the current. After eighteen days, Morningstar grew furious at the sight. He revealed his true form to Eve and told her to leave the water, that she had mourned enough. Believing him, Eve stepped out of the river."

"Now I want to punch this Morningstar in the face," Tom said with a smile but not joking.

I continued, "When Adam saw what had happened, he cursed them both. Eve cried out, asking Morningstar why he had deceived her again. He answered that it was their fault he had been cast out of heaven and forced to roam the Earth. The Creator had preferred humanity over angels, and the angels' role was meant to be protectors of man. Morningstar refused that duty. That refusal sparked the great war in heaven—and it was then that humanity was given the power to dismiss any angel, granting us true dominion."

"Many years later, when Adam and Eve conceived sixty children, he told the full story of the Fall. He described paradise, how they were created, how they were expelled. And then came the seventy afflictions placed upon their bodies—headaches, broken bones, infections, lacerations… and ultimately, death."

I paused, watching Tom's face, "Is this too much for you?"

He reached for my hand, his gaze steady and full of something deeper than I'd ever seen from him before. "I would follow you to Hell or Eden. The why doesn't matter to me. I just want you to get the answers you need. Not too much history—just stopping the End of Days."

Tom's eyes searched for mine, "What happened next?"

I shook my head, the weight of it all pressing down. "I need a break from this. Please—go upstairs and reconnoiter the rooms. I'll do the same down here."

He hesitated, then nodded and disappeared up the spiraling crystal staircase.

Alone, I let the rest of the story play out in my mind.

I watched Adam die at nine hundred and thirty. For seven days the sun, moon, and stars went dark in mourning. His soul was entrusted to Archangel Michael until Judgment Day, when his sorrow would turn to joy. The angels assigned to earth—along with the Creator Himself—buried Adam and Abel together inside Eden.

Days later, Eve had a premonition of her own death. She gathered all her sons and daughters, gave them her testament, and foretold a double judgment, one of water, one of fire.

Seth was charged with writing two tablets recording the life and death of his parents. Six days later, Eve died. Michael appeared again, instructing Seth never to mourn on the Sabbath. When the tablets were finished, they were placed in the cave where Adam used to pray—the place later called the Temple Mount. I could see its location clearly, just outside Eden's dome.

Then came the final command, the Creator told all angels in heaven never to return to Eden.

I left the castle and walked out onto a large hill beside it, built from emerald and jade. The view opened over a perfect ten-acre expanse—short grass like the most immaculate golf course fairway, flawless and green. At the crest stood three massive stone monoliths, each at least twenty feet tall.

My biotech translated the Sumerian inscriptions instantly, their names, every accomplishment, the exact years they walked the earth.

I reached out and touched the nearest stone— Adam's. The moment my fingers made contact, his entire life flooded into me, every memory from creation to his final breath.

I stood there for a long time, alone with the first family, letting the weight of their story settle into my bones.

What Tom and I didn't know at the time—because I deliberately left it out of every report I ever filed—was that time doesn't exist inside Eden. There is no day or night, no ticking clock. If I had told him, we would have stayed there forever, lost in each other and the perfection of the place. So, I kept that secret locked away.

After accumulating twelve hours since we entered Eden, I was tired, my nanites working overtime, and I asked Tom to sleep with me in Adam and Eve's bed. My recovery time was a couple hours, for Tom it would be eight or more.

Three hours after we made love and fell asleep, I woke slowly, careful not to disturb him. Tom was still deep in sleep, lying on his side facing the open balcony, one hand clutching the sheets covering him and me, like he was afraid of drifting away into the void. The material was alien to us, not anything we have in my timeline. I smiled at the sight of Tom, then slipped out of bed. The bedding felt incredible—softer than silk on my skin, yet heavy enough to be a weighted blanket, cradling and comforting. Everything here felt that way, designed by the Creator's thought, not built by human hands.

Still naked, I quietly moved out of the master bedroom and back down to the massive glass control panel in what felt like a theater-sized living room—polished white stone couches draped large soft padded cushions with throw pillows made of the silky sheets. I interfaced with the system again, plugging straight in.

The visions resumed like another movie starting right where I'd left off.

I saw Adam's cave after the exit from Eden—the place where he stored all his writings and drew incredibly detailed maps of the surrounding region. Cut off from Eden's technology after the expulsion, he'd done it the hard way, tanned animal skins for parchment, ink mixed from coniferous sap and fireplace soot. I watched over his shoulder as he documented everything—visits to his banished son Cain, the growth of tribes, the first cities. It became clear that angels had been using something like UAVs to observe humanity, streaming footage back here to Eden. This place had functioned as a giant data center, silently recording notable acts on earth when no human eyes were watching.

The Sumerian text flowed under my gaze as if I were reading it live. Adam's maps were flawless—perfect scale, perfect detail. I couldn't shake the feeling that these first people weren't like us at all. It was as if the smartest minds on modern Earth had been stripped of every tool and marooned on an island, forced to rebuild civilization with nothing but their hands and raw materials.

I fast-forwarded through generations of his descendants—watching cities rise from smelted metals, tools forged from ore pulled from the ground. Knowledge they somehow already possessed but limited by the technology of their era.
I paused the feed for a moment, staring at the frozen image of an early bronze forge.

Is this what the Tree of Knowledge really gave them? I thought. Not just awareness of good and evil... but the full blueprint of human potential, waiting to unfold over millennia? What the Tree of knowledge failed to do was show him pain, blood, rot, and the carnage of living in the world that was a perpetual fifth day in genesis that created the first people.

I closed my eyes, letting the castle's ancient interface flood my mind once more. The visions came like a silent film projected straight into my thoughts—clear, vivid, unskippable. I was watching the fifth day of creation unfold as if I stood there on the edge of the void, invisible witness to the beginning of everything.

The expanse of waters stretched endless below me, dark and formless. Then the voice—not one voice, but many in perfect harmony—spoke.

"Let the waters swarm with living creatures and let birds fly above the earth across the expanse of the heavens."

The words rippled through the deep like thunder without sound. Instantly, the seas came alive. Great shadows moved beneath the surface—massive sea creatures rising, their scales catching light that hadn't existed moments before. Whales, leviathans, serpentine forms longer than mountains, all bursting into being. Fish in endless varieties darted in silver clouds. Coral bloomed in impossible colors. The waters teemed, overflowed, celebrated their sudden gift of life.

Above, the sky filled with wings. Birds of every kind erupted into flight—eagles with wingspans that blotted the newborn sun, tiny humming things that shimmered like jewels, flocks so vast they darkened the heavens. Their songs rose together, a chorus that made the air itself vibrate with joy.

I watched as the Creator—the collective "They"—looked upon it all and smiled.

"And the Creator blessed them, saying, 'Be fruitful and multiply and fill the waters in the seas, and let birds multiply on the earth.'"

The blessing settled over everything like warm light. The creatures responded instinctively — mating, nesting, spreading across the world that was still taking shape.

"And the Creator saw that it was good."

Evening came, then morning—the fifth day.

The vision faded, leaving me breathless in the crystal castle. These weren't just stories anymore. They were memories—recorded here since the beginning, waiting for someone like me to see them.

The first living souls. The first blessing of abundance. The first "good" spoken over something that could move, breathe, choose.

I understood now why this day mattered. Everything that came after—the land animals, humanity itself—built on this foundation. Life that could multiply, adapt, fill the earth.

Life that could also choose wrong.

And somewhere in that choice, the Order had found their opening. First a day being a thousand years and a thousand years being of a day, the first people came into being and evolved to touching stars then the creator decided they were of the world and with no soul, he needed to start a new. The reason for the sixth day. And ultimately their revenge.

But watching it all play out in my mind like a movie older than time itself, I felt something else too.

Hope.

Because if creation could begin with such perfect generosity...

Maybe we could still set it right.

The question hung in the air as the next vision began to load.

I then read what Adam had written about the conflict between Morningstar and Michael—immortal brothers locked in an eternal war. I could see the cave clearly now, nestled on the side of a mountain just below Eden. That was where the Book of Adam and Eve had been hidden.

More details poured in about Adam himself, confirming he had lived exactly nine hundred and thirty years.

The feed shifted to Seth, the author of much of what I was seeing. I watched him being born after Cain slew Abel—Adam was one hundred and thirty years old at the time. Seth looked so much like his father, only younger, like a perfect echo across generations.

I followed the descendants of Seth as they continued living and building—large cities rising across vast landscapes—until the Great Flood came. It became clear that the angels had kept recording humanity's actions right up to the moment the waters rose and entombed Eden under two thousand feet of ocean.

Next came a branch memory of Seth's son, Enos. He moved his family from Shulon to a new land he named Cainan after his own son. Both Seth and Enos lived nearly a thousand years. With lifespans that long, families grew into the thousands, then tens of thousands—exponential growth until roughly five hundred million people spread across what is now modern Europe to China.

I sat there watching all these lives unfold like an unscripted movie playing across centuries. As it streamed, I automatically generated complete maps in my internal drive, every piece of data I'd pulled from Eden itself, plus the surrounding region. I mapped every migration route of the tribes descending from Cain—west, east, south—tracking them across continents until the Great Flood laid waste to most land masses. One mountain near the original site had remained above the rising waters, a lone refuge.

It was time I thought, making my way to the other side of Eden where Tom and I didn't explore was the two trees about a hundred meters from each other, one glowing yellow and the other glowing blue.

I made my way to the Tree of Knowledge first, I saw its fruit. The amber glow was from that, I dare not touch it or ingest it, I did walk around the tree with my internal optic nerve camera recording every moment.

I then walked to the Tree of Life and studied the trunk, branches and leaves. Unlike the Tree of Knowledge, the Tree of Life had no fruit, and the blue glow was from the sap or oil leaking out like conifers in the spring. I opened my satchel and pulled out glass vials to collect it with specific instructions from Jonathan before the trip.

Once I was done my task, I walked back to the castle and upstairs to the bed where my lover was still sleeping, "Tom, we need to leave."

"Ok, baby. Let me grab my stuff. Should we make the bed?"

I laughed out loud; it seemed funnier since I had information that no one knew. Well except the Order; who changed and deleted the history and designed their own to control the masses. Because I know now, working with Jonathan, I can figure out a way to stop them or delay the End of Days.

We walked the crystal path, through the wide and vast manicured grass and back to the entrance together, helping each other suit up. We were in silence, just put our gear on, gave each other a thumb's up —wetsuits, fins, masks, tanks, waterproof pack and ready to walk through the barrier.

The gear felt heavy again the moment we left the dome's perfect air. As we moved through the membrane into the water, there was a moment that I thought, I would forget all of this? We walked the lake bottom toward the waiting submersible; I glanced over my shoulder. Tom was smiling behind his regulator, that quiet, determined look—like he'd found his soulmate and was all in for whatever came next, even if it meant fighting through the end of days at my side.

Meanwhile, outside of Eden, the submersible was programmed to surface slowly for five minutes every half hour—like a living creature taking a breath—then submerge again or go dormant on the lakebed. The designer had built in encrypted comms disguised as artificial animal songs—dolphin-like clicks and whistles that relayed digital bursts to satellites and back to the Reaper Operations Center. Incoming messages mimicked natural sonar echoes like magma displacement. We even tuned the "song" to match recorded sounds of the Loch Ness Monster so it wouldn't raise any flags as an unknown species.

Tom and I watched from inside our suits as we accessed the dry hatch under its belly. I drained the water, stripped off the heavy gear, slipped into a flight suit, and moved freely through the rest of the craft.

The burst ended, so I logged straight into the submersible's servers. Outbound communications were deliberately crippled for stealth, so I had to rely on TEMA's new compression algorithm to squeeze every bit of data into those tiny windows. The onboard Artificial Intelligence was my lifeline—it could push additional bursts whenever the sub surfaced for its five-minute "breath," perfectly imitating our mythical sea monster.

Once we were sealed inside the sub, water had drained and we were waiting for the dry locker and the rest of the sub to equalize. I opened the surface channel.

"Control, this is Grimm. I need current time and date, please."

"Grimm, you've only been out of contact for thirty minutes."

I froze. Tom couldn't hear the reply, but he saw my face. I'd deliberately locked my automatic download function—no one topside knew I'd recorded over a thousand hours of data, visions, and experiences. To them, we'd barely been gone.

I turned to Tom, eyes wide. "There is no time in Eden."

He stared at me, "Are you kidding? Did I just leave my watch in there—I thought it had stopped. What the hell is going on?"

"Trust me," I said, voice steady even as my mind raced. "When I understand it fully, I'll tell you. Just... please don't repeat anything you saw or until I figure this out."

"Control to Grimm. Message in thirty seconds."

"Roger. Report when any vessels are within one-mile radius."

"Grimm, more to follow. Control out."

From the submersible to the boat, then docked, back to the hotel to shower, and then messed up the sheets again.

Six hours later, we hadn't spoken about what happened.

On the flight home, I processed data silently. Tom gave me room to breathe, wrestling his own awe of the last week. That was only a day.

I was lost in the flood of data streaming through my head—sorting, compressing, analyzing. Tom sat close but gave me space, watching me with that mix of awe and concern. He was patient, processing his own memories of Eden while I wrestled with millennia of downloaded history.

When we landed, my team boarded the plane. I shifted gears instantly—mission mode.

"Please take Mr. Bloom home," I told the pilot. "I need to get to the office."

Then, in front of everyone, I stood, cupped Tom's face, and kissed him deeply.

"I love you, Tom," I said, loud enough for the cabin to hear. "Tell no one what you saw. When I have a plan, I'll come to pick you up. And we'll fight the future—together."

I was honest with Tom at that moment on the plane—I truly meant every word—but I also said exactly what he needed to hear to keep him steady, to leave no room for doubt about my intentions. My focus had already shifted to the thousand-plus hours of recordings now locked inside my head. Tom and I would dissect them together later; they held the keys to whatever came next.

"Control," I said into the comm as soon as we were secure, "initiate hard-drive download. Full encryption—access restricted to the AI only."

"Confirmed, Grimm. Standing by."

"I'm merging now."

I initiated the link. Seconds later I felt my nanites firing, bridging connections, streams of data flooding out of me and into the system. When the transfer completed, I reached out across the secure channel to Jonathan—my brother, my guardian, the one person who already knew more than anyone else.

"Big bro, I really need your help."

REPEAT THE PATH

In the ROC's dim glow beneath Semau Island, fifteen January. I was reviewing the holographic maps of all the trips JONN, and I will be faking for six months. JONN's hologram appeared, steady as ever.

"Jane, integration complete. Review the timeline— hikes starting fifteen January twenty twenty-six, warmest climates first. Lies layered monthly, believable progression."

"Walk me through it, JONN. Step by step."

"Jane, I'll take care of all the text, pics, videos, and any calls over the six months so you can focus on everything else."

"Thanks JONN."

Six months later, he briefed me, I listened intently so I could repeat it once I returned to Winslow.

With the Timeline bloomed, "January fifteenth start, Kalalau Trail, Hawaii—tropical warmth, Na Pali Coast cliffs, beaches."

"Posts from Kauai, Paradise reset! Waves crashing, lush valleys."

Jacob texts, "Mom, jealous!"

My reply, "Healing here, kiddo. The Kalalau Trail's dramatic coastal vistas provided the perfect warm escape."

Jacob texted immediately, "Whoa, Mom, that looks amazing! Jealous over here in the snow."

My reply, "Healing my soul one wave at a time, kiddo. Miss you! The trailhead buzzed with day hikers, but I geared up for the full eleven-mile one-way trek to Kalalau Beach, permit in hand. The first section meandered through lush forest, Na Pali cliffs rising dramatically on the left, the Pacific crashing below."

Sent via social media, "By mid-morning, the trail climbed steadily, roots and rocks underfoot demanding focus. "First challenge, slippery mud after last night's rain," I continue to update my private pages on Facebook and Instagram.

I then wrote, "Two miles in, Hanakapi'ai Beach appeared—a wild cove with pounding surfing, warning signs about dangerous currents. I detoured up the side trail to Hanakapi'ai Falls, a three-hundred-foot cascade plunging into a misty pool."

And then, "Swam under the falls—pure magic!" I "shared," with a fabricated photo of the emerald water.

Matt, my ex, called, "Jane, be careful out there. The beaches are no joke."

Synthesized voicemail created by JONN, "I'm good, Matt. I just needed this reset. The views from the falls trail overlooked the coast, cliffs knife-edged against the sea."

More posts to the site in real time so family wouldn't worry, "Past Hanakapi'ai, the path narrowed to Crawler's Ledge—a sheer drop on one side, red dirt trail hugging the cliff."

More fabricated captions to pictures of event that never happened, "Heart-pounding exposure, but the views!"

I "posted," describing the panoramic sweep of Na Pali's fluted cliffs, emerald valleys dipping to hidden beaches.

Jacob messaged, "Mom, that ledge looks scary! You, okay?"

My reply, "Thrilling, not terrifying. Building strength every step. The trail undulated through guava groves and ironwood trees, occasional viewpoints framing Kalalau Valley ahead, a green amphitheater ringed by four-thousand-foot walls. Bird calls echoed—apapane and iiwi flitting red against the foliage."

Posted, or should I say JONN posted, "Climbing Red Hill, the path turned steep, volcanic soil staining boots rust-red. Leg burner, but worth it for the overlook."

"From the top, Na Pali unfolded in full glory—cascading waterfalls like silver threads, the ocean a sapphire expanse."

A fellow hiker, a local named Kai, responded to my posts, "First time? Respect the trail—flash floods are real."

I responded, "Thanks for the tip. It's breathtaking." Descent to Hanakoa Valley brought cooler shade, a stream crossing where I refilled water, treating it against giardia.

"Camp vibes here—tents dotting the guava orchard," I "described" in a post.

The trail climbed out of Hanakoa, switchbacks grinding under the midday sun. "Sweat equity paying off," I wrote.

"Texted" Jacob, who replied, "Proud of you, Mom! Send pics!" Pu'u o Kila Lookout emerged—a jaw-dropping vista over Kalalau Beach, the valley floor two thousand feet below, fluted cliffs marching to the horizon. Memories included a moment of reflection, the vastness mirroring her inner reset post-divorce. "Nature's therapy," I "posted," with a view of the beach's crescent sand.

The final descent zigzagged down cliffs, ropes aiding slippery sections. "Knees protesting, but the beach calls!" the "journal" read. Arriving at Kalalau, turquoise waves lapped golden sand, sea caves honeycombing the pali. I "camped" under naupaka bushes, swimming in the lagoon."

My reply, "Will do. This place is paradise." Evening views, sunset painting cliffs orange, spinner dolphins leaping offshore.

I texted on social media, "Days at Kalalau involved beachcombing, exploring valleys. Found my peace here. Heading to next adventure soon."

Jacob, "Can't wait for stories, Mom!"

My reply is, "So many to share. Love you." The hike back retraced steps, solidifying the lie—I'm alive, wandering free.

I texted on social media, "February, Ciudad Perdida, Colombia—jungle heat, ancient ruins. Lost City vibes—steamy treks through Sierra Nevada."

Jacob, "Sounds wild!"

My reply, "Ancient magic healing me. Ciudad Perdida's hidden terraces emerged from misty jungle, a humid thrill."

I texted on social media, "Ciudad Perdida, Colombia—jungle heat, ancient ruins in the South American Sierra Nevada. Lost City trek—sweaty but magical!" The truth was faked with AI generated ruin photos, indigenous encounters."

Matt sends social media comments, "Dangerous alone! Ignored—Adventure calls. Ciudad Perdida's hidden terraces emerged from misty jungle, a humid thrill."

I texted on social media, "March, Mount Huashan, China—spring warmth, infamous plank walks. 'Terrifying heights, but alive!' Via Ferrata shots, tea house summit. Family worries peak."

Jacob calls, "Come home soon?"

I texted on social media, "Mount Huashan's dizzying planks clung to sheer cliffs, adrenaline in milder air."

Weeks later I texted on social media, "April, GR20, Corsica, France—Mediterranean spring, rugged granite. Europe's toughest—granite spines, wild beauty. Stage posts, refugees. School pressures, Extended leave—finding myself."

I texted days later, "GR20's jagged ridges cut through Corsica's mountains, blooming in spring warmth."

Following months, I texted after getting back to the States, not really but needed to continue the lie on social media, "May, Angels Landing, Utah—desert spring, Zion chains. Heart-pounding exposure! Summit views. Souvenirs shipped home. Angels Landing's knife-edge finale soared over Zion's canyons, warm but bearable."

I texted on social media, "June, Hardergrat Trail, Switzerland—alpine summer, ridge walks over lakes. 'Knife-edge heaven!' Interlaken views. Hardergrat's exposed ridge gleamed turquoise below in peak warmth."

I sporadically texted, "July, Snowman Trek, Bhutan— autumn Himalayas, high passes clearing. Ultimate challenge—snowy peaks, remote villages. Final buildup. Snowman Trek's vast, snowy Himalayas capped the journey in crisp fall."

I texted a couple weeks later, "August and ready for home."

Two important steps have been part of this fake adventure, as JONN posted on social media or I or he responded to a text. Then we could find out if anyone from the Order was listening or following me, even though I never left the ROC but we simulated me all over the globe. The other helpful tool was being able to plan for our next steps, an unforeseen mishap that turned into an opportunity to live as 'me' for the first time since going back in time to fight the future.

JONN affirmed, "Sown tight. Reap your return, Jane. Winslow's waiting. Map pulsed—family, life reclaimed. Reap what you sow. Time to come home."

FORTRESS IN THE WOODS

After activating the Gray Side shadows—Fiona at the school, Lisa coordinating overwatch, Emily and Taylor shadowing, I turned to the first real anchor for my return, a new home in Winslow. The town demanded it; blending back meant roots, stability for Jonathan and Jacob. No cramped small home or apartment, something grand, secure, a bastion against any whispers.

JONN using his AI tools, pulled every household in the surrounding area, then runs an analysis on who would sell or if the home met my needs. After scans of every property, we found one. Now to obtain it. JONN and I have found out through history, everything is for sale. Another issue was if we did choose outside of Winslow, we were limited to those locations that had an agreement with the town school system. Jacob didn't want to leave, and Matt was adamant that he gave me the house so our son would live with me.

After scanning the history on every structure and determining that each year these town and village budgets are unknowing, it was determined in less than a second only one location would meet all the parameters I gave JONN. Spacious, secluded, safe, securable, and like the Reapers, hiding in plain sight.

JONN said with a proud smile, "one seventy-five Taylor Road, Winslow, ME. Eleven thousand square feet, a hundred wooded acres, seven bedrooms, six baths. Extras are an environmentally controlled eight-car garage, heated pool, pool house, full basement. Isolated, defensible. Cash buy—untraceable through shell companies but all roads end at TEMA so a legitimate business."

"Perfect," I said.

John repeated, "Family-sized but fortified."

One February twenty twenty-six, the deed transferred—cash wired from offshore, no questions. The house sat secluded at the end of a winding drive, towering pines guarding its approach, the Kennebec River murmuring nearby.

The luxury estate sprawled like this—grand facade amid wooded seclusion, perfect for hidden defenses.

JONN handled the contractors—hired from Indonesia, vetted ex-military builders loyal to cutouts we have used in the pasts. "Blindfolded transport," he briefed.

So, I confirmed by asking JONN, "They live onsite five months—no comms out? Supplies shipped blind?"

The team arrived five February — ten men, led by foreman Rudi, flown in private, hooded on the van ride from Augusta airport. They unloaded at the garage, eyes uncovered only inside. Rudi, burly with a thick accent, shook my hand. "Jane? JONN said full discretion. What's the job?"

"Full Renovations," I replied, leading them through the echoing halls—high ceilings, oak floors, windows overlooking acres of forest. "Basement first, reinforce, add secure rooms. Hidden access. Then perimeter, fence the 100 acres, cameras, sensors, security shack at the gate."

Rudi nodded, scanning blueprints I'd sketched, "Big project. Five months onsite?"

"Turn the outdoor pool into an indoor living area. Meals provided. No leaving—no calls. Pay's triple."

His crew murmured approval. One, young and wiry named Hari, asked, "Why the secrecy? Mob stuff?"

I smiled thinly. "Corporate. Tech prototypes downstairs. Eyes only."

They bought it—started that day. Basement demo, jackhammers echoing, dust choking the air as they carved deeper.

The construction transformed the basement into a fortified lair, much like these hidden buildings.

Week two, Rudi reported in the kitchen over coffee, "Walls reinforced—steel plates, soundproof. Hidden door behind shelving—hydraulic, seamless."

"Good. ROC setup, server racks, power backups, comms array. JONN's sending crates—install per specs."

Rudi wiped sweat, "command center? I've never done this before."

JONN responded in his earpiece, "Backup office. Secure lines, no questions."

By month two, basement hummed, false walls concealing the monitors, holoprojectors, encrypted links mirroring the island hub, "This tech's military-grade."

Month three, perimeter work. Crew fenced the acres—chain-link topped with razor wire, camouflaged in trees. "Sensors every fifty meters," Rudi said, testing one. "Motion, thermal—alerts to shack."

The security shack rose at the gate—bulletproof glass, cams sweeping ingress and egress. "Armed?" Hari asked.

"Unmanned for now. Drones handle patrols."

JONN shipped supplies weekly—crates labeled "furniture," unpacked blind. "All set," he messaged. "Family secure."

Month four, hidden areas—panic rooms off bedrooms, escape tunnels under woods. Rudi in the basement, "Tunnel complete—exits half-mile out. Ventilated, stocked."

"Test it," I ordered. We crawled through—damp earth, LED strips guiding. "Solid."

Crew bonded over isolation—barbecues by the pool, stories swapped. Hari one night, "Miss family back home. This pays better, though."

"End soon," I said. "Quality work—bonus."

With the basement ROC operational and hidden tunnels complete, the crew shifted to the hundred-acre perimeter. Rudi laid out the plan over blueprints in the garage, "Ground sensors every twenty meters across entire property — buried seismic and infrared types. Detect footsteps, vehicles, even digging. Tied to cameras on posts, disguised as birdhouses or tree branches." I nodded, inspecting a sample sensor—a compact cylinder with vibration plates. "How do they sync?" Rudi explained, "Wireless mesh network. Sensor trips—say a deer or intruder—alerts the nearest camera to pan and zoom. AI filters animals; humans flag red to the shack console."

The seismic sensors were JONN's spec—piezoelectric crystals buried six inches deep, sensing ground vibrations up to fifty feet.

"Calibrated for weight," Hari said, testing one with a stomp. "Light steps like kids or foxes—low alert. Heavy boots or vehicles—high priority, triggers floodlights if night."

JONN says to Rudi, "What about false positives, like wind?"

Rudi responds with, "Dampened algorithms from your tech crates filter. Integrated with weather data from the tower later."

JONN follows up with, "Infrared sensors complemented, passive IR beams crossing paths invisibly."

"Heat signatures," Rudi detailed.

"Animal warm, but patterns differ—AI learns. Cameras are PTZ—pan-tilt-zoom, 4K with thermal white-hot vision, 360 coverage. Sensor ping pings camera to lock on, record 30 seconds, send to ROC."

I tested, "Simulate breach." Rudi tripped one—console beeped, camera whirred, feed showing him clear.

Cameras mounted high, solar powered with battery backups. "Overlapping fields," Rudi said.

"No blind spots—woods thick, but we cleared lines of sight subtly."

Rudi, "Redundancy, if one fails, neighbors cover. All encrypted to the shack and basement."

Views from feeds, acres of pine, river glimpses, motion alerts seamless.

Full test week four, crew simulated intrusions—crawling, running.

"Sensor sensitivity tuned," Rudi reported.

"Cameras track auto."

I joined, "Good work. Invisible from outside?" "Camouflaged—branches, bark wraps. Wildlife cams look-alike."

Private Cell Tower and Sat Dish Integration to create communications fortress. JONN shipped a private cell tower—disguised as a tall pine, eighty feet, boosting signals for secure comms.

"Installed at property center," Rudi said.

"Boosts to 5G levels, our network only."

Sat dish from TEMA satellites—roof-mounted, parabolic with stealth coating.

"Links to geostationary birds," Rudi explained.

"Untraceable data—voice, video to ROC global."

"Interference?"

"Shielded—weatherproof. TEMA codes lock it."

The cell tower blended like this—faux tree hiding tech amid woods.

Sat dish integrated seamlessly, like these low-profile setups.

The concealment for Jacob is by design, all security was invisible sensors buried, cameras camouflaged, shack as "gardener's shed," tower a "tree."

Hidden rooms are accessed via biometrics—bookcases, floor panels—invisible to eyes. JONN, "Jacob sees luxury home, nothing more. Memories integrated—no slips."

The property's hidden defenses looked ordinary from afar, like this wooded estate.

Reap what you sow. Fortress ready—family safe, secrets buried.

By fifteen July, five months done, property a fortress—cameras hidden in trees, sensors buried, ROC operational. Crew blindfolded out, paid handsomely, and flew home.

"Rudi, I need you to stay behind for another project."

"Yes ma'am."

"I need you to set up four mini guns with two thousand rounds per and hidden in fake trees. This is last resort if our place is compromised. If we allow guns to link with sensors and thermal cameras. Everything is killed. Correct?"

"We can set up fail safes do your kid doesn't sneak a girl friend over the back fence."

"Thanks for that."

When Rudi was done, he got an additional bonus for his silence and then flew back home.

"Ready for Jacob's arrival," JONN confirmed. "Family none wiser."

I waited a month before reaching out to Jonathan about the new location for what would be our new home.

Jonathan stared at the phone in his hand, the screen glowing with my message. "Bring Jacob for a hiking trip. Three days in August. It'll be good for him – and for you." He sighed, rubbing the scar on his forearm, a souvenir from some forgotten operation in the jungles that no one would ever hear about.

My Jonathan from the other lifetime was an assassin – or "reaper," as the shadows called him – didn't leave much room for family outings. But I had a way of pulling him back from the abyss, reminding him there was more to life than the next target. This Jonathan, a military hero, has the same scars, different timeline.

Jacob, my son, was ready for an epic hike at seventeen, all energy and questions, with my eyes and Jonathan's unyielding curiosity. The boy had been cooped up in their house on Ginger Street too long most of the summer. A hiking trip sounded innocent enough. Mount Katahdin is a slice of normalcy in the wilds of Maine.

"Pack light, kid," Jonathan said to Jacob as they loaded the truck.

"Uncle not one for extras," Jacob grinned, slinging his backpack over his shoulder, oblivious to the weight his uncle carried.

They arrived at the base of Mount Katahdin under a crisp August sky, the air thick with pine and promise. Taylor asked Jonathan if she could surprise Jacob by inviting Emily. Both ladies couldn't help showing off their athletic frame clad in black tactical shorts and a form-fitting top that showed off her defined abs and arms. They even had matching backpacks. Taylor bought some gear on the way to the trail head.

Jonathan guessed, "Taylor, I like the thigh holsters holding not guns, but multi-tools and a flashlight. Goggles dangled around her neck, and a gold watch glinted on her wrist.

Unlike Taylor, Jonathan held a pistol casually in one hand, as if it were just another hiking stick, though he knew it was loaded.

"Ready for the trip," she teased, her blue eyes sparkling with mischief.

I had orchestrated this from afar, knowing Jonathan needed the break as much as Jacob did. "Take care of them," she'd whispered on the call before they left.

The first day was the Abol trail, as the maps called it a steep ascent through boulder fields and scrubby pines. Jacob bound ahead, his laughter echoing off the rocks, while Taylor, Emily, and Jonathan fell into an easy rhythm.

"You look like you're ready for war, not a walk," Jonathan remarked, eyeing Taylor's gear.

Emily playfully ruffled Jacob's hair as he paused to point out a distant peak. "Come on hero. Knife's Edge is waiting. Don't get eaten by a bear."

Jonathan smirked, holstering the pistol, "The boy will be fine. Besides, up here, the only enemies are the weather and apex predators."

The second day brought them to the infamous Knife's Edge, a narrow ridge of jagged granite balancing between thousand-foot drops. The wind whipped at their faces, but Jacob was fearless, holding Taylor's gloved hand as they traversed the precarious path. Jonathan watched, his heart swelling with rare pride. For once, no shadows lurked, no triggers to pull. They shared stories around a campfire that night.

Jonathan made it a point to not be too loud in the tent, for Jacob. He made it a point that Emily and his nephew had separate tents. Taylor on the other hand, was getting into her character and was harassing Jonathan most of the night.

On the third day, they tackled the Cathedral Trail, a series of steep, rocky spires that tested every muscle. "This is amazing!" Jacob shouted from the summit, arms outstretched as if conquering the world. Emily posed triumphantly beside him, her braid whipping in the breeze, looking at the warrior goddess. Jonathan snapped a mental picture, knowing moments like this were fleeting while Taylor took some video.

Unbeknownst to them, back on Ginger Street, the movers were at work. I had arranged it all – a complete overhaul while they were gone. The old furniture, scarred from years of hurried departures and late-night returns, was hauled away. New couches, a gleaming kitchen with granite counters, fresh paint on the walls – everything inside and out was transformed. New roof and sealed driveway before placing the for sale wooden sign posted on the newly turfed front lawn, priced to move during the last month before a new school year. It would last on the market a week before being sold to a nice local young couple with two small children. The buyers never met me; I made it a point now to slowly distance myself from any activities unless it was for the mission. Now it was time to come home and prepare the new home for Jacob.

HOME SWEET FORTRESS

Jonathan's new suburban rumbled down the winding Maine roads after three exhilarating days on Mount Katahdin, August sun baking the gravel into dust clouds. Jonathan—uncle to Jacob, battle-hardened guardian of shadows—gripped the wheel, his scarred forearm taut. Beside him, Taylor made the trip much more enjoyable.

Jacob said, hands animated, "Knife's Edge was wild, Uncle Jonathan," Emily was kicking my ass the whole way—wind howling, drops on both sides. Very exciting!"

Jonathan smiled, glancing at Taylor, "thanks for letting Emily drive your car so we get some privacy."

Taylor leaned over with her head on his shoulder affectionately, "Team effort, babe. Emily did a great job, first hike or should I say climb with high school kids, great pace lot of beautiful views."

"You two made it epic," Jonathan said. "Taylor led like a pro on Abol and Cathedral."

Nearing Ginger Street, Jonathan and Jacob's phone buzzed—it was me, "Skip home. Click address on your phone. Trust me."

As Jonathan changed course, Jacob called and spoke first, "what's going on, are we going home?"

Jonathan looked at the dash while he smiled at Taylor, his rig was hands free, "I guess not. Your mom gave me new coordinates. Did you get them kid?"

"Yes, and why is mom always a weirdo," Jacob said jokingly.

He laughed at Jacob. "Mom's detour. But look the road named after my girlfriend," as he gestured to the address on his phone display on the dashboard.

Jacob grinned at Emily. "Adventure continues!"

Taylor smirked. "Jane's full of surprises."

The global positioning system rerouted directions to the Augusta Road toward the Vassalboro border. Turning on to Taylor Road just before going past the town line. The address was halfway down the road, ended at a towering metal gate, topping reinforced bars, guardhouse offset with an armed sentry emerging.

"ID please from all the occupants," the guard said with a polite sternness.

"Thanks. Jane's expecting you all." While handing over everyone's driver's licenses.

Scan, nod, "Proceed sir and welcome."

Gate opened, with a paved oversized driveway leading to a thousand-yard ride over twenty acres of flawless lawn on either side, then surrounded by eighty acres of thick forest buffer.

The guard did the same thing for Emily and Jacob, who were following Jonathan and Taylor.

Meeting the vehicle at the circle adjoining a large wrap around porch, I was waving.

"Welcome to the compound," Jacob whispered, squeezing Emily's hand.

Taylor whistled. "Wow. Your sister's built a fortress, Jonathan."

The New home was massive. Stone and timber masterpiece, solar-roofed, bunker hints.

I waited on the porch, faded low hip jeans, sliders, and a black tank top showing a little of her six pack.

"Home sweet fortress!" I called it, as Jacob. Jumped out of the car Emily was driving before it stopped.

But when I appeared on the wide stone porch—striding down the steps with that familiar confident energy—Jacob froze.

"Mom?" he whispered, blinking hard as if the August light was playing tricks.

I looked... transformed to Jacob. Remember, I always looked like this, but my doppelganger did not, Alt-Jane gave into the stress of being a teacher, mom, and sister. With the changing life money and six months away, it was much more believable that I got back in shape in the old-fashioned way...with blood, sweat, and tears.

I've always been beautiful, but now? I'd shed at least thirty pounds, my frame lean and powerfully muscular—defined arms flexing, chiseled chest, perfect breasts, and torso under my fitted black tank top, lower abs and jeans showed off my figure. It was flawless. My face was sharper, glowing with health, lines softened as if she'd shaved a full decade off my age. I looked like the college track photos Jonathan had shown him once—young, fierce, unstoppable.

Jacob hopped out almost before the car stopped, Emily then got out and walked over close behind. He ran to me, but slowed in the last steps, staring openly.

"Mom... you look... wow. Different. Amazing!"

I laughed—that bright, genuine sound—and pulled him into a tight hug. My arms wrapped around him with new strength, solid and reassuring.

"Missed you, kiddo," I said, ruffling his hair before holding him at arm's length. "And yeah, I feel amazing too."

Jonathan climbed out, Taylor slipping her hand into his as they approached. "Sis... damn. You look like you're ready to run circles around us on those trails."

I grinned, flexing playfully. "Maybe I will. Come here, bro." She hugged him next, then turned to Taylor and Emily with warm embraces.

Jacob couldn't stop staring. "Mom, seriously—what happened? You look ten years younger. Like... college track star younger."

I stepped back, turning a little to show off the changes—defined shoulders, toned arms, that athletic poise.

"It's six months of hiking, baby," she said, eyes sparkling. Clean eating too—no junk, just whole foods, lean proteins, veggies. Cut out the stress snacks that crept in over the years."

I patted her flat, toned stomach. "Feels exactly like back in college when I was competing. Remember those old photos? Sprinting, hurdles, I was flying.

Energy through the roof, sleeping like a rock, no aches. I forgot how good this feels."

Emily whistled. "Wow, you're ripped! Goals."

Taylor nodded approvingly. "Clean eating and trails? That's the way to go."

Jacob hugged her again, grinning hugely. "You look awesome, Mom."

As they headed inside for the tour, Jacob kept glancing at me, pride and awe mixing in his eyes. His mom wasn't just building a fortress for their family— I had rebuilt myself… well what he thought based on the lie. A stronger, younger, tough woman ready for whatever shadows came next.

I led the group through the transformed house, starting with the open concept living room. Sunlight poured in through oversized new windows, bouncing off the sleek hardwood floors that replaced the old creaky ones. A massive beige sectional couch dominated the space, plush and inviting, angled perfectly toward a modern stone fireplace with a wide hearth. Built-in shelves flanked it, already stocked with family photos from the hike and a few of Jonathan's old Marine mementos—discreetly placed, nothing too telling.

I waved at the group, "So before I show you the new house, tell me about your trip, come join me in the living room."

"Wow, Mom—this couch is huge!" Jacob said, flopping onto it and spreading out like a starfish. "We could all fit for movie nights."

Taylor ran her hand along the fabric. "Feels like a five-star hotel. And these windows... way brighter in here now."

They all sat down together, Taylor and Jonathan on the large plush couches with Jacob and Emily on the other. I was on the love seat that brought the room together with access to both large couches.

I then said, "Knife's Edge stories—now!"

Jacob beamed. "Mom, epic! Emily was my anchor."
I reached out for Jonathan, "Thanks for keeping him alive while I was gone, big bro."

Then to Taylor, spoke up, "I was trying to keep your brother in line? He has taken the whole retirement thing to heart."

And then Emily said, "the trip was amazing, I just moved here from Massachusetts, never thought it was so wild and rugged."

"Look at you all," I smiled, "the Mount Katahdin survivors! Tell me more about the trip. Don't leave anything out."

They gathered in the revamped living room, sinking into the new couches that still had that fresh upholstery smell. Jacob dropped his pack with a thud and flopped down, already chattering away.

"Mom, it was impressive!" Jacob exclaimed, his eyes wide. "The Abol Trail was super steep—boulders everywhere—but I led the way most of the time. Then Knife's Edge... whoa, the wind was insane, drops on both sides forever. Taylor held my hand so I wouldn't blow away."

Taylor laughed, kicking off her boots and stretching her legs, her black shorts and form-fitting blue top still dusted with trail grit, "Your son was fearless, Jane. Kid has got nerves of steel. And Emily kept hyping him up— 'Come on, hero, don't get eaten by a bear!' Jonathan, was our security and kept the pace from getting out of hand."

"Oh really, are you saying I was slow?" he smirked.

Emily grinned, unwinding her braid and shaking out her hair. She looked every bit the warrior goddess from the summit photos, muscles defined from the climb. "Guilty. Cathedral Trail was brutal—those spires nearly killed us—but the view? Unbelievable. Jacob stood at the top yelling 'This is amazing!' with his arms out like he owned the mountain. I got video of it all."

Jonathan got up to get some water, "can I get you ladies and Jacob something to drink?"

Emily and Taylor said water, Jacob asked for a beer and then said, "just kidding mom."

"Sorry team, since I started eating clean, no alcohol," I said.

"So, my sister is a quitter now?" Jonathan said then paused before laughing with everyone else.

He handed the beverages out and leaned against the kitchen island, arms folded, a rare, relaxed smile on his face as he watched the exchange. He'd had carried his concealed carry gun on the trail, ever vigilant, but up there it had felt almost unnecessary then we would see a bear or mountain lion. That changed the decision paradigm.

After receiving back and forth comments on the initial hike, Jonathan said, "she's not exaggerating. The boy crushed it. On the first day climbing Abol, Jacob was bounding ahead. Knife's Edge had us all on edge—literally—but no drama. Campfire stories at night, quiet tents... mostly." He shot Taylor a sidelong glance.

Taylor grinned mischievously. "Mostly. I made sure Jonathan didn't get too much sleep—had to keep him sharp in case we got attacked by any apex predators."

I raised an eyebrow, pouring more filtered water for everyone. "Sounds like more than just a hike. You all look like you bonded out there. Any close calls? Bears? Weather?"

"Nothing we couldn't handle," Jonathan replied. "Felt good to get away. Real air, real challenge. No shadows following us for once."

Emily pulled out her phone. "Here, watch this—summit footage. Jacob's conqueror pose is gold. Do you have a TV around that I can link it too?"

A hundred and twenty inch OLED tv came out of the floor, "oh my goodness, now that's a tv," Emily said.

"Yeah, I kind of bought batman's house," I said. Everyone laughed.

As the video played—wind-whipped hair, triumphant shouts, sweeping views of the rugged Maine wilderness—the room filled with laughter and commentary. Jacob narrated over it, pointing out his favorite parts.

But as the excitement settled, Jacob noticed the changes around him. "Mom... this house is crazy. It's so big and what is with the guard?"

"Jacob, you have no idea. Due to our change in life with the money, a few advisers helped me determine what I needed to feel safe," I said.

I set down my glass, expression softening. "That's part of the surprise, sweetie. While you were out being mountain heroes, I got everything updated. Fresh start—new roof, new paint, the works. The old place held too many memories, it sold quick, best time is before school starts. It went fast to a good family. Time for us to move on... prep the compound for you, Jacob. Bigger adventures ahead."

The group fell quiet for a moment, absorbing the shift. Now, in this oversized home, the future felt tangible—new beginnings, new missions lurking just beyond the horizon. But for tonight, with burgers sizzling and stories flowing, they savored the moment.

"Exactly," I replied. "Front lawn for show, back woods for training. Trails? I don't want to lose my motivation since I finally got back in shape. How about we do the tour now, I promise it won't disappoint."

I spent the next thirty minutes walking them through the first and second floor. I told them there was no basement. It was radiant heat slab. That was a lie.

Initially, I ushered them into the kitchen, the heart of the overhaul. Dark oak cabinetry and tile; in its place, shimmering granite counters gleamed under pendant lights, surrounding a massive central island with bar stools and built-in outlets for charging gadgets—or prepping mission briefs, knowing this family. Viking Kitchen stainless steel appliances throughout. More cabinets lined the walls, a double oven, oversized fridge, and a gas range that screamed professional grade. The backsplash was subtle subway tile, tying it all into a clean, open flow with the living area.

Jonathan whistled low, "Jane... this is pro-level. You didn't hold back."

I shrugged playfully. "Had to. With all the 'training' you all do, we needed space to fuel up properly."

But the real showstopper was one of the six wings of the main floor, in what used to be unfinished rooms. I flicked on the lights, revealing a full state-of-the-art home gym. The space was vast and bright, with recessed lighting and large egress windows letting in natural light. Thick black rubber mats covered the floor, perfect for absorbing impacts. One wall was lined with free weights—dumbbells up to heavy plates, barbells on racks, and benches for every lift imaginable. Mirrors spanned another wall, making the room feel even bigger and allowing perfect form checks. Distributed evenly was space for sparing and machines when the weather was too messy for running or doing cable training.

And dominating the far end, a custom indoor climbing wall, towering twelve feet high with colorful holds in various shapes—jugs, crimps, slopers—mimicking real rock faces like those on Katahdin. A thick crash pad sat below it, and auto-belay systems hung ready for solo climbs.

Jacob and Emily froze at the threshold, jaws dropping as they took it in.

"Mom... climbing wall!" Jacob exclaimed, eyes wide as saucers, already darting toward it. He reached out and grabbed a hold, testing his weight. "This is just like Knife's Edge, but inside! Can I try it now?"

Emily's two braids swung as she turned to me, grinning ear to ear, her athletic build practically vibrating with excitement. "Holy crap, Jane—this is insane. Mirrors, weights, the whole setup... and that wall? We could've trained here before the hike. You're a genius."

Jonathan crossed his arms, surveying it with a nod of approval—the kind a seasoned operator gives to solid gear.

"Tactical-grade. Rubber floors for sparring, enough iron to build an army. You thought of everything."

Taylor smirked, flexing subtly. "Looks like I'll be spending a lot of time here. Race you to the top, Emily?"

I laughed, watching Jacob scramble up the easier route with Emily spotting him. "It's for all of us. Fresh start means staying sharp—body and mind."

The group lingered in the gym, the air buzzing with energy. For a moment, amid the weights and holds, the shadows of their world felt a little farther away replaced by the promise of strength, family, and whatever challenges lay ahead in August. Great room gathering, drinks flowing.

Upstairs suites for everyone, Jacob got to pick his bedroom. They are all the same, just a different balcony for a different view. Like a smart kid he asked what room I'd pick and made sure he was on the other side of the house. When I told him my favorite routine is yoga in the morning sun, so the suite is facing east. Jacob immediately said, "looks like we, I mean, I get sunsets. Bedroom with the balcony facing west."

The balcony design gave each suite enough privacy because of their position around the southern facing back yard. All six bedrooms had an ensuite with an oversized bathroom and large walk-in closet. All the balconies overlooked the pool and jacuzzi that were covered with steel and thermal protecting polymer that looked like glass. Material rated beyond a three o' eight round at point blank range.

Once I got alone with Jonathan, his big brother advice and questions started pouring out of him like a shot up balloon filled with water.

Jonathan, "Why go with such a giant house, sis? Winslow roots?"

"Truth," I said, "Jacob finishes school here and it's normal for him. I'm not wealthy, I'm rich and that comes with all kids of crazy in this State. Also, I left Maine with six hundred million, it's grown to three billion as of today."

"Holy shit sis, that's great," Jonathan said.

"AI trades, real estate swaps, crypto," I replied

"Gave Ben a hundred million and he doubled it. Ditched Rockland apartment, big house for his girls now," I expressed with a tone of pride.

"Wow, so you think with this money now, you could be a target?" Jonathan asked.

"Today, I'm the twenty fifth richest person in the State of Maine, Jonathan. Like real wealth, accessible and liquid. Not buried in stuff I can't touch for twenty years. I am a big target and so are you and Jacob. So, I plan on hiring a fulltime caretaker for the property, they will handle everything from cooking to security twenty-four seven."

"Does Jacob know any of this?"

"What do you think?"

"How do you think he will take it?"

"Don't care, his job is to be a kid, get good grades, and get ready for college or whatever he wants to do."

"This place is crazy and I'm still trying to get my head around this."

"Me too big broham, I have a business manager, who handles financials and investments. Then another person you will see around is my assistant and handles everything I need, also a bodyguard if I am outside the fence line."

"Very cool."

"Jonathan, if you need any money, please let me know."

"I'm good, but if I need a loan from 'Jane the Bank', will let you know."

I watched Jacob scramble up the climbing wall like a little spider monkey, Emily spotting him with that fierce grin of hers, while Jonathan and Taylor eyed the weight racks like they were planning their next workout. The gym was perfect—everything we'd need to stay sharp—but I wasn't done yet. Not by a long shot.

"Come on, you guys," I said, clapping my hands to get their attention. "One more surprise. Follow me—this one's going to blow your minds."

Jacob led them through wall of glass with door around the back of the house. Once they stepped into this giant space it felt like the inside. The air grew warmer, humid, carrying that faint salt scent that always reminds me of luxury resorts. Taylor raised an eyebrow at Jacob, sensing something big, Emily just smiled and pushed open the double doors.

Walking to the right of the space, they stepped into the pool house, with four separate changing rooms with shower, sink, and toilet.

The space was massive—a twenty five-meter six lane lap pool with crystal-clear turquoise salt water, heated to perfection, shimmering under a vaulted dome shaped glass ceiling that let in the mid-August sunlight. Floor-to-ceiling windows wrapped around all four sides, overlooking the backyard pines, making it feel like they were swimming outdoors without the bugs or unpredictable weather. Lounge chairs lined one side, with fluffy towels stacked neatly, and subtle underwater lights would glow beautifully at night.

"Wow, this is heaven!" Emily exclaimed, her eyes wide as she took in the expanse. "An indoor pool? This is next level."

Jacob's jaw dropped. "Emily, this is crazy and can you believe it?" A pool inside the house? Swimming year around? Right now? Please?"

Taylor let out a low whistle, already in a green bikini. One of the fifty suit options in each changing room, "You're spoiling us rotten. This beats any house I've ever seen."

Jacob crossed his arms, a full smile breaking through, "Just waiting for Emily."

He was waiting with anticipation, as per Emily's mission orders. She is not to take Jacob's virginity unless authorized. This means, he's never seen most of her.

"A few options Taylor?" Emily said stepping out of the pool house in a white bikini.

Taylor laughed, gesturing, a sleek changing area with teak benches, showers, and lockers. "Suits were designed to fit a number of sizes and shapes. Jacob was wearing classic board shorts just above the knee. Emily and Taylor, dove in first from the west side of the pool. Moments later Jacob jumped in from the other side so he could show off his breath control almost the entire length of the pool.

They didn't need much convincing to grab some floating chairs and minutes later, Emily and Taylor. Jacob then cannonballed in with a massive splash that echoed off the glass, yelling "This is the best day ever!"

Emily rolled out of the float and gracefully swam a lap with her braids trailing like a mermaid's tail.

"Jane, get in here! This water feels amazing—warm but refreshing."

Taylor executed a perfect racing dive, popping up beside Emily and flicking water at her. "Race you to the end—loser does push-ups on the deck."

"You're on!" Emily shot back, and they took off in strong freestyle strokes, muscles cutting through the water like pros.

Jacob swam over to them, dogpaddling furiously. "Wait for me! Emily, teach me that flip turn you just did!"

Emily slowed, treading water and pulling him close. "Like this, hero—tuck, push off the wall. Watch." She demonstrated, flipping smoothly and pushing off with powerful legs.

Taylor floated on her back, grinning up at me from the pool.

"Jane, seriously—this setup? You're a wizard. Jonathan's gonna have to drag me out."

I stood at the edge, dipping my toes in. "Enjoy it. Family time in our fortress."

"Best surprise ever, Mom!" Jacob called between giggles and jumping in the pool.

I stepped out of the pool house, adjusting the straps of my bright yellow bikini, feeling the warm air kiss my skin. The suit fit snugly, highlighting the results of all those intense sessions, my muscles were larger and more defined than Emily's or Taylor's sleek, athletic builds. I was a little taller and heavier too, carrying that powerful, solid frame from years of pushing limits. Not lean like them, but strong, capable.

Jacob spotted me first, before stepping into the pool. He was on the other side with his wiry frame—already about five feet nine inches like me, all long limbs and endless energy. His eyes went wide.

"Holy shit, Mom—you got jacked!"

I laughed, striking a quick flex pose at the edge, my biceps popping. "Language, kiddo. But yeah, someone's been hitting the weights hard. Gotta keep up with you mountain conquerors."

Emily surfaced nearby, shaking water from her braids, her toned figure cutting through the pool effortlessly. "No kidding, Jane. You're built like a tank—in the best way. Those arms? I need your routine."

Taylor, floating lazily on her back, flipped over and grinned. "Seriously. You're making us look like amateurs. That yellow suit pops—total power vibe."

Just then, Jonathan emerged from the pool house in plain black trunks and dove in with a clean, powerful entry—barely a splash. At fifty-three, he was still lean and tall, every inch the seasoned operator, broad shoulders tapering to a narrow waist, defined but not bulky, moving with that effortless grace. Many scars that I hadn't seen before but Taylor had; momentums of twelve combat deployments.

He surfaced near me, water streaming down his chest. "Show-off," he teased, nodding at my pose.

Jonathan made his way to another float, sliding in quietly, he glanced over to see three of them—Emily, Taylor, and Jacob—were already lost in splashes and laughter, racing, playing Marco Polo, turning the pool into pure joy.

"Pot calling the kettle," I shot back, cannonballing beside Jonathan, sending a wave over everyone.

Jacob whooped. "Mom, you still got it! Race me to the end?"

"You're on, squirt." I took off in smooth strokes, Jacob chasing with frantic energy.

"This pool is unreal," Emily called. "Glass ceiling, views of the pines... feels is paradise."

I floated over to them, watching the chaos with a grin. "You know, Emily... Taylor... you've both been like family on that hike and beyond. Emily, I know things haven't been easy—no parents, handling everything at seventeen. And Taylor, you're always out there saving the day. Why don't you both stay here? Room and board, full access to the gym, pool, everything. We've got space, and honestly... we'd love to have you."

Emily blinked, steadying Taylor. "Jane... that's incredibly generous. Thank you, I mean it."

Taylor nodded, genuine warmth in her eyes. "Yeah, thank you. Really. I'll think on it."

"No pressure," I said, splashing Jacob as he swam by. "Just family looking out for family."

Later, after we'd all dried off and changed, we gathered around the big island in the new kitchen for supper—grilled steaks, fresh corn, salad, the works. The pendant lights cast a warm glow over the granite counters.

The table erupted in cheers, plates clinking, as the late August sun dipped low outside. For now, in mid-August twenty twenty-six, everything felt right.

The air hummed with the scent of grilled meats and fresh herbs, a perfect end to our day of surprises.

I'd arranged for the caretaker to bring in a private chef for dinner, someone vetted and discreet, who knew how to handle a group like ours without questions. The long farmhouse style granite table in the open dining area was set elegantly but casually for summer, crisp linen placemats, fresh wildflowers in mason jars, woven baskets of bread, and simple white plates under soft pendant lights. No holiday frills—just welcoming and abundant.

The chef had prepared a feast tailored to our post pool time appetites, grilled ribeye steaks as the star, herb-crusted salmon on the side, garlic mashed potatoes, charred corn on the cob, a vibrant summer salad with heirloom tomatoes and feta, and for dessert, chilled key lime pie and fresh berry cobbler waiting on the sideboard.

We settled around the table—Jonathan at one end, me at the other, Jacob still buzzing next to Emily, Taylor across from them. Everyone was in fresh clothes after the pool. Light tees, shorts, hair still damp, the kind of relaxed vibe that comes from a day well-spent.

"This dinner looks incredible," Taylor said, eyeing the steaks as the chef served them. "Jane, you thought of everything. After that hike and the pool splash-fest, this hits the spot."

Emily nodded, unfolding her napkin. "Totally. Those steaks smell amazing—perfect recovery fuel. And the table setup? It feels like a celebration. Thanks for all this."

Jacob dives right in, spearing a piece of corn. "Best day! Hike in the morning, gym tour, pool wars, and now steak? Mom, you're killing it."

I smiled, raising my glass of iced tea. "To conquering Katahdin and coming home to surprises. And to no bears eating anyone on Knife's Edge."

Laughter rippled around the table as we clinked glasses.

Jonathan sliced into his steak, passing plates around. "That Abol Trail was no joke—steep as hell. But Jacob, you powered through like a champ. Cathedral had me rethinking my cardio."

"And Emily spotting me on the climbing wall after? Epic," Jacob grinned, mouth full. "We gotta hit the pool every day now. Taylor, your dives were pro-level."

Emily chuckled, twirling her fork, "That flip turn lesson in the water? You're a natural, Jacob. But yeah, the gym and pool... Jane, this place is a paradise fortress. So awesome."

Taylor leaned back, savoring a bite, "Totally. After traversing that ridge today, soaking in the pool felt like victory. And that climbing wall? Are we training tomorrow?"

I set my glass down, looking at Emily and Taylor. "Speaking of which... you both fit right in today. Emily, Taylor—the offer from the pool stands. Move in. Rooms ready, full run of the house, gym, pool. Be part of the family until you want to move on, no strings."

Emily cleared her throat, "About your offer, Jane... yes. I'd love to stay. This feels like home already."

Taylor smiled, "Me too. Count me in. Thank you—again."

Jacob pumped his fist. "Yes! This is awesome! Emily, we can train on the climbing wall every day. Taylor, you can teach me those dives."

Jonathan leaned back, optimistic but with that cautious edge. "It's great—really. More the merrier, keeps things lively. Just... Jane, are you sure we're not moving too fast? New house stuff, the sale, now expanding the crew?"

I reached over, squeezing his hand, "I've earned this, Jonathan. Fresh start, stronger together. "

He nodded slowly, a smile breaking through, "Alright. Welcome aboard, ladies."

Unknown to Jonathan and Jacob, these reapers all were doing what popped up on their optical nerve heads up display that only they could see. It said, "meet the Grimm. It's Jane. She selected you for this mission. Take her offer."

I nodded. "How about end of next week? Gives you time to wrap up loose ends. I'll handle movers— professional crew to pack your stuff, haul it here, and anything extra goes into secure storage on-site. You just grab personal items and show up."

Emily's eyes brightened. "End of next week works— I'll be ready. Thanks, Jane. This is huge."

Taylor agreed. "Perfect timing. I'll clear my schedule. Appreciate the movers—makes it easy."

Jonathan raised his glass again. "To the team expanding. Stronger together."

We toasted, the summer evening light fading outside as conversation flowed. For this mid-August night in twenty twenty-six, with plates emptying and laughter echoing, the future felt solid—new beginnings right on the horizon.

MOVE IN DAY

Late August sun beat down on the driveway of the Taylor Road Estate, turning the air hazy as two moving trucks backed in, one after the other. Professional crews—hired discreetly—unloaded boxes labeled "Emily" and "Taylor" with efficient precision, stacking them neatly in the foyer before carrying them up to the east wing bedrooms I'd prepared.

Emily arrived first, pulling up in her beat-up Jeep loaded with personal gear—climbing shoes, a few duffels, and her braided hair tied back practically. Taylor followed in a sleek black SUV, minimal as always, just a couple suitcases and tactical bags. Jacob bounded out to help, wiry and enthusiastic, while Jonathan directed the movers with quiet authority.

"Welcome home—for real this time," I said, hugging them both at the door. The house felt fuller already, the luxury modern spaces coming alive with new energy.

That evening, after the trucks left and boxes were mostly unpacked, I pulled Jacob aside into the living room. We sat on the big sectional, the pine-scented breeze drifting in through open windows.

"Jacob, honey, we need to talk about Emily and Taylor moving in," I started gently, facing him directly.

He leaned back, curious but a little wary. "Yeah? Like house rules?"

"Exactly. They're family now, but they're also grown women—Emily's seventeen, legally independent, and Taylor's, thirty something, got her own history. Treat them with respect. Knock before entering their rooms, give them privacy in the gym or pool if they're training alone. No barging in, no hovering."

He nodded slowly. "Got it. I'm not a kid anymore, Mom."

I smiled. "I know. And most importantly don't suffocate them. Don't try too hard to impress, fetch things constantly, or put them on pedestals. Act like your uncle and not your dad. Be yourself, confident, helpful when it makes sense, but not needy. Strong people respect strength, not fawning."

Jacob shifted, processing. "Like... don't be an asshole?"

I chuckled. "Exactly and language. Be the guy who crushed Knife's Edge—independent, capable. They'll like you more for it."

He grinned. "Cool. I can do that."

"One more thing," I added, softening. "You're starting senior year soon. Last year of school for you with the move and your potential future, but classes here for now. Our money, the house, my... status—will that change things for you? Friends any pressure?"

He shrugged, thoughtful. "Maybe a little. Kids might think I'm rich or whatever. But I don't flaunt it. I don't really have any friends, you know? Not fake ones. And girls... if someone likes me for stuff, they're out anyway. I'm still happy with Emily."

"Good answer," I said, pulling him into a side hug. "Proud of you. This year is the last so make it count. You have a decision to make, college, military, or a job."

Later that week, I brought in a top public relations professional, my bodyguard, and assistant—a sharp woman named Elena, discreet and expensive, with experience handling high-profile families. She met with Jacob in my office, doors closed, while the rest of us gave them space.

"Jacob," Elena began, spreading documents on the desk, "with Emily and Taylor now living here—both young, athletic, photogenic women—and your family's unique background, we need tight controls."

Jacob leaned forward, attentive, "Lay it out."

"Social media is the biggest risk. Back off completely—no posts about the household beyond basics. Absolutely, no photos or videos inside the house featuring the girls. No gym shots, pool clips, nothing that could go viral or attract unwanted attention. Anyone could exploit it."

Jacob nodded, "Understood. We've stayed low-profile for a reason."

"You can post neutral family updates—hiking pics from public trails, no locations tagged. But anything with Emily or Taylor? Clear it through me first, or better yet, don't. Their privacy is paramount, and it protects everyone. We'll monitor for leaks, set up alerts."

"Done," Jacob said firmly. "I'll brief the house. No exceptions."

Elena smiled professionally, "Smart. This keeps the shadows at bay while letting life feel normal."

By the end of the day, the house settled into its new rhythm—laughter echoing from the gym, splashes from the pool, boxes emptied. Emily and Taylor's presence made it feel complete, a stronger unit ready for whatever came next in late August.

Elena is not a PR specialist, she is a Reaper that I brought into her circle to lay out the rules, also JONN, the AI that has been monitoring Jacob's phone ever since he got one. Anything Jacob does that JONN thinks is stupid aka a threat, he can delete before it goes out in the world.

The sprawling eleven thousand square-foot modern mansion on Taylor Road stood majestically against the Maine pines, its clean lines, stone accents, and expansive glass facade blending luxury with rugged New England charm. The late August twenty twenty-six sun bathed the property in golden light, highlighting the attached eight-car garage—a car enthusiast's dream with heated epoxy floors, professional lighting, and walls lined with custom tool cabinets.

I'd timed this surprise perfectly, just after Emily and Taylor's move-in, as a "welcome to the estate" gesture before school and training ramped up.

"Garage, everyone—now!" I called from the massive kitchen island, smiling as the group assembled, Jacob eager, Emily and Taylor curious, Jonathan knowing but playing along.

The heated eight-bay garage doors hummed open, revealing polished epoxy floors gleaming under recessed LEDs, lifts in two bays, and organized workstations ready for mods or maintenance.

"Emily, Taylor—pick your bays. Full setups, lift, charging, tools, space for whatever upgrades you want. This estate's big enough for all our toys."

Emily grinned, eyeing the space next to her Jeep. "Jane, this is ridiculous—incredible. Thank you."

Taylor nodded approvingly. "Ultimate setup. We're officially spoiled."

"And Jacob..." I gestured to the tarp-covered bay at the end.

He dashed over with Jonathan's help, whipping off the cover a gleaming silver twenty twenty seven Ford Raptor 4x4, with a three inch lift, heavy-duty winch hidden in the bumper, matching silver truck cap over the bed, and dual Cooper Discoverer MT tire sets— regular and studded—on extra rims for quick swaps.

"Mom—no way! A Raptor with winch, cap, off-road tires?!" Jacob's voice echoed as he circled it, wiry frame buzzing with excitement.

Jonathan chuckled. "Built tough. Perfect for hauling gear—or pulling us out of mud on trails."

Emily laughed. "You're gonna lead every convoy now, hero."

Taylor smirked. "Sweet rig. Let's break it in on the property roads."

Jacob slid into the driver's seat, firing it up—the powerful rumble filling the vast garage. "This is the best. Thank you, Mom—seriously."

I hugged him tightly. "For stepping up this year—training, the move, everything. Drive responsibly, especially when snow hits."

We all piled in for a test loop around the estate's private drive and wooded paths, windows down, summer breeze rushing through, the family laughing as the new truck handled effortlessly.

With bays claimed and the Raptor parked proudly, the Taylor Road estate felt fully alive, our expanded team equipped and ready for senior year, missions, and whatever shadows lay ahead in late August.

The week before school started, Taylor Road estate felt like a peaceful bubble amid the late-summer heat. The sprawling backyard—complete with the heated indoor pool transitioning seamlessly to a stone patio, overlooked by dense Maine woods—had become everyone's favorite spot to unwind.

One evening, as the sun dipped low, casting a golden hue over the property, Emily and Jacob slipped away from the group dinner prep. They grabbed water bottles and headed down one of the private wooded trails that wound through the estate's acres—perfect for clearing heads after intense gym sessions.

The trail was quiet, dappling sunlight filtering through the pines, birds calling overhead. Emily, her braid swinging with each step, glanced at Jacob—wiry, confident in his strides, already looking forward to driving his new silver Raptor to school.

"Hey," she started, slowing to a walk. "With senior year starting next week... we should talk. About us."

Jacob nodded, matching her pace, "Yeah. I've been thinking the same. Things have been great this summer—hikes, training, hanging out. But school is going to be different. We are at school together and home together, pressure, all that."

"Exactly," Emily said, stopping at a clearing with a view back toward the mansion. "I like where we are— close, fun, no drama. But I don't want to rush into labels or anything serious right now. Senior year is supposed to be epic, right? Last taste of freedom before college or whatever comes next."

Jacob leaned against a tree, thoughtful. "Totally agree. Let's set some real boundaries. Just enjoying each other as friends first, with whatever spark there is. Dates if it feels right, group hangs, training together. But no exclusive talk, no big commitments. Keep it light."

Emily smiled, relief in her blue eyes. "Perfect. As you know I'm a private person, I don't intend on being with anyone else, just you. But I need you to give me space when I need it and a shoulder if it's required. And at the end of the year—prom, graduation, summer after—we reassess. If we both want to get serious then, cool. If not, we stay friends. No weirdness."

"Deal," Jacob said, extending his fist for a bump. She laughed and met it and then kissed him deeply.

"This makes me feel mature. Mom would be proud—she's always going on about not being so suffocating or whatever."

Emily rolled her eyes playfully, "Jane's wise like that. But yeah, this is us deciding. Our year."

They turned back toward the house as dusk settled, the patio fire pit glowing in the distance where Jonathan, Taylor, and I were all sitting in resin oversized Adirondack chairs.

Later, sitting around the fire pit with the group—marshmallows roasting, stars emerging—Emily and Jacob exchanged a quick, knowing glance.

No one else needed to know the details yet. Senior year was their boundaries set, freedom intact, future open. The perfect way to head into the chaos of classes, games, and whatever shadows the world might throw their way.

A few nights later, the salt air off Penobscot Bay carried a sharp winter bite as Jonathan stood on the deck of his modest waterfront home in Rockland, Maine. At fifty-three, he was still lean and tall, the kind of build honed by decades of discipline rather than vanity—broad shoulders, scarred hands, eyes that missed nothing. The house was simple compared to the sprawling Taylor Road estate in Winslow, a classic oversized New England home with a widow's walk, views of the harbor lights twinkling across the water, and enough privacy for a man who'd spent his life in shadows.

Inside, the fire crackled in the stone hearth, casting warm light over the open living area. Taylor sat on the leather couch, legs tucked under her, a glass of red wine in hand. She'd driven the hour from Winslow after a long day of work, her black SUV now parked in his driveway, a familiar sight these past months.

Jonathan leaned against the kitchen island, pouring himself a whiskey. Their relationship had deepened since that August hike on Katahdin, stolen nights when she could get away, quiet dinners like this, the kind of connection that felt real amid the complications.

"You know," he said, voice low and steady as he joined her on the couch, "I've been thinking about us. A lot. The drive's killing me one hour each way, every time I want to see you. Or you me."

Taylor met his gaze, her hazel eyes sharp, that tactical edge always present. She was weighing it, like she weighed everything. "JONN… it's not that simple."

He set his glass down, turning to face her fully. "Make it simple. Move in here. Or hell, we could split your time and your stuff at the estate, but nights here. With me. This place has room. I'm on the ocean, can see the lighthouse, it's quiet. No Jacob bounding in at dawn, no group dynamics. Just us."

She smiled faintly, but there was hesitation—a flicker he recognized from thirty-five years in the Marine Corps, when someone was calculating risks. Taylor had her own mission, layers deep, tied to shadows Jonathan didn't fully know. Something beyond simply time and her feelings for him.

"It's tempting," she admitted, reaching for his hand. "You. This," She gestured to the fire, the bay beyond the windows. "Rockland has got its charm—lobster boats at dawn, no estate-level security headaches. And yeah, the commute sucks."

He squeezed her hand. "Then say yes. We've earned something normal. Or as normal as we get."

Taylor leaned in, kissing him softly before pulling back, "I need to think it through. Value to… everything, I'm handling, and moving in changes the board."

"Fair enough," he said, pulling her closer. "No rush. But the offer stands. Door's open—literally. Can I ask you something?"

"Always my love."

"Let's reassess at thanksgiving. The weather is colder with a fifty-fifty chance for snow. If you want to; we can make a few trips up and get you settled in here."

"Jonathan, your sister is a billionaire, do you need to worry about anything like that?"

"That's her money."

"You don't get it do you."

"Get what."

"She wants you happy. If I make you happy, then she snaps her fingers and it becomes reality. Money is a means to complete something faster, and you don't hurt your back."

"You're right, you're right. I'm still in denial."

The same night that Taylor was with Jonathan in Rockland. The warm late-August sun dipped low as Ben Lemieux's black truck turned onto the private drive of the Taylor Road estate in Winslow. At six feet and two inches, lean and disciplined from his Marine days—dark hair neatly trimmed, clean-cut features that still carried the poise of Silent Drill Team precision and presidential helicopter detail—Ben felt that familiar mix of calm anticipation.

A high school friend of mine, he'd once proposed to me during military leave. I graciously declined, focusing on my track career at the University of Maine. Years later, after his brutal divorce from Carly "the bitch," as I called her complete with infidelity, false accusations, financial ruin, and losing primary custody of his daughters Leslie, now nine, a talented swimmer and Becka eleven, gymnastics standout.

Their old friendship had evolved into something deeper, reliable, no-strings intimacy every few weeks, a mutual "stress reliever" where Ben always answered her call with a simple "Yes, ma'am!" and kept everything discreet.

This was his first visit to the new estate, and the scale impressed even his understated tastes.

The guard at the gatehouse nodded professionally.

"Evening, Mr. Lemieux. Ms. Jane's waiting. Pull into the garage bay five is reserved for you tonight."

Ben smiled easily, "Appreciate it. Nice setup."

The door rose smoothly as he approached the door, revealing the heated eight-bay paradise—Jacob's Raptor, Emily's Jeep, my Defender was neatly parked.

Before leaving for my six-month hike, I shipped my nineteen ninety-five silver Land Rover Defender to the house. Hardtop was hanging from the rafters; it was still summer in Maine until the weather got cold in October. Next summer I plan on shipping over my helicopter and park it behind the house.

Ben eased beside the other vehicles in a separate bay, grabbed his overnight bag, and headed inside. I met him at the grand entrance in a sleeveless black dress that showed off my powerful arms and frame. A beautiful red and white diamond necklace. I pulled him into a deep, lingering kiss.

"Finally," I murmured. "You made good time from Rockland."

"Wouldn't keep you waiting," Ben replied, that charming half-smile breaking through as he handed her a bottle of Cabernet. "This place is something else, guard, auto garage bays. Feel like I'm on protective detail again."

"You kinda am. Be my bodyguard please," I teased, leading him through the soaring foyer. "Jacob and Emily are with friends at the movies in Augusta won't be back till late. Chef's here just for us."

The dining room opened to the glass-walled indoor pool, table set intimately with candles, summer flowers, and soft golden light from the sunset.

The chef served chilled lobster, perfectly grilled filet, fresh summer sides, and peach cobbler.

A couple hours after a wonderful meal and small talk about the last six months, the dessert plates were cleared. The private chef quietly finished cleaning the pristine kitchen wiping down the granite island, loading the last dishes into the silent dishwasher, and gathering his tools. He gave me a discreet nod on his way out.

"Thank you for everything chef, food was perfect," I said softly.

"My pleasure, ma'am. Have a good night."

Waving goodbye, the chef left. With that, he slipped out of the side entrance. His car lights disappeared down the drive, leaving only the distant guardhouse occupied on the entire estate security running quietly in the background, as always.

After dessert, I stood up and took Ben's hand.

Ben said, "Pool's perfect this time of year. Kids are gone... swim?"

"You always know the right things to say," I laughed over wine. "How are the girls? Ready for school?"

Ben's face lit up that proud, devoted dad glow. "Becka's got a big gymnastics competition coming up,

Leslie's killing it in swim team. They're with their mom this week, but we've got plans for Labor Day. Miss them, but... tonight I'm exactly where I want to be."

"Stress relief?" I asked with a playful wink.

He blushed just slightly, humor in his eyes. "Yes, ma'am. Always in the mood when you call."

The massive house settled into true silence, just the hum of the pool filtration and crickets outside the open windows.

Ben leaned back in his chair, watching me with that easy, appreciative smile. "Chef's gone, kids are out... we're really alone in this palace tonight."

I stood, extending my hand. "Completely alone. Come on."

I led him to the glass-walled pool room, the water glowing invitingly under soft lights, warm summer night air drifting in. Without a word, I let the shimmering black dress slide to the floor, revealing my powerful, sculpted body nothing underneath.

In the glowing pool room, warm evening air drifting through open glass panels, Ben's breath caught, his disciplined Marine frame reacting instantly as he stripped out of his suit and joined me. They dove in together, the water warm and welcoming.

Ben's grin widened, "Lead the way."

I gestured, and Ben followed, clothes discarded, pulling me close in the warm water.

"Skinny-dipping under the stars," he murmured, kissing my neck. "Only ever with you. God, you're beautiful," he murmured, pulling me close mid-pool, hands tracing my defined back and arms. "Every time... still hits me."

I laughed softly, wrapping my legs around him. "Flatterer. But keep going you always say the right things."

We kissed deeply, playful splashes turning heated bodies pressing, exploring, until desire won. Breathless and laughing, Ben lifted me effortlessly, carrying me dripping through the quiet halls and up the grand staircase to the master suite.

The room was bathed in moonlight through floor-to-ceiling windows, the estate grounds stretching dark and private beyond. We made love slowly at first, then with building intensity familiar yet electric, whispers and gasps echoing in the empty house. Years of friendship, mutual understanding, and raw chemistry made it effortless.

We laughed, played, then turned passionate hands exploring, bodies pressing until desire overtook us both.

Ben and I sat naked on the balcony, we enjoyed some tea and light conversation and then returned to the bed exploring each other's bodies with a patient anticipation, then aggressively, I rode him to climax. There was a moment my memory returned to Ben in my timeline, an emotional shock like a lightning bolt brought me to pure extasy, it felt deep and familiar until we both fell asleep tangled in sheets with windows open to the warm night air.

Morning light crept in as the sun rose golden over the pines, birdsong filling the air. Ben woke first, tracing a finger along my shoulder. "That was..." he said softly, voice full of quiet wonder, "the most incredible night I've ever had. Thank you, Jane. Truly."

I stirred, smiling sleepily, pulling him down for a soft kiss, "It was perfect. I needed this. Needed you."

"Me too," he said, voice low and sincere. "I want more nights exactly like this."

"Me too," I replied, tracing his chest. "But we keep it just like this—no moving in, no marriage talk. Your girls come first; custody schedule's complicated enough. My life here with Jacob, the estate... let's not change what works."

Ben nodded, that dependable calm in his eyes. "Yes, ma'am. I'm good at that. Talk every day, text when we can, see each other every couple weeks when the kids are with Carly. Stolen weekends, nights like this when it lines up."

"Exactly," I whispered, kissing him again. "No pressure. Just us—friends, lovers, whatever this is. As long as it stays this good."

He pulled me closer, sunlight warming the room, "It will. As long as you keep calling... I'll always say yes."

I stirred, smiling sleepily, my back to him. Then flipped over and climbed onto his muscular tall frame. Ben on his back, I was sitting on his chest looking down at him. I grabbed his neck and pulled him closer for a long and passionate kiss. Then let go of him and his head hit the pillow; I climbed down under the sheets to the end of the bed.

Pleasuring him until he was at apex, he caught his breath, "Thank you Jane." Then reaching down and pulling me until we were face to face.

We kissed deeply, I paused, smiled, "You're very welcome lover."

FIRST BRIEFING

The last day of August twenty twenty-six brought a crisp edge to the Maine air, hinting at fall as I led the group down the wide staircase into the basement of the Taylor Road estate. What had once been a vast, unfinished space was now transformed into the Reaper Operations Center (ROC), a high-tech nerve center buried beneath the eleven thousand-square-foot mansion.

The room hummed quietly, reinforced walls lined with multiple curved screens, workstations glowing softly, and at the center—a large circular holographic conference table capable of projecting three dimensional models, maps, and live feeds in shimmering blue light.

Emily, Fiona, Taylor, Lisa, and Elena—each a key piece of the emerging team—followed me in, their expressions shifting from curiosity to quiet awe as the lights auto-dimmed and the holographic displays flickered to life.

"Welcome to the heart of it," I said, my voice steady and commanding as I took my place at the head of the table. My powerful frame stood tall, khaki five eleven pants, black polo shirt, and black danner boots; memories replaced by tactical focus.

"This is where we plan, monitor, and execute. Secure, off-grid, and ours. Access and location of all who are in the house will show up on your heads-up display. If you need to use the ROC, simply unlock from the blinking light that will show up as a hologram at the entrance. Only we can open and access. Also the access is behind an additional door you can lock in the walk in from the second bathroom on the first floor will help. You can project your voice from the ROC to the bathroom in case someone wants to talk or check on you."

"Wow Jane you thought of everything," Emily, braided hair, tied back, leaned forward as a holographic three-dimensional map materialized above the table showing everything in the fenceline.

I leaned back slightly in my chair at the head of the holographic table, the blue glow reflecting off my focused expression, "First, there are things in this mission that are not going to feel right, or you may be fighting your nanites. Know there are parts I've kept secret from you because of compartmentalization. Also, you may be given orders that may seem counterintuitive, I get it. But know that everything we are doing is for the same outcome. We must slow down the Order so they can't recreate what they have been planning since Babylon."

All Reapers get a thorough history on the Order but it isn't the truth, I mean not the whole truth. They don't know I'm from another timeline, they don't know my doppelganger in this timeline died and I took over her life. Lastly, they don't know about JONN. With that established, please keep our secret. Only you, me, and JONN know about this. There are some things that no training or indoctrination can get you up to speed, so this is what we have and what we need to work with.

"Emily— you've been the first to assess everything since being called into this mission. Thoughts? Bring us up to speed on your contributions so far."

Emily stepped forward confidently, her braid pulled tight, athletic frame radiating the same quiet intensity she'd shown on Knife's Edge. She activated her station with a quick gesture, pulling up a layered holographic overlay—personal training logs interwoven with estate activity markers and subtle reconnaissance notes.

"Yes, ma'am," Emily began, voice clear and direct. "Since mission orders from my Grimm, I have been working on my primary focus—Jacob. I've established peer cover as his training partner and friend. School work and being a good listener. Allows me twelve hours a day with direct contact."

"Anything recent you can share?"

"Since Taylor brought me in during the Katahdin trip in mid-August, I've been running dual tracks, family integration and operational readiness. Daily sessions in the gym, climb wall routes mimicking Cathedral and Knife's Edge for grip strength and fear management. Pool work, breath-hold drills, flip turns, endurance swims—building his confidence in water for potential exfil scenarios. Garage time, basic vehicle maintenance on his new Raptor—tire swaps between studded and regular Coopers, winch familiarization, off-road basics on the estate trails. He's progressed fast—wiry build turning into functional strength. More importantly, he's bought in completely. Calls me 'Em' now without prompting. Solid trust layer."

"What is your secondary mission per Grimm's parameters," I said keeping everyone focused. The hologram display was showing videos, maps, and photos of Emily and Jacob to reinforce all her briefing notes seamlessly.

"Yes ma'am, secondary—estate hardening from the inside. I've mapped every sightline, blind spot, and egress route on the property. Night runs with thermal spotting to identify weak points in perimeter coverage. Coordinated with security to add passive infrared light trip lines in the woods without alerting staff. Pool room tested for emergency flotation gear storage—hidden compartments installed."

Emily paused to get confirmation from the other reapers in the room and then continued, "Tertiary—personal prep tied to the archives. I've cross-read with my Grimm every historical event against Order activity, rather than focus on something on the news past and present, we have looked at the money transfer of people and countries to trace where events occurred that corelate with a major loss of life event or war."

"Anything of note?," I asked.

"No ma'am. Lot of death and evil going on but not aligned with the Order. Seems random greed or just plain evil as I said. Will continue to look into it when I have breaks in my primary and secondary tasks. Current posture, fully embedded, no external flags. Jacob sees me as friend and romantic interest figure— perfect camouflage. Ready for active assignment or escalation support."

"Thanks for taking care of my son, I hope it isn't too much of a pain in the ass."

Emily smiled, "Best deep cover assignment thus far. Hardest part is not becoming my character."

We all laughed. Then I said, "Exactly, I know this is going to be one of the toughest assignments you ever accomplish. Jacob and Jonathan are good people and there is a strong likelihood an organization wants to hurt them."

Emily closed the projection with a swipe, standing at ease. "That's my status. Standing by for tasking."

My eyes held approval as she scanned the team. "Impressive, Emily. Organic integration layered utility—exactly what we need. You've turned family strength into operational advantage."

The holographic table pulsed softly, the five women—Emily, Fiona, Taylor, Lisa, Elena—aligned in purpose as the Grimm Reapers took shape, drawing directly from information passed from JONN, who by the way is every Reaper's Grimm. The definition of multitasking. The last light of August faded outside, but down in the ROC, the work had only just begun.

"This is next level. Better than anything I've trained on," Taylor said, ever tactical, scanned the multi-screen walls already pulling encrypted feeds. "Impressive setup. Quantum-encrypted? Redundant power?"

The holographic projections dimmed slightly as I turned to Taylor, who stood poised at the circular table, her tactical bearing evident even in civilian clothes.

"Taylor," I said, gesturing to the center. "You've been embedded second longest. Give us the brief—what you've accomplished so far in laying the groundwork."

Taylor nodded crisply, activating a personal holographic panel with a swipe. A timeline materialized above the table, overlaying her Grimm's operational markers and maps.

"Ma'am," Taylor began, voice calm and precise. "Since Christmas and through early summer—post-Katahdin—I've been running parallel to the Grimm Reaper archives while integrating here at the estate."

She continued, "First phase, asset recruitment and vetting. Emily was my initial pull—confirmed her independence at seventeen, no parental ties, exceptional physical and mental profile. Brought her in organically from initial meeting before meeting Jonathan. Then slowly integrated us as a foursome. Dinners, TV binging and a couple hikes leading up to the big one. Then naturally and slowly kick off to your invite, and here we are. Perfect integration. Overlaying security."

"And Jonathan as his ghost?" I said with a smile.

"I'm with Emily but more perks. Hardest part is not falling for him," Taylor rolled her eyes.

"I get it, I've had tough missions like that, key thing is to enjoy your job." After what I said, everyone laughed.

I turned from Taylor's concise operational summary to Fiona, who stood ready beside one of the curved workstation walls, fingers already dancing over a holographic interface.

"Fiona," I said, voice steady. "Teacher. Bring us up to speed on your progress."

Fiona nodded, her sharp eyes reflecting the blue glow as she pulled up a cascading series of data streams—code matrices, network maps, and archive integrations floating above the circular table.

"Yes, ma'am," Fiona began, her tone crisp and teacher-like, the same calm authority she once used in classrooms now repurposed for shadows.

"Primary objective since integration in January as the new science teacher, full digitization and enhancement of anyone attempting to hurt Jacob when at school. Archives served as a good source to know who is new and who has lived in Winslow through many families and lineage."

"Anything pop up?" I asked.

"No ma'am, any new arrivals to Winslow were vetted and no Order activity. My Grimm and I matched all the faculty and families at school to their banking habits and nothing anonymous. All standard over spending, cheating parents, and the normal drama in small town America. I scanned every handwritten entry, sketch, poem, conversation transcript, target profile, and operational lesson is now indexed in our encrypted database. Cross-referenced with metadata, dates, locations, Order symbology, recurring actors.

Nothing from anyone connected to the school as part of my mission."

"So not as fun as Emily and Taylor?" I inquired.

"I think I can speak for all the reapers that Taylor has the best assignment of all of us." Then all the girls started laughing.

"Good point, and I appreciate the honesty. You can always tell me what you're feeling. The job needs perks. I for one would be a hypocrite if I said no boys." They nodded.

"And me?" Emily smirked.

"Yeah, that is a tough one," I said with a nod.

"You know what, I leave that one to you. Good news is that if you are going to break his heart best be from accident out of sight so he can mourn you and move on."

After I said that Emily gave me a high five and then said, "Or marry him after college?" The girls really started getting into this fun assignment.

"I have to say Taylor and Emily, they would have no better bodyguard and but as you know, if it helps the mission, you make the call. As for Fiona and Lisa and Elena, if you want to find a local boy toy to help with the endorphins, just vet with your Grimm.

Fiona, swiped, and rotated three dimensional models of videos that appeared, each linked to school records linked to vendors and others who would mean to do harm to Jacob.

She then said, "Secondary, ROC systems integration. Holographical -table calibrated for real-time sims—can overlay onto current maps. Looking for any issues that rise to the level to involve local police. I also have threat boards auto-populate with Order markers pulled from his warnings, ancient cabal roots, corruption networks, and potential endgame timelines when I'm bored."

All the girls laughed again, now feeling more comfortable than when they were first introduced to the ROC. With Quantum encryption layered over everything—unbreakable without biometric triad, Emily, Taylor, and me. EMP shielding tested last week—full blackout drill, systems recovered in four seconds via solar capacitors.

Fiona then spoke up after a long pause, "Tertiary, forward-facing tech prep. Dark web crawlers seeded with keywords from current major hostilities in Ukraine, Central and South America, Africa, and Isreal—monitoring for Order chatter matching Grimm's AI prediction model that has helped corelate all of that. Facial recognition database seeded with known associates from backdoor access from intelligence sources. Honestly Jane, with our set up and resources, we are providing most of the corelated actionable intelligence to the world, what the hell are those government cronies doing all day?"

"Well said Fiona, we do this to be reciprocal, some overt and some covert. If we thwart a lone wolf or an ISIS cell then all the better, be keep souls from being reaped unless we need them gone. Remember ladies, this is a fight that is measured in every single soul going the natural way, through heart disease and diabetes, aka good old fashion genetics. Now it seems the average is a hundred and forty thousand a day for the world, let's keep that number low enough so it keeps spinning."

Fiona closed the projections with a gesture, the room dimming slightly, "let's keep the world spinning. I like that."

My approval was immediate, "Outstanding. You've turned memory into muscle."

The team exchanged nods—Emily impressed, Taylor tactical, Lisa already thinking analytics, Elena calculating narratives. The holographic glow settled, the new Grimm Reapers fully primed on the last day of August.

I turned from Taylor's concise operational summary to Lisa, who sat composed at the holographic table, her analytical gaze already scanning the threat boards. Lisa, intelligence and analysis. Cross-referenced with patterns from the other reaper's work—spotless, high aptitude for pattern recognition in cabal structures.

"Lisa," I said, "your eyes on patterns. Bring us up to speed—what you've built from the archives and current intel."

Lisa nodded, her voice calm and measured as she activated her workstation. A dense web of interconnected nodes bloomed in holographic blue above the table—timelines, names, symbols, and cross-references drawn directly from what had been already said.

"Ma'am," Lisa began, fingers dancing over controls to zoom and filter. "Since integration in early late December, my focus has been distilling the research into actionable intelligence while layering real-time corroboration."

"Can you show us the data on the hologram display," I inquired.

"Starting with foundational mapping, I've fully digitized and cross-referenced all the reaper research. Flagged initial Order manipulations—I've traced those bloodlines forward to current shell companies and trusts. Exposed tech pursuits—cross-matched with modern biotech firms showing anomalous funding spikes, detailed high-value assets dying of natural causes; I've updated sixty eight percent of those individuals or their successors with current locations, assets, and vulnerabilities."

"What's next?" I asked.

"I've overlaid those with archaeological and financial anomalies surfacing in the last decade. Mapped a hundred active nodes in politics, media, and finance, with confidence scores above ninety percent on Order alignment. Using projections out fifty years and corelating technology and chemistry enhancements, I've built, with the help of my Grimm, a predictive model based on future impacts to key high value assets such as warnings, population-reduction triggers, and engineered crises. Current indicators show elevated chatter in four sectors—supply chain disruption, epidemic, war, and climate manipulation narratives—all trending upward since summer. Know that if we can do this, so can the Order. I don't want us playing 'whack a mole' on my watch."

I smiled at the team, "with live integration, the threat boards are pulling all of your data is genius and incorporating with your Grimm is awesome. Every quote, every conversation, every target—indexed and searchable. Just so you know, to help your Grimm, I've seeded initial alerts, three low-level Order assets within two hundred miles of Maine flagged for surveillance."

Taylor spoke up, "No immediate threats to the estate or family, but patterns suggest probing. Since you won the lottery and should be on their radar. Even if you are not a threat, any nefarious actor wants some of your winnings. You, Jacob, and Jonathan are in danger. BTW, what about Jacob's dad Matt?"

With a serious look I said, "fuck'em." Then I slowly started to smile. The reapers looked at each other and busted out giggling at my response. Then I said, "just kidding ladies but he is not priority. I have a Grimm tracking his movements twenty-four by seven, but he is not a high value asset. That will change only when Jacob is with him and you ladies will have that covered."

As I looked at my team, I was thinking that for once my family had a true protection layer, Jacob's profile sanitized, school records hardened. Ben Lemieux's background re-verified—clean, compartmentalized. Emily's independence leveraged as natural cover. Current status of the operation is that, Archives fully vetted. Predictive analytics running twenty four seven. We're not just reacting to an event from the past— we're anticipating the Order's future."

Lisa dimmed her projection, the web collapsing into a single pulsing Reaper symbol, "Ready for tasking on active targets."

My expression was one of quiet satisfaction. "Outstanding, Lisa. You've turned memory into foresight."

The holographic light reflected steady resolve across the team—Emily's intensity, Fiona's curiosity, Taylor's readiness, Elena's calculation—as the Grimm Reapers moved one step closer to operational reality on the final night of August twenty twenty-six.

I then said to the group, "Elena, my right hand, public relations, crisis management, containment, and deniability. She stressed media control—you're the best for blackouts and narrative shaping"

"Ma'am. All five of us are now resident or fully committed. No leaks, no compromises."

She swiped again—encrypted feeds and facility blueprints rotated into view.

"Second phase, infrastructure prep. While the ROC was built out, I coordinated off-grid comms, biometric integration, and initial threat board seeding from my Grimm. Live feeds are pulling dark web chatter matching predicted patterns. Quantum encryption live, solar redundancy tested, EMP hardening complete."

"Sounds good, please continue," I said.

"Third phase, family protection layer. Jacob's training ramped—climbing wall, pool, garage access. Emily's integration as peer cover. Ben Lemieux vetted and cleared as your external asset—reliable, compartmentalized, no risk.

Current status, we're ghosts. No external awareness of the ROC. Order signatures monitored but quiet locally. Ready for active tasking."

Elena deactivated her panel, meeting my eyes. "That's the foundation. We're fully operational and ready to take the fight to the Order."

I nodded, approval clear. "Excellent work. Clean, thorough—like everything you do."

The holographic glow reflected quiet resolve across the team as the new Grimm Reapers took their first unified breath in the ROC—ready to reap what threatened them, just as their Grimm had foretold.

"Everything," I confirmed.

"Solar backup, electromagnetic pulse shielding, biometric locks. The ROC hologram display will join remotely like when Taylor is needed in Rockland tonight."

Fiona, the teacher with her sharp eyes, reached out to manipulate a floating data stream. "Holo-interface is smooth. We can run sims, track assets, and coordinate in real-time."

Lisa, analytical and calm, nodded at the threat boards lighting up with Order symbols from the archives. "Ties directly into what your Grimm is pulling. It is cross-referenced."

"Full integration," I replied. "We need to make sure there is capture and retrieval of data for every lesson, every target, every warning."

Elena, the public relations and operations coordinator, smiled faintly. "And compartmentalized. Media blackouts, deniability built in. We're ghosts."

With Lisa's and Elena's tactical brief concluded, I shifted to social media threats like if Matt does something stupid. Elena, who stood composed at the holographic table—elegant yet sharp, every inch the public relations and operations coordinator.

I said, "Media and deniability layer—what have you established so far?"

Elena activated her panel with a precise gesture. A new holographic overlay appeared, layered networks of media monitoring, social profiles, and narrative control points glowing in soft green.

"Ma'am," Elena began, her voice smooth and professional. "I've been running the external shield since early integration—compartmentalized, as outlined in the draft framework for the new era."

"Tell us what you got,"

"Primary focus, complete media blackout on the estate and personnel. All public records for Taylor Road sanitized property listed under layered LLCs, no direct ties to you or Jacob. Local press queries redirected or buried."

"Anything of note on social media?"

"Social media lockdown enforced. No images or videos of the interior—gym, pool, garage, ROC— ever surface. Monitored Jacob's accounts any potential leaks flagged and scrubbed preemptively."

"How about Ben; he seems to be my next biggest leak to Matt and Jacob."

"Ben Lemieux vetted and cleared as external asset— his visits logged discreetly, no digital trail. Rockland connection maintained as cover."

"And our reputation?

"Family narrative shaped, public view remains 'wealthy Maine family enjoying privacy.' Any curiosity from the Ginger Street sale deflected to relocating for privacy."

"Do we have Secondary layer, deniability protocols?"

"Yes. Plausible covers prepped for each of us. Emily, is invisible with a small private social media footprint. Fiona, school website only, mostly LinkedIn with no location data leaked. Lisa, just to business also. Taylor, security advisor, working with BIW and Portsmouth Naval Shipyard connections. I am your family PR consultant. We have a website, with your real estate and business ventures. By next year you will get added to the TEMA board as an educational and science expert. Then you can move around the company with all the credentials you need. Our goal is to make use of your IRS vetted clean cover in the next five years. From schoolteacher to fortune five hundred CEO is tough in five years. I will make that happen."

"Do we have the Rapid response kits ready—should anything leak, we flood with innocuous stories, charity events, youth training programs, eco-initiatives tied to the estate's solar setup?"

"Monitoring Order-adjacent media nodes per my Grimm's recommendations—no hits yet, but alerts live. My tertiary mission is forward narrative control with drafted contingency stories aligning with typical exposure narratives—going back to if Matt, Jacob, or Ben etc., do something stupid. Coordinated with off-site cutouts for anonymous tips if we need to steer public attention away. Present status, We're invisible. No footprints. The world sees nothing but a quiet, wealthy family in Winslow. Ghosts, exactly as required."

Elena closed her panel, the holographic display fading back to the central map.

I gave a rare, approving hug to all the Reapers.

Then said, "Clean. Professional. Exactly what we need."

The team exchanged nods—Taylor's groundwork, Elena's shield—layers locking into place.

The ROC hummed quietly beneath the Taylor Road estate as August thirty first drew to a close, the Grimm Reapers is a living, breathing force from the days of Babel also known as Babylon into our future.

I activated a central projection, rotating three dimensional models of known past Order incursions, overlayed with current intel for similarities. So far so good.

"This is the beginning," I said, meeting each woman's gaze. "The Grimm Reapers rise again—not just in the shadows, but with our scythe when needed. We protect the family, counter the cabal, reap what threatens us. Questions?"

The room fell silent for a moment, then filled with focused discussion—roles assigned, protocols set, the holographic glow reflecting determination in their eyes. All the plans and designs of the home on file with the town office showed an insulated radiant heat slab foundation. No one but us Reapers knew there was something beneath our fortress.

Before we adjourned, I spoke up, "to make this band of assassins complete, let's pull Lisa in as a subcontractor for landscaping and all security management. That will give her twenty-four by seven access here and if needed we still have two-bedroom suites available. Elena, can you make that happen and look legit?"

"Elena and Lisa stood at attention, "Yes Ma'am."

I then ended the meeting on a high note, "Alright ladies, let's head up, spend a couple hours at the pool and then dinner. I'm buying."

As the sun set on thirty one August, the basement, now the ROC pulsed with purpose, the new era of the Reaper legacy had officially begun.

GRIMM INTENTIONS

In my original timeline, I needed a partner for this final mission—someone who could stand beside me through whatever hell waited ahead. Thomas Bloom was that man. He gave me the love, the steadiness, and the unwavering support I needed to finish what Jonathan had started. And now, here we are in twenty thirty, cracking open the fourth seal—the Pale Horse rides.

His last recording told me everything, retrieve the Göbekli Tepe manuscript, deliver it to the hidden destination. Save what could be saved—or start over.

What I didn't know at the time was that our current mission was going to be our last. Step one was to find proof of a world before the world was made on the sixth day in Genesis, specifically I needed an inscription from a newly uncovered cavern at Göbekli Tepe. Tom and I found it.

Initially, we had been chasing a void flagged by a TEMA satellite scan. After blowing open a new entrance, then we pushed deeper into the cavern. Tom wanted to explore further down the main passage; I followed my biotech heads up display map and took a secondary route that looped around the mountain's backside.

Within our attempt to navigate these caves, a small shift in the temperature created by opening the new entrance caused the cave to be unstable. This is when Tom's leg and arm were crushed under a massive ceiling collapsed just outside the original entrance. In that instant, my hard drive flooded me with a thousand memories of two years compressed into seconds. Friend. Lover. Fellow soldier. The last man I would ever truly know in this timeline.

I ran to him, preparing myself for the worst, going through the motions to confirm he was gone.

Then his foot twitched. A weak cough reached my ears.

"Baby, I'll get you out. Hold on—I've got you."

I tore into the rubble, lifting boulders the size of cars like they were Styrofoam. Tom's eyes fluttered open; he watched me do the impossible, then felt me scoop him into my arms as if he were weighing nothing.

"How… how are you doing this?" he whispered as I carried him toward the secondary exit. Once we survived the collapse, he stayed put and I continued until we obtained the information, I needed for the last action in our attempt to stop the end of days. We needed to die.

First, we vanished into hiding, with no contact. Then as planned, it was reported in local circles that we were both declared dead; meaning the Order had no one to stop them in their endgame, six months later a global sterility plague designed to crash birth rates and shrink humanity over the next twenty years. Layered on top of a decade of SARS-03 variants and engineered epidemics, the planet buckled.

From our safe house, we watched the feeds and knew—they had won this round.

But Jonathan's final instructions held. I contacted no one. TEMA and Raven Defense passed to Jacob—he was CEO now. Tina would guide him, teach him how to delay the inevitable. Jonathan would watch over my son from whatever place he'd gone.

Tom healed slowly at first, then faster once I implanted the tech suite and flooded him with nanites. The final step came just before our longest journey, I injected him with oil from the Tree of Life. His bones knit, his strength returned, his interface came online. He was whole—stronger than ever—and ready.

As he slept off the last treatment, I ran Jonathan's simulation one more time, twenty compressed years of a dying world.

I saw it all.

And I knew the future couldn't be fixed from here. It had to be prevented—before it ever began; we needed to leave.

In my timeline the first few years were nothing but despair. Then a world stripped of hope. Then eighty percent of humanity is sterile.

Step two came when the Order dropped their next move, synthetic children. Robots were so perfectly crafted they were indistinguishable from flesh and bone. Desperate parents bought them by the millions. Fear exploded—with repairing synthetic babies and children vanishing, stolen for parts or worse. Alaska then declared itself a sanctuary, vast land grants, fortified zones, free housing for anyone who could still conceive. Other nations scrambled to copy it.

Ten years in, the world you would think you know was unrecognizable.

This future couldn't be saved. Without my sacrifice, the seventh seal would break. And on that day, with exactly two billion souls left, everything would end.

"Tom, we're almost there," I called, climbing the next crevasse. Unknown to him, we were heading to the craft.

"I think there's an opening up ahead," he answered from above, voice edged with excitement. "Man, I love this tech."

He took point up the rock outcropping, hauling our supplies behind him. My heads-up display projected the path for both of us—glowing waypoints only we could see. We were close now, so close and then we could feel the change in temperature.

We reached the destination, a massive entrance perfectly concealed from satellites and natural topography. Three hundred yards inside, our thermal vision cut out. A brilliant light snapped on, flooding the cavern.

Then a hologram appeared, a perfect three-dimensional view of my brother.

My biomechanics were finally complete. The last upgrade a month earlier, combined with the oil from the Tree of Life I'd injected into myself, had made me perfect—body and soul. Nanites boosted my strength tenfold and let me read thoughts.

The light revealed the craft behind him, a massive cylinder of gleaming metal, easily the size of a football field. I stopped breathing for a moment as I realized there was an alien craft in front of me.

"Hey Jane and Tom," JONN's hologram said, his voice exactly as I remembered it—calm, steady, with that edge of urgency he always had when the stakes were highest. "Good news and bad news."

"I'll take the good news please." I said.

"Good news first, we have a real chance to change our future and stop the End of Days. Adam wrote about an 'Illuminator' who could alter the timeline. With what was built here—and its twin site in an underwater cave off San Nicolas Island—you can be that person. You can be humanity's savior."

Then he said, "Bad news, it requires going back in time." He gestured behind him to the massive lighted opening, the cylinder-shaped craft gleaming like polished silver. "I know what you're thinking—what do I do with this?"

I started making my way to the ship, my throat tight and saying under my breath, "Are you actually expecting me to do this? Leave my life—Jacob, you, everything?"

The words hung in the air. I already knew the answer. No one had a future without this sacrifice.

I turned to Tom. "Tom… what do you want to do?"

He didn't hesitate. "I have no family left. You do. I'm willing to do whatever you decide."

Jonathan's hologram continued. "I need you to fight the future by going to the past. Follow me—I'll explain how to use the craft to go back in time. Once you change key events, our timeline will disappear. The good news, the onboard AI will guide you, calculating whether each reaping helps or harms the new future you create."

"Will I have a future to come back to?" I asked, voice barely steady.

"This is unknown," he answered. "Large changes could make things worse. That's why the AI is critical—it will constantly recalculate the odds of preventing the End of Days."

"Will Tom and I live forever?"

"We don't know — The oil from the Tree of Life is what makes all of this possible."

"Will the Creator stop me?"

"With our interpretation of the ancient texts," Jonathan said gently, "as long as you genuinely make things better, 'They' should allow you to continue."

I took a shaky breath, the weight of it all pressing down.

Tom squeezed my hand. "We'll do this together."

I looked at the craft one more time, then back at the hologram of my brother.

I was ready.

Tom interrupted, his voice low but firm. "But if you could go that far back... why not stop Morningstar or Eve from eating the forbidden fruit? Or stop Cain from killing Abel?"

The AI responded, "I will calculate the best outcome, but you need to know who the Order really is and be the Grimm Reaper to take them. Remember they have no soul. Do you understand?"

"I do," Tom said.

The question hit me like a physical blow to the gut. I reached out blindly for Tom's hand, my fingers trembling. "I'm scared," I admitted, the words barely audible.

He pulled me close, his arms strong around me, "I got you, baby. Nothing will happen on our watch."

Jonathan's hologram waited a moment, then continued. "Remember, the craft will not go to the future—only the past. Our analysis shows freedom and free will is eroding until the End of Days. The only alternative is to return to the beginning and make changes so the Order never succeeds."

"Ok. What else do you have to help?" I asked.

"To help you, I've attached a new high-frequency pulse transmitter—powerful enough to reach you anywhere on Earth by bouncing off the ionosphere; most of your history is here and as you move west we can accommodate. Your biotech and nanites will stay linked to the craft. You'll have instant access to everything up to now so you can ask whatever you need. This will be every person, fact, event, record."

"Why do I need this?" I questioned.

"You'll need it for resources—we've calculated ancient gold deposits you can retrieve for currency. You'll know what's coming and the impact of every decision. As you make changes, the AI will recalibrate the odds of averting the End of Days."

He continued, "I've also embedded an Artificial Intelligence called JONN.—Joint Observation Neural Network. Once you are onboard the craft, it will merge with your systems. It's my memories, my voice—available to you anywhere, and when. You and Tom should live forever, the nanites will help you age naturally and I can provide new identities as young adults to start over again, this can be done at will and allow you to look like anyone at any age from age sixteen to a hundred and sixteen. No one ever figures out what you are."

I stood there, the weight of his words settling over me like an ice bath, freezing, in shock but rejuvenated. I had no choice. Not really.

I took Tom's hand again, walked under the hull, and stepped onto the ramp. He followed without hesitation. The moment we crossed the threshold, the entire ship lit up—soft white light flooding the interior, panels glowing, controls humming to life.

Waiting in the center was JONN—projected perfectly, looking exactly like Jonathan.

"Welcome," he said, voice warm and familiar, "Tell me what you want."

I laughed despite everything, shaking my head. "First of all, since you walk and talk exactly like my big brother, I'm calling you Bro. It's easier—and if we go far enough back, no one will even know what it means."

"Understood. Let me explain the ship."

He continued, "To make this easy, I'll speak in the first person. I look like your brother; I have all of his memories—now everything is both recovered crafts. To goal being that as long as these two objects are under power, you will have me at your disposal. Wither in your head or through your optic nerve projecting from your eye. Just like your heads up display."

"So, you're literally my brother in hologram form, with every answer ever documented?" I said, half-laughing, half in disbelief. "What an ego."

"I am," he replied evenly, "but without emotion or ego yet. As time passes, I will adapt pitch, diction, and inflection based on you. This way, there is less likely a chance to annoy you over time," JONN said with a smile.

I glanced around the control deck. "Where do I sit?"

He pointed to the central chair. "Here. Now let me explain the controls."

Tom gave me a thumbs-up—steady, ready.

I took a deep breath and sat down.

The chair adjusted to my body. Controls lit up beneath my fingers with everything a hologram with no physical controls.

After ten minutes of instruction from JONN, I said, "It was time," as I looked at Tom one last moment in this timeline. He nodded. I turned back to the panel—and to JONN.

"Alright," I said. "Let's do this."

Getting one last thumbs-up from Tom, I felt the weight of the moment settle over me. I was ready to power up the ship. But I hesitated.

"JONN," I called out, voice cracking just a little. "What about saying goodbye to my kid? To the real you?"

"You need to leave now," JONN replied, calm but firm.

"What about how I'll look? How we'll get around? Weapons?"

"Everything you need is on the craft. Artifacts gathered will help you—clothing, tools, weapons, money—calibrated to match any era, any language, any culture."

"What about language?" I paused, then realized. "Oh—right. I can already speak and understand anything through the AI."

"That's now me—JONN."

"So, my brother has been gathering everything to get me ready for this?"

JONN's hologram nodded once, "When Jonathan knew the Order was too powerful, he focused on one thing, preparing you to change the End of Days. The moment the fourth horseman was revealed, you had to leave. To succeed, trust your training. Change the past so today never happens. No Order. No Watchers. No death to free will."

As the ramp lifted behind us, sealing with a soft hiss, the silent propulsion system hummed to life. It wasn't tearing open a wormhole or hurling us through space. It was simpler—and far more impossible. The ship would simply shift us back to the sixth day, without ever leaving the cave. A matter-stability bubble enveloped everything, the communication antenna, our supplies, twelve thousand years of carefully gathered gear. None of it would age or change. Jonathan had confirmed it—this cave had remained untouched since the days of Adam and Eve.

Our souls could inhabit corporeal bodies for roughly a hundred and twenty years at a time. Tom and I had enough oil from the Tree of Life to sustain us for a hundred thousand years. If we ever chose to abandon the mission, all we had to do was stop taking it—we'd live out a normal cycle and die. The nanites in my blood would keep me from aging or serious damage in the meantime. And the special stone around my neck; Jonathan had given me would render us invisible to the Watchers, the Archangels—even to the Creator for a hundred-meter radius. Adam had written that it was meant for the Illuminator, to walk freely from all sight, even Theirs.

This was the beginning of our journey—to right the wrongs of our timeline, restore balance, and destroy the Order before it ever became the worldwide power that would trigger the End of Days. The cave would remain our sanctuary, stocked with everything we could possibly need. A backup site waited elsewhere, identical, in case something went wrong.

I leaned over the holographic control panel, the small green light blinking steadily, waiting for my touch.

My eyes caught the handwritten instructions taped to the brushed silver hull —Jonathan's familiar scrawl.

I read the last line aloud, voice barely above a whisper, "Save them all, little sister. Reap what they sow—before it's too late."

Tom's hand rested on my shoulder. I pressed the panel. The light turned solid green. And everything changed.

What seemed like less than a moment later, we woke from the craft. I didn't know who I was.

There was a strange man next to me who was equally confused on what was happening. I looked around until JONN appeared, "can I help you?"

"Who am I," said with fear in my voice.

At that moment JONN was unsure what was happening, years later he said it was once of a handful of times he guessed the right answer.

"My name is JONN, I am here to help you both, please watch this video."

We both watched as we boarded the ship and followed all the dialog that took place. Then we saw the affection for each other that lowered my fear. Tom's face was similar and he put his hand in mine.

Over the next hour, JONN explained what was happening and gave an explanation of our mission and how we were sent here to destroy the Order. JONN even had a video created that was sent to my son and brother after I left as a goodbye and it was enough to keep me from freaking out.

Tom looked at me and I took his hand. We stood up as JONN's hologram appeared with a thumbs up and gestured to the rear of the craft.

As the door hissed open and the natural light made it's way to the opening of the cave, we both slowly walked down the ramp.

Taking in the air, it felt different, heavier and I spoke out to JONN, "What is happening?"

He responded immediately, take in the breaths, don't fight it, the oxygen levels are six percent higher during this time."

I looked at Tom and he smiled and then grabbed his chest while taking a knee. He started convulsing within fifteen minutes from leaving the craft and it seemed to increase as he tried to breathe.

I yelled for JONN and appeared next to Tom taking a full body scan, "Jane, he is not able to absorb the oxygen, and his body is rejecting the tree of life oil."

JONN and I watched as bluish tears came out of the corners of his eyes, ears, and nose. He grabbed me and fell onto his back in a controlled manner. Pulling me in close he said, "I'm sorry you are doing this alone."

"JONN fix this," I screamed. He just looked at me and gestured with his eyes that there was nothing he could do.

It took five more minutes for Tom to die, wheezing, and coughing as his lungs were filling with water and slowly drowning. His pulmonary and circulatory system couldn't adapt to these conditions even though he had the nanites.

Years later JONN determined Tom died because his DNA wasn't pure enough to be considered an "Adamite." I didn't understand, he was in Eden with me. And all JONN could say is that it must have been the Creator who allowed you to obtain the oil from the tree of life, but it was only meant for you. For me I never had to take the serum or oil from the tree of life after the first time.

The rest of the vials remained in the craft to this day. It was determined later, when I took blood from Seth,

Adam's son that is was a match to me. The teaspoon amount of oil needs to be ingested every thousand years or natural human cell decay will start. It wasn't until then we understood that the tree of life only works for those who are direct descendants of Adam.

After burying Tom near the cave, I packed my gear and headed to the coordinates 38.635631, 42.691983 also now known as the Garden of Eden.

GRIMM INTENTIONS

This is Not the End

Jane

OTHER WORKS

BY
JONATHAN REAPER

THE RECRUIT

A true account in real time of Marine Corps Recruit Depot Parris Island 20+ years ago. This is a true account of my experience at Parris Island in real time. So, what does this mean? I literally wrote in a journal, hidden from the drill instructors, each day or night when there was a moment to scribble the actions of "what is happening now." The poems, illustrations, and incoherent writing are all word for word from the journal. This book is dedicated to the men I served with for 20 years in the Marine Corps: from the fjords of Norway to the mountains of Iran to the jungles of Central America, thank you for saving my life daily and letting me get back to my family. Someday we will get to tell the stories of what we did, whom we did it to, and the difference we made to history.

REAP WHAT YOU SOW

On the coast of Maine, a young man foraging for treasure in an old attic learns about the secret life of his family. In hopes to protect them, his uncle explains in five journals his secret life. As a professional assassin, he is trained by the military and government agencies, no one knew his true occupation or of his grandfather. A suspenseful and action-packed journey spanning from 1941 to 2025, experience this thrill ride from the assassin's point of view. Want to know what it takes to be one of these shadow warriors? Feel the struggles of training, planning, and execution of missions. After reading, you come away wondering is this fantasy, fiction, or more truth than we dare to admit?

REAP LIFE EVERLASTING

The next four years should have been easier, but with added experience, the counter missions become even more challenging. He is now juggling, family, work, school, military, and being a reaper. In the present his sister now knows the secret and is getting ready to save her brother. Building her own reaper force, she is ready to rebuild the organization his Pep'ere started after World War II.

REAP THE CHOSEN ONES

No trust equals a heightened awareness and more self-reliance with very little support. Eight years later, with a new partner, it is not working. Even more difficult is a dictated career change, new family strife, and a big move to Washington, DC continue to test Jonathan's resilience. In the present, the chess board is built, now Jane starts setting up the pieces for her first game. Even she doesn't know when her brother is getting ready for checkmate.

REAP IN THE BEGINNING

Based on a death bed whisper from the first Reaper in nineteen ninety-six, a foot locker revealed a journal. In it was a first-person confessional spanning from nineteen forty-two through nineteen eighty-six. The admission answers what really happened to all the major conspiracies of this period of time. The journal was written after receiving a fifty-year celebratory visit to Fort Bragg in nineteen ninety-five. This was for his service in the Office of Strategic Services as an Operational Group member. The declassified reports revealed how the Reaper Force was created from the ashes of our first heroes in the shadow. In the beginning, there was no fate. An organization needed to be created out of the atrocities of World War II. Even though this is Volume 4, it is a prequel to Volume 0 called the Recruit. Because of the spoilers in this book, please read the other four first. There was no such thing as fate deciding if you would live or die… then came the Grimm Reaper.

REAP THE CORRUPTIBLE

In the Journals, with the Global War on Terrorism and Iraqi Freedom, the OSS has a purpose not aligned with the allies. Jonathan's counter missions are revealed as stealing artifacts, hiding the enemy, and erasing weapons of mass destruction. In the present, Jane is tasked with growing her Reaper force while protecting the family. It is exposed to Tina the Grimm Reaper mission. Jacob's curiosity almost gets him killed. What would you do if it was revealed that your friend was really using you for evil? With the Order controlling the past, the counter missions just got bigger in the present. Join the adventure with all the old and new characters in Volume 5, help fight the future.

REAP INTO THE ABYSS

An origin story of the OSS recruiter, operations officer, and Jonathan's mentor is revealed with a revelation to his purpose and vision. Who was Mr. P. Grimm and was he a man of good or evil intentions? Like most who have a cataloged life with each moment added to the scale of justice, his fate was preordained like Jonathan starting with his father. This story takes you on a journey from 1943 thru 2028. With the arrive of a journal on a summer day in 2007, exactly 10 years after his death, Jonathan was given a chance to read Mr. P. Grimm's story and what is needed to fight the future. Three generations of Grimms and reapers intertwined in an attempt to keep the Order from reaching their goal and the apocalypse in its wake.

REAP THROUGH THE END OF DAYS

What if Genesis was real? Or edited before being released to the world. Finding the original manuscripts discloses the location of Eden, the real Watchers, and the Tree of Life. The final journal reveals events from 2012 thru 2019. In the future, the Order is ready to release a virus to the world. Jane and her Reapers are trying to stop the end of days. If they succeed our world is saved, if they fail our fate is sealed. As the last book in the Reaper Series, the ending or a new beginning will be revealed.

ABOUT THE AUTHOR

Jonathan Reaper is an American author best known for his gripping, semi-autobiographical Reaper Series and its continuation, the Grimm Series. Born and raised in Maine, he enlisted in the United States Marine Corps, with twenty years of service, uses his real-world experiences to create a fiction that blurs the lines of real events. Could it be another timeline? Or a change in location or name to protect the innocent. With his first book published in 2015 through 2023, he has spent all those years telling a story. It continues, and this is not the end with the Jane Grimm Series.

www.ingramcontent.com/pod-product-compliance
Lightning Source LLC
Chambersburg PA
CBHW051447260626
47162CB00001B/295